CHRISTABEL WAS A MINE—AND A MYSTERY

Slope Dugan had walked across the country to sell his stock in the Christabel mine back to Bonanza Chris, who had sold it to his father years back. He was offered $1500 dollars for the "worthless" stock. Red knew more about life than most boys his age; he'd learned to live by his wits and wear an alias. He knew no operator like Bonanza would *give* away money.

To protect his gullible friend from being bilked, he worked out a plan. Slope would refuse Bonanza's offer, then Red, Slope and their new friend Blondy would explore the mine for themselves. If rumors were true, they might end up millionaires. But they might also end up—dead.

MAX BRAND

TRAIL PARTNERS

WARNER PAPERBACK LIBRARY

A Warner Communications Company

WARNER PAPERBACK LIBRARY EDITION
First Printing: April, 1974

Library of Congress Catalog Card Number: 56-6286.

This Warner Paperback Library Edition is published by arrangement with Dodd, Mead & Company, Inc.

Cover illustration by Carl Hantman

Warner Paperback Library is a division of Warner Books, Inc. 75 Rockefeller Plaza, New York, N.Y. 10019.

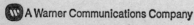 A Warner Communications Company

Printed in the United States of America

CHAPTER 1

What's the grandest thing you ever clamped eyes on? Some of you may pick out a mountain, or an iceberg sailing green and blue through somebody's midnight, or a river turning loose in the spring with everything that it had forgotten all winter. To others it will be a fine bull terrier, or a great horse that seems the smashingest thing, or perhaps a hawk against the wind, or a tall ship, but of all the great things that I ever saw, that stops my heart beating and makes my eyes jump, remembering, there's nothing in a class with "Slope" Dugan.

I had been seeing men enough, for that matter. The hobos on the Southern Pacific, in those days, were men, all right. They printed their thumb marks and their toe marks, too, all over me, and they used indelible ink, blue and purple, for the job. I was a fairish size for a kid, but those shacks, they kicked me all over the map because I was trying to ride the rods or the blind baggage on the fast trains. Where the tramps left off, the station and the yard cops came in and carried right on. Any station cop could kill three hooligans with one hand, and one brakeman could handle any three tramps. That gives you a sort of idea of the measuring rod that was in my mind for the judging of men, but still Slope Dugan beat everything that ever came my way.

For one thing, I could see him stripped for action, and in action, too. That makes the difference. The shirt had been torn off him, and the electric light in front of the station house flashed on the sweat that ran on him as though he were covered with grease.

Then he was up against a man that would've made a

7

background for a whole mountain, six feet anything you please, and over three hundred pounds, maybe, with a short, curling black beard and the look of a fellow that would hit a thunderbolt on the point of the chin and bounce it back into the sky harder than it came.

That Slovak, he was a man, all right. But he was nothing, compared with Dugan.

I can't go describing Slope to you. You gotta use your imagination some when I'm talking about him. I mean to say, there was six feet of him—he wasn't so awfully big, but inches had nothing to do with Slope. Bit by bit, he looked heavy, sluggish, and muscle bound, but take him all together and he swept into the picture like a race horse moving. When Slope got into action, he was like a terrible machine. Something had to give way. I mean, if you ever seen a hydraulic jack working on a big scale, lifting half a mountain, maybe, then you know what I'm talking about when I say machine.

There was a chance for Slope to move this evening that I'm talking about. The Slovak, when he makes his first rush, beats down Slope's guard and dodges his first pass. Then he leans on Dugan and laughs down at him, like he was just about to enjoy himself and swaller the feller whole.

Dugan didn't seem very mad, either. He had the same bothered, thinking-of-something-else expression that was on his map most of the time. I mean, with wrinkles wiggling across his forehead, and his eyes a little dull, like the eyes of a statue that's only half come to life.

No, he didn't seem very mad, but when the big Blackbeard laughed, Slope picked up that quarter ton of meanness and threw it right through the station-house door. As he did this, Blackbeard grabbed hold of Slope's shirt to anchor himself to the ground. So the shirt went along with him, and he landed on his back.

He thought it was magic, I guess, and he got up and charged out of the blackness with a roar. But when he clamped his eyes on Slope again, he understood. The whole crowd that was gasping and enjoying this free fight, it could understand, too, because there was Slope with his shirt off, and if you could see his muscles working, you didn't have to see the working of his mind.

Blackbeard saw that he had started trouble with a combination of Texas mule, mountain lion, and grizzly bear. That's the best I can think of for meanness, and the mule comes first.

But that Slovak, or whatever he was, was game, all right. He stuck out his jaw, his teeth showing through the black mist, and he came at Slope. But Slope wasn't where Blackie expected to find him. Blackbeard slammed at the air with both fists, from a good stance that showed he knew a lot about boxing, but Dugan was just nacherally faster than an electric timer could catch. A cat's-paw was slow compared with him. He steps around and winds up behind Blackbeard, lifts him up, and heaves him back through the doorway again.

I kind of laughed and kind of groaned, and so did the whole crowd, because we all of us seen that Slope didn't know nothing about boxing. His idea of putting the other fellow out was to pick him up and sling him out of bounds. Only, there wasn't any bounds here, and Slope was too clean-hearted to rush in and take advantage of a man that was down. He just stood around and waited for Blackie to get up and mix again.

Well, it made me laugh, but it made me mad, too. I mean, you can't take and juggle a whole piano crate full of exploding Slovak through an entire evening. You just give out or the floor gives way under you!

Back came the Russian revolution with its eyes red and blood spouting out of its nose, that had bumped on the floor.

And Slope stood there, thoughtful, but not working out a solution of the problem. There were two parts to that problem. The first was what to do with Russia; the second was how to keep his pants up. Slope had a length of machine belting or something around his hips by way of a belt, and when he lifted Poland the second time that belt busted with a pop.

Now Slope lingered around, using one hand to hold up the trousers, and the other hand to stop the landslide.

We howled. We all howled, because we didn't see how the thing could be done.

But Slope stopped the next rush, all right. He just stepped between Blackbeard's driving fists and put the flat of his hand on Lithuania, and pushed Russia, staggering, back into the Pacific Ocean, if you know what the map of the world looks like.

Well, you can't keep a grizzly off with caresses, I guess. And Blackbeard came back. He was beginning to roar, and he was blowing the blood out of his beard in showers.

This time he landed a punch. It was a good, solid sock, and it whacked on the side of Slope's jaw. I kinder squinted. Then I opened my eyes to catch a sight of the big fellow as he sailed right through the air.

But he wasn't sailing. No, sir; he was just standing there, a little bit puzzled, still holding up his pants and brushing aside Russia's two sledge hammers with his one hand—just heading off the punches up in the air, the way that a cat bats a ball of cotton around above its head.

Well, you can't catch a whole shower of brickbats, and one of those punches slipped through again and banged Slope on the same side of the same jaw, a little nearer the point.

This time he sat down, and Blackbeard rushes in, yelling blue murder, to finish things off.

He oughtn't to 'a' done that, not considering how far west it was. And a little guy, with a rod of blue revolver in his hand, steps out and says: "Back up, beautiful. You ain't hittin' a gent that's down."

Russia backed up and stood still, waved his elbows, and roared some more. I didn't understand his language, but there was a lot of it. I guessed that he was telling Slope to stand up and get killed.

And Slope stood up, all right. Maybe you've seen people and nacherally get up on their feet, not touching the ground with either hand. People do things like that to show off in gymnasiums, but Slope done it nacheral and easy.

He stood there, and still he kept one hand for his pants

and the other in the air for a guard; just the flat of that second hand.

"Darn your pants! Fight in your B.V.D.'s!" yells a big cowpuncher that looked half crazy, he was so mad and excited.

"The trouble is that I haven't any," says Slope, and turns toward the puncher.

While the big fool's head was still turned, of course, Russia takes a run, a jump, and a half turn, and slams Slope right on the button again.

I thought that even India rubber would break in two then, but I give you my word that the fist of Russia bounced more than the head of Slope did. He didn't fall; he just sank slowly and sat on his heels.

It was a lot too much for me. I dived between two pairs of legs and dropped on my knees beside Slope, while the gent with the revolver starts counting to ten, keeping time with his gun.

I cupped my hands at my mouth and yelled: "You big stiff, hit him with your fist!"

"What?" says Slope, quiet and concerned, looking hard at me.

"Hit him with your fist!" I screamed.

"I don't want to hurt him," says Slope.

The whole crowd heard him say that. And it knocked the spots out of everybody; they just stood flabbergasted.

But I shrieked into the feller's ear:

"Do what I tell you, bozo!"

"Oh, all right, then," said Slope with a sigh, and he stood up.

He did, too. It wasn't much of a punch. It only traveled half a foot, maybe, but it knocked the head of Russia against the small of Russia's back. He turned a fast somersault and tried to balance himself on his face, failed, and rolled over with a flop.

They got two trucks and about ten men to freight that half ton of jelly out of the way of the trains.

CHAPTER 2

Now that the fight was ended, I watched to see Slope stand around and receive a lot of admiration, but he didn't do that. He just picked up the spoiled rags that had been his coat and shirt, and dragged them onto his shoulder, then slipped away into the darkness.

That impressed me a whole lot. I've tried to be modest, but I can't manage it. Every time that I do something that calls for extra attention, I've gotta stand around and wait, and if it don't come my way, I'm mighty sore. But Slope, he just faded away into the night while the fellows were still flocking around to congratulate him and offer him drinks. They wanted to find out his name, too.

I went after Slope. When he turned into the lunch counter, I stood in the doorway and sized things up. Just then I was flush. I mean, a week or so before, I'd sneaked two nice new bicycles out of the stand they were in and I rode one and steered the other to the next town. There I sold 'em both and raked in twenty-nine dollars in hard cash. I was still flush, but there was only one way into or out of that eating room, and I hate to get in that sort of a pocket. I was still peeling my eye for a railroad cop that might come into the lunch counter, or an elbow that might've shadowed me for the stealing.

But I couldn't see nothing. Down in the smoke cloud that kept boiling up around the big, black face of the stove, where hamburgers and such things were frying, I saw a couple of stiffs drinking coffee. That was about all there were in the dump.

Only Slope was sitting at the counter.

He pulled a nickel out of his pocket and spoke to the

waiter: "Do you mind telling me what I can buy, and how much, for five cents?"

The waiter, he picked up a cleaver—just in case. But when he seen the dull, polite eye of Slope and the nickel in his hand, he says: "Sure, brother! You can buy a whole loaf of stale bread and a glass of water for that nickel, if it's honest."

"Thank you very much," says Slope.

The waiter was a tough bird, and he gave Slope another look, but when he made out that the dummy was in earnest, he fishes out the loaf and he planks a dripping glass of water on the counter.

Slope thanks him again and takes a sip of that water like it was wine, half closing his eyes on it, if you know what I mean. Then he breaks off a wad of that bread and feeds it into his face, and my jaws, they fair ached to see him work on it. He was patient. He didn't ask for nothing. He just took the socks as they came.

Says the waiter with a snarl: "There's more water behind this, brother, if you want it. There's a whole barrelful."

"You're very kind," says Slope, and douses that glass of water down his throat in one wallop.

The waiter gives him a long, hard look. Then he fetches up a quart dipperful from the barrel and puts the dipper in front of Slope. Slope lays his lips on that water and pours it down in eight seconds flat.

"Delicious, really," says Slope, and smiles like a baby at the waiter.

That hash slinger gives him another look and plants another dipperful in front of Slope.

"When did you drink last?" says he.

"Yesterday evening," says Slope, "I found a spring. But the water was very alkaline. I could only drink a little of it."

"Holy smoke!" says the waiter.

Then he busts out: "Where was you yesterday evening?"

"Between here and a town named Coleman. Do you know the place?" says Slope.

"A hell hole!" says the waiter. "How long was you on the way?"

"Three days," says Slope.

"You had a fast hoss, brother," says the waiter with doubt in his eyes.

"No," smiled Slope, beginning on the bread again, and acting like it was tenderloin steak. "I didn't have a horse."

"Rode the rods, eh?"

"I walked," says Slope.

"Brother," says the waiter, resting his knuckles on the edge of the counter, "that's two hundred and forty miles of anybody's feet."

"It was quite a long walk," says Slope. "It just about wore out my shoes."

The waiter said nothing. He started to swab up behind the counter, and after a minute he growls: "Well, I'm darned!"

I was digesting the same sort of ideas. Two hundred and forty miles, and likely on one drink of water!

"Look," says the waiter, "they's two houses spotted along the last hundred miles. Didn't you see 'em?"

"Oh, yes," says Slope.

"Then why the devil didn't you ask for water, will you tell me?"

Slope got red to the eyebrows and above 'em. And he says: "I couldn't very well do that. If I asked for water. I might have been offered something more, you see."

"What? A slam in the eye?" says the waiter. "Oh, I see what you mean," he goes on, and gapes at Slope like a fish out of water.

I was gaping, too, as I came into the joint.

The waiter saw me and shook his head at me.

"It's got everything stopped," says he.

"It sure has," says I.

Slope sees me and smiles at me.

"I'm glad to see you again," says he.

"That goes two ways," says I.

"Two ways?" says he, without a flash in that dull eye of his.

"It's an even split," says I.

"Ah, yes," says he, blanker than ever.

I gave a look at the waiter, and the waiter gave a look at me. Then I went back to the cook. "Lemme have a look at a chunk of beef in your cooler," says I.

He batted a few tons of smoke out of the way and looked through the hole at me.

"You're a fresh kid," he told me. "Get out of here before you're kicked out."

"I'm paying my way," said I, jingling the coins in my pocket. "You ashamed to show me that you only got dog meat in your cooler?"

He was a big, tattooed bloke, looking like a sailor, and he reached over the counter before I knew what he was about, and dragged me by the neck to the far side of it, shoved me down a short hall, and opened the door of the cooler. It was a little room, with the sound of water dripping all around it.

"Does that look like dog meat?" says he.

There was about half a steer in there. It looked right, and it smelled right.

"Brother," says I, "carve off two slabs of that tender-loin about a foot thick and get it onto the stove; serve up ten pounds of french-fried potatoes and any other little fixings that you got around. Boil up a gallon or two of coffee. I'm gonna eat."

He gave me a look, fingering my neck like he wanted to twist it. So I remarked, with a hook of my thumb over my shoulder: "I got a friend out there at the counter."

"The bum that walks a thousand miles a day?" asks he with a grin.

"I just been seeing him chew up a ton of corrugated Russian iron over at the station," said I.

"Did he slam that Polack over there?" says the cook, letting go of me.

"He threw that freight car around for a while," I answered, "then he poked him just once, and Blackie, he dissolved like sugar in coffee."

The cook laughed. "That big ham has been looking for trouble," said he, "but I thought it would take a few

15

sticks of dynamite to break him up to pick-and-shovel size. I'm gonna fix a couple of steaks that'd crowd the jaws of a grizzly bear. Go on out of here and spread the word to bread and water out there."

I went out and took a seat on the left flank of Slope, where I could see the button that Russia had slammed three times with all his might. But all I could see was a little pale-purple patch, with hardly no lump at all rising.

I looked real careful, but I made sure that I was right. India rubber, that was what he was made of, and iron inside the padding.

"Friend of yours, Red?" says the waiter to me.

"Yeah," says I.

Slope already had half of that dry loaf down his throat, and he turns and smiles at me, not pretty, but pleasant.

"Certainly," says he, when he can speak again.

"And what's your moniker?" I asked.

"Moniker?" repeats Slope.

I looked at his lifted eyebrows and the dull eyes under them. "Yeah," said I, "what's your tag, handle—name, if that's the word you're waiting for?"

"Oh, my name?" said the dumbbell. "It is really Edward Dugan, but since you seem to use nicknames a great deal here in the west, I suppose I should say that I was recently called Slope."

"You were?"

"Yes."

"How come?" said I.

"By a man who passed me on the train the first day out from town; the second day I passed him, and it was then that he referred to me as Slope. I don't know why."

I looked at the waiter, and the waiter looked at me.

"Maybe he thought that you were walking pretty fast?" said the hash slinger.

"Could that be it?" says Slope. "Ah, well, perhaps."

"Ah, yes, I think so," said I.

The waiter grinned, but Slope didn't get me at all.

Just then the cook walks out of his own cloud of smoke and brings along a pair of platters loaded to the top deck. I never seen such a pair of steaks; there was an ox in each platter, you might say.

Slope looked at him with a puzzled frown.

"It's all right, chief," said I. "It's on me, that one."

"On you?" said Slope.

"I'm paying," said I.

Confound it, I forgot about his fool pride.

He got as red as a beet again.

"Thank you very much," said he. "I really couldn't eat it. The bread is quite enough for me."

I got into a sweat. I looked at that idiot of a waiter, but he couldn't help me out.

Then I had an idea.

I said: "Look here, Slope. Do me a favor. The crazy cook down there, he made a mistake. He thought I ordered two steaks instead of one. If I don't pay for these two steaks the boss will fire that cook. You wouldn't wanta be the cause of a man's losing his job, would you? You see that I can't eat more'n half of one of these slabs, don't you?"

He looked at me, and then he looked at the steak. He bit his lip and then stared at me again, with a plea for honesty in his eye.

"Is it really so?" said he.

"Sure," said I. "I'm only thinking about that blockhead of a cook. He don't know very much, but I don't want him to lose his job."

The cook heard every word, and I thought that he'd throw a pan at me. But he held himself in, because Slope had been persuaded and was starting a frontal attack on that chunk of beef.

CHAPTER 3

I've seen a lot of hungry men eat and some that prided themselves on the poundage that they could get around. But I never seen none that could hold a candle to Slope.

He walked right through that steak of his, and I carved off half of mine and passed it onto his plate while his eyes were hidden by his coffee cup. And he didn't notice any difference. He went right on, drank coffee, ate meat, and stoked up with potatoes. Then all but one thin wedge of an apple pie went down that throat of his.

When the thing was over, I asked for the bill, and I found that it was only twenty-five cents.

I didn't dare to make a fuss in front of Slope, but I went down the counter and said to the cook: "What's the main idea? I can pay for those steers you've just cooked for us."

"Shut up," says the cook. "You can't pay for nothin.' I would've bought tickets to see that show."

"The boss'll kick you out on your red face," says I.

"You wall-eyed little lump of poison," says the cook, "I'm the boss my own self. I own this joint."

So I paid him twenty-five cents and tipped the waiter another twenty-five cents, but he chucked the quarter after me, and I had to catch it out of the air.

That's the way in the West, if you know how to take people. The latch is left outside the wallet, and you can help yourself most of the time.

I stepped out on the street with Mr. Edward Dugan.

"Good night," says he, "and thank you for the cook's mistake. I've rarely enjoyed a meal so much."

"You ain't been overworking a knife and fork lately, I guess," I says.

"Eating, do you mean?" said he.

I almost laughed in his face. "Yes, that's the general idea," said I.

"No," he admitted. "Not for the last three days."

"Nothing—for three days?" I asked.

"Nothing," he said. "Good night again, Red. A very choice bit of fortune for me that I happened to meet you. I should thank you, too, for the advice you gave me earlier in the evening. But I hope that the other man was not hurt."

"He was only kind of generally dislocated all over," said I. "I hope that they have to put him in a plaster cast from his head to his toes."

I looked at Slope and tried to swallow the idea of him, but I couldn't. A man that goes for three days with one drink of water and then ties five hundred pounds of Sandow in knots—well, what are you to think about that?

I saw the champion heavyweight fighter of the world standing there alongside of me—I seen him in a kind of electric light of glory; and me not able to say no word to him.

He held out his hand. I took hold of it and didn't let go.

"Where you bound, Slope?" said I.

"Yonder," said he.

"Meaning where? One of them stars?"

He smiled in his childlike way.

"I'm walking through that pass between the two big mountains," said he.

That was about eighty miles off—just a step for him!

"You don't stop to sleep?" I asked.

"Oh, yes," answers he. "I stop and curl up somewhere. The nights are very warm at this time of year."

"Look here," said I, "why don't you come up to my room in the hotel and bunk there?"

"Sleep there?" said he. "I couldn't pay my half of the expense, and I really couldn't dream of—"

19

"The way of it is this," said I; "my partner ain't in town just now. And there's his bed not working at all. Besides, I'm mighty lonely."

"Oh?" said he, biting his lip and trying to think, but not getting very far along the trail with his ideas.

"Yes," says I. "I'm afraid of the dark, in fact."

I waited for him to laugh, but he didn't.

"I remember," said he, "that my brother was troubled that way when he was about your age. Of course, if that's the way of it, I'll be very glad to go along. The very thought of a real bed, in fact—"

He did laugh, in a foolish, apologetic way, this time, and so I walked up the street with him to the hotel.

I didn't even know that there was a hotel, but pretty soon I seen the sign around a turn in the street, and I says to Slope at the door: "Wait here a minute and look at that sign there, over the blacksmith's shop across the street. I'll tell you a story about that."

I went inside and up to the desk, where I asked the clerk for a room with two beds.

"For who?" asks he.

"For a friend and me," says I.

"What kind of a room?" he again asks.

"A bedroom, you ham!" says I, a little peeved by the way he looked over my clothes.

He leaned across the counter, but I back-stepped too fast for him.

"I got a mind—" he began.

"How much is the room?" says I.

"Only a dollar and seventy-five cents," says he.

That was a pretty fairish price in those days. But I slid the money over the counter, scrawled William Vance in the ledger, and then went out and found Slope standing obediently just where I had left him.

A kind of pity came over me as I looked up at his handsome face, his thick shoulders, his dull, patient eyes. I wanted to take care of him somehow. I dunno how to put it. My heart kind of ached for him.

"I've been studying the sign, Red," said he.

"Well," said I, "tomorrow, when it's light, if you look

at that sign, you'll see a half inch hole bored right through the middle of one of the letters, the top half of the letter B. That bullet was fired a whole block away, from the hip, out of a Colt revolver, and there was a five-hundred-dollar bet won on it!"

"Well, well!" says he. "How extraordinary. I must note that down in my diary."

He swallowed that stuff of mine without any trouble at all.

"You keep a diary, eh?" I asked, as we turned into the lobby.

"Yes," said he, "so that I can have everything up to date to tell mother and father in my letters home."

He went up to register, me beside him; while that fool of a clerk sneered at the rags of big Slope, I wondered what the Dugan folks must be thinking about this fellow who walked two hundred and fifty miles in three days on one drink of water. What a pile there must be in his letters home!

Well, I got up to the room with Slope, and it was a good enough place, with two beds, a washstand, and such things.

Slope undressed and gives himself a sponge bath and a scrub that pretty near took the skin off his body. Then he gets himself dried off, sits down, and says that he must make his entries for the day.

So he squats cross-legged in his bed, and I crawl in mine and look him over. He frowns, puts his head on one side, and spells out the words he writes down, one by one, moving his lips like a kid studying his lessons.

Now and then, while he thinks, he stares blankly across at me, and once he actually sees me through the mist of his thoughts, and he says:

"Delightfully comfortable, Red, don't you think?"

"Yeah, I think," said I.

He went on pushing his pencil over the paper of his notebook, and then I saw his head beginning to nod. Pretty soon he slumped quietly over and went to sleep.

I got up to put out the light, but first I looked over his shoulder to see the account of the terrible march across the desert and the fight at the station. This is what I read:

Arrived in the town. Found the rabbits extremely tame along the way. One hopped some distance, keeping just ahead of me. How did they know that I carried no gun?

Accident to coat in station. The tear can be sewed up.

Met William Vance, and heard extraordinary dialect of the country.

Alert blue eyes. Red hair, sticking up at the crown. Brisk but friendly manner. Delightful—

There he had stopped writing.

Where was the desert? Where was the fight? Where was the starvation?

CHAPTER 4

Before I went to bed I looked at Slope's shoes. They were worn to shreds. And he couldn't go barefooted. I wondered how I could get him into decent shoes that would fit him and went to sleep on that problem.

I dreamed about a fight for the heavyweight championship of the world, and my man was Slope Dugan. I was in the newspapers as the boy manager, and I wore a diamond stickpin with a rock in it as big as your thumb nail. I stood close to Slope's corner, and opposite him was "Demon" somebody or other—I couldn't get the last name in my dream. I stood close to big Slope before the gong, and I said: "Go out there and let the big stiff sock you a couple of times!"

"Sock?" says Slope, blinking.

"Hit!" said I, stamping with impatience. "Go out there and let him hit you a couple of times, and it'll break his dirty heart when he sees that he can't put a dent in you. Then go in weaving, like I taught you to do, and let his punches glance off that cast-steel dome of yours. Get in close, and then you'll tear him apart!"

That's what I said in the dream, and it came out that way. About two minutes later the Demon sailed over the ropes and draped himself over a silk hat and a mean reporter, and there was Slope standing in the middle of the ring with his hands full of nothing but the championship of the world and not knowing what to do with it.

Pretty soon I made up my mind that while I was managing the world's champion I'd salt away some dough, go back to school, and make something out of myself. Just about the time I hit those good resolutions I woke up, with the pink morning light glimmering outside of the window, and I looked across and saw that old Slope still lay in a heap just where he had sunk, writing his diary. He couldn't budge.

I judged that he would be out for about a couple of hours, and so I dressed, hopped downstairs, and found a Negro cleaning up the lobby.

I asked him where there was a secondhand shop for clothes, something that might be open at this time of day. He said nothing was open, but that Ben Sill's second-hand store was right down the street, that Ben slept in the second story, and that he would get up at midnight to bargain about the sale of a paper of pins.

I found the place, all right. When I banged on the door, I found Ben Sill already up.

I showed him one of Slope's shoes. He said that he could match it, and he did.

He had about a hundred pairs of shoes and boots in rows along some shelves, and it beat me to see how little worn all of those shoes were. I never knew where secondhand shoes come from. Nobody ever gives away his shoes or sells them, but somehow or other there's secondhand shoes to be had!

I got a good strong pair, with hobnails sunk in the heels, and soles about half an inch thick, because the way that foot calvary slid across the country, he had to have something that would stand the rub.

Then I went back. The sun was just up, and when I stepped into the room I was carrying the shoes, and big Slope was sitting up in bed, stretching his arms.

What an arm he had! It was a cross between a cat's forearm and a walking beam!

I busted in in a rush, and yelled out: "Hey, Slope! Look what they've done!"

I showed him the shoes.

"Well, well?" says he, a little startled.

"They've gone and mixed up your shoes with some of another gent that left on the early train; and he's gone off with yours in his bag, I guess. You better kill that fool of a porter for mixin' 'em up!"

"That's too bad," says Slope. "My shoes, you know, were not in very good condition. We'll have to find out the name of the other man and—"

"You can't find out his name," said I. "He's some thug that give a faked name. When the proprietor found out about it, he asked him to move on, so he left this morning early."

"That complicates things!" says Slope.

"Yeah, it knots 'em all up," said I.

"I don't know what can be done about it," says Slope. "We'll have to leave the shoes here for him to claim when he returns."

"He'll never return," says I, thinking about the two dollars and fourteen cents that I had paid for those shoes. "And you can't go barefooted. The porter'll be fired if you walk out in your socks, and the proprietor begins to ask questions."

Slope shook his head.

"I seem to be thoroughly entangled," says he.

"You are," said I. "There's only one thing to do."

"What is that?" says he.

"Put those shoes on and wear them, and when you're flush, one of these days, give away a good pair of shoes to somebody that needs 'em."

He thought a moment, and then his face brightened.

"That's a very far sighted idea, Red," said he. "Or should I call you William?"

"Why William?" said I.

"That's your name in the hotel register," said he.

I choked a little. "Oh," said I, "I've been called Red so long that I wouldn't know how to answer to William."

"At any rate," says he, "I don't see what I can do except to follow your advice."

"Hurry up," says I. "We're pretty nearly late for breakfast, and I'll bet you've got an appetite."

"I have," he nodded, and then his smile went out.

"Look here. The fact is, I'd like to have breakfast with you, Red," says he, "but you've already done far too much for me, and I cannot really accept——"

"Aw," said I, "what are you acceptin'? This here is American plan, this here hotel. If you don't eat one of the breakfasts that're lyin' around loose down there in the kitchen, it'll just be money throwed away. Me and my friend, we're all paid up in advance."

He rubbed his chin and thought this over. Finally, in a troubled way, he admitted that it seemed all right. He said that he was always walking into good fortune in my company, and then he got up, shaved, washed very careful, and dressed. You could see, with half an eye, that baths meant a lot to him.

Speakin' personal, a good swim is a handy thing, but I never took much to soap and a scrubbing brush. I guess my skin is delicate.

So we slid down into the dining room, and I got the Negro waiter cornered and told him to fry half a dozen eggs apiece for us, and slice up about two sides of bacon. I wanted Slope to start his campaign with something in his locker to go on.

Slope looked a little surprised when he saw that breakfast begin to flock onto the table, but I spoke up and said: "This here hotel caters to the miners and the lumberjacks. They don't eat very good up there in the mountains, and when they come down here they expect to lay into the grub."

"That fellow in the corner," says Slope, with his eyes wide, "seems to be eating only two eggs."

"Sure," said I. They got some cheap skates in here that get a room and grub at cut rates. They only get one third of everything."

Pretty soon Slope said: 'I don't wish to pry into your affairs, Red, but may I ask you about your friend who lives here in the hotel with you?"

"He's by name of Benderberg," said I. "Julius P. Benderberg, of Akron, Ohio."

"Yes?" said Slope, smiling with interest.

'Yeah," said I. "His pa was German, and his mother was French, and he used to be called Bunderberg, sounding like oo in fool. But he found a lotta people that wouldn't pronounce him right, so he changed the way he spelled the name, you see."

He waited for a moment, thinking this over. Then he nodded.

"I dare say he's a rancher, or some such thing, Red?" says he with a diffident air.

"Nope," said I. "Mining is his long suit. Mining and lumbering and such."

"Ah, a very wealthy man," suggested Slope.

"Wealthy?" said I. "I've seen him light a cigar off a twenty-dollar bill!"

"Ah, what waste!" says Slope, amazed.

"Yeah. He was plastered that day," said I.

"Plastered?" queried Slope.

"Tight, all wet, soggy, on the slide," said I.

"Tight—wet—soggy," murmured Slope.

"Drunk," said I.

"Ah, yes, drunk," said Slope.

"Ever tip 'em over yourself?" said I.

"Tip them over?" says Slope, polite but baffled.

"Yes. Ever get swamped now and then on Saturday night? Ever get plastered yourself—drunk I mean to say?"

"Never, I believe," said Slope. "Once I was a little dizzy, and yet I don't think that it was—"

"No, it wasn't," said I. "It wasn't even near the real

thing. Gee, you been around a lot of corners and never seen what was on the far side!"

"I don't quite understand that," says Slope.

"Maybe you don't," said I, "but say, leave Benderberg rest and tell me something about yourself, old-timer. Why are you walking, and where from, and where to?"

He sorted out the questions.

"I left Boston two months ago," said he.

"What train? Through Chicago, eh?"

"No, on foot."

"All the way on foot?"

"Oh, yes."

I leaned back in my chair and just looked at him. I saw that he had the world beat and stopped ten ways from Sunday.

CHAPTER 5

What would you do with a man that walks across these United States the way that you or me would walk across the street? You couldn't do nothing but hold on and hope that the dream would come true. So I asked him: "Slope, what started you?"

"Ah, that makes a story," says he.

"Go on and tell me," says I.

"It begins, oddly enough," said he, "with a mine."

"Sure," I answered. "That's where a lot of stories begin, and end, too."

"My father," said Slope, "when he retired from the practice of law, invested a large share of his earnings in mining stocks promoted by a certain Henry Christian."

I didn't get the name all at once, though it rang a bell

somewhere in the back of my mind. Then I popped out: "Hold on! You mean Bonanza Chris, or I'm a liar!"

"Bonanza Chris?" said he, batting his dull eyes at me.

"Oh, go on, go on," said I. "That doesn't make any difference. Your old man bought a lot of mining stocks, and after a while it was a question of where are the mines?"

"As a matter of fact," said he, "the mines seemed to peter out. All of them were quite worthless. And that was extraordinary bad luck."

"If you call it luck," said I, "it's the kind that Bonanza Chris deals every time."

"Really?" said the dumbbell.

"Yes, really," said I. "Go on."

"There was only one mine that was worth anything. My father had bought quite a lot of stock in it. It was the Christabel."

"Yeah," said I, "Bonanza generally hooks part of his own name into everything. That sounds like one of his beauties, all right."

"There seemed to be some value attached to the shares and father bought in the Christabel."

"Go on!" said I. "What makes you think that?"

"Why, we received a letter from Mr. Christian saying that he regretted our bad fortune in the other mining ventures father had invested in, and, in one case, at least, he would like to help us out. He said that he was re-organizing his company, and wished to try to develop the Christabel again. He would pay us fifteen hundred dollars for our shares in the Christabel mine, though as yet it had not shown any real promise."

"Did Mr. Christian offer you hard cash for that, or more shares?" I asked.

"He offered twice that much in other shares in his ventures. But we thought that the fifteen hundred in cash would be more worth while," says the dummy.

"Yeah, you bet it's more worth while," said I. "Hold on. How much did your old man sock into the Christian companies?"

"Sock?" says Slope.

"Yeah. How much did he invest?" says I.

"About two hundred and fifty thousand dollars," said Slope.

That was a sock for me. But, then, the farther off "Bonanza" Chris found a sucker, the deeper he hooked him, as a matter of fact.

"That's a tidy lot of cash," said I.

"It was," said poor Slope, "and I had a particular interest in the sum, because, as it turned out, it would have belonged to me."

"Oh, would it?" said I.

"Yes. Some time after my father retired he called a family meeting and I came with my sister and brother. He pointed out to us that he had divided his estate fairly among us all, according to his stock holdings. He retained about half a million for myself and my stepmother. To my half brother and sister he apportioned two hundred and fifty thousand each; and to me he gave the same sum."

"Jiminy, Slope," said I, "you're rich, then!"

"So it would appear," says he, carefully. "And so it appeared to me, at the time. However, you will soon see that I was not quite as well off as you imagine. For he had assigned to me all of the mining stock that afterward turned out to be worthless."

The hair, it rose on my head. I got goose flesh all over.

"What bad luck I had! Don't you think so?" says Slope, shaking his honest head and smiling a little.

"Bad luck?" said I. "Yeah. It was bad luck, all right! Lemme ask you something, will you?"

"Of course," said he. "You show so much interest, Red, and you have led me into so many bits of luck, one after another, that it really is a pleasure to talk things over with you."

"Yeah?" said I. "Well, then, this stepmother of yours, what sort of a picture does she make?"

"Oh," says he, "she has a charming face."

"I'll bet that she's a charmer, and then some," I told him. "You mind telling me when she got hold of your father?"

"You mean, when he married her? No, I don't mind telling you. My mother died when I was born, and my poor father felt very helpless in dealing with a small infant. Naturally, being a business man rather than a family man, he looked about for help. And it was because I was such a problem to him that he married at once."

"I'll bet that his second wife was a help," said I.

"Naturally," says Red, "he could not have got along without her."

"How old are your half brother and sister?"

"Just a year and a half younger than I," says Slope.

"What made them fall out with you?" said I.

"Fall out?" said he.

"What made them so mean to you?" said I.

He looked at me with a frown and shook his head. "I'm sorry," said he, "that I've told you that, too. I didn't intend to go quite so deep. But, as a matter of fact, they have quick and alert minds, just like their mother. And they could hardly put up with me. Perhaps you may have noticed that I am not exactly alert?"

He looked at me with a sort of dull hope in his eye. I looked him back in the face.

"No," said I, "I never noticed anything like that, at all. I thought you were way above par."

It did me good to see the smile that came all over him at once. He shifted in the chair. He got a little red in the face.

"There appears to be a sort of sympathy between us," said he.

"You bet there is," said I.

"Perhaps you are not very quick about some things?" he suggested timidly. "Such as school work, I mean to say?"

"I was always a rummy in school," said I.

I didn't mind taking a whack from him, poor devil.

"Ah, well," said Slope, "so was I. I managed to do my work fairly well for the examinations, but during the term I was almost always a week or two behind the rest of the class. I used to irritate the teachers a great deal, and therefore, it's not strange that I should have upset my stepmother, who had to see me every day at home, except when she sent me away to boarding school."

"She sent you away quite a lot, didn't she?" said I.

"As a matter of fact," said he, "I was generally away."

He nodded, as innocent as a bird. He couldn't put two and two together any way you looked at it.

"Well," said I, "it's too bad that she hated you so much."

"Oh, not hate, not hate!" he broke in. "I never wish to give that impression of her. As a matter of fact, she actually wept when I left home on this trip. She told me how bitterly she felt because the money that was to come to me was all lost, or all except the fifteen hundred dollars."

"Yeah, I'll bet it hurt her a terrible lot," said I.

"It did," said he. "She is a woman with a good heart. I was surprised by her depth of feeling."

"Did she know that you were coming West?" said I.

"Oh, yes. Of course."

"Was she so sorry for you that she offered to buy you a railroad ticket?" said I.

"As a matter of fact," said he, "it didn't occur to her. And I did not ask. Otherwise, of course, she would have given it at once!"

"Yeah, of course," said I. "Your half-brother, too. He forgot to offer anything?"

"Ronald," said the dummy, "mentioned the matter when he said goodby to me. He was very much moved, too. I had hardly thought that he was so fond of me. But it happened that all of his money was tied up, and his checking account, as a matter of fact, was already overdrawn."

"I'll bet it was," said I.

"I've had the same thing happen many times to me," says Slope. I give a sigh.

There ain't any words to say what I wanted to say.

"And what started you West, really?" said I.

"Well," says Slope, "the proper thing for a business man to do is to look after his estate personally, don't you think?"

"Yeah. I guess so."

"And the only estate that I had was the stock in the Christabel. So I left home and came to the Christabel. Tomorrow I shall be there."

He leaned back in his chair, with his fourth cup of coffee inside of him and the world's record breakfast. He smiled at me, pleased as a pup with the logic and the beautiful clearness with which he had worked out his position.

And me? Well, I was thinking about him going up against the most famous crook on the whole range—Bonanza Chris! It made me kind of dizzy. I didn't know what to say; I didn't know what to think.

"One thing is clear," said I at last, "Bonanza Chris has found something in the Christabel, or he never would've offered spot cash for your interest. Got a controlling interest in that hole in the ground?"

"Yes," says the dummy.

"Then it's probably worth walking across the continent to get to it," said I. "But when you buck up agin' Bonanza —well, you'll find him quite a stack."

"Stack?" says Slope.

I saw it was no use, and then I got another idea.

"Benderberg ain't coming back for several days," said I. "If you don't mind, I'm gunna walk along with you to the Christabel."

"You?" he cried, astonished.

"Yeah. I need some exercise," said I.

"True," says he, his face lighting up. "Walking is a splendid exercise. And it will be delightful to have company along the way, Red!"

CHAPTER 6

It was splendid exercise, all right. We went to Potts Valley, near where the Christabel was supposed to be, in two days. And it was a hundred miles.

I mean, mountain miles. Slope loved mountains. He walked faster uphill than he did down. When he got started at a real cliff he turned himself into a mountain goat and jumped from rock to rock.

I was numb from the hips down every day, an hour after the start. I was running a lot of the time. At that, he cut down his pace a good deal; by half, maybe. And so we managed to get along. I never walked like that before, even with the cops after me. And I've never walked like that since. I don't mean to, either. I can stand on the record that I made to Potts Valley.

It wasn't so bad either, when we got on top of things. The pines was big, there in the middle of the pass, and with the smell of them in the lungs, the cleanest in the world, I made me a smoke and looked down into the valley.

You know what a place looks like after a mining rush —I mean, the sides ripped out of the hills here and there, and the old bones of the mountains showing through where the green skin had been. Since old Tom Potts hit gold a few years back, there had been plenty of scratching around by prospectors, and plenty of real digging, too. Pottsville itself was in the middle of things, stretched out long and narrow, and looking somewhat like a real town at this distance. Two ways from it went to the wagon roads, and through that clear mountain air I could see the long freighting teams as they worked down the windings and the grades of the roads. You could see the big covered wagons, too, and the thin dust clouds behind them. You could almost see them sway, almost hear the creaking of the wheels on the axles, and the cussing of the mule skinners as they rode along.

"That ain't so bad," says I, sitting down in a lap that the root of a tree made, putting its knees out of the ground.

"Bad?" says Slope slowly, and he rubs his hand across his forehead. "Ah, no, Red! I think that I should like to pass on into such a scene, all the days of my life, and go deeper and deeper into it—new mountains and greater ones, new heights and loftier ones. Perhaps it's a foolish thing to say, Red, but it seems to me almost as though one's soul is washed cleaner in the blue of these mountains. Life is no longer hot and grimy, Red, with snow like that to see. Yes, and to touch, if you please!"

I batted my eyes a couple of times, hearing him run on like this. It was a new chapter in him, to my eye. I begun to guess that there was more to the book than just the cover and the title. And I was right in the guess. I says to myself maybe he wasn't so dumb, but different.

"Would you walk, I mean to say," says I, "to get next to that picture that you're talking about?"

"Walk?" says he. "Yes, of course."

"Then you walk alone," says I. "I've done enough walking the last couple of days to suit me. I'll put my mountain scenery in lavender from now on, and keep it handy. I'm gonna take up the reading of books of description. Doggone me, if there ain't something in it, after all!"

He looked helplessly at me.

"I don't quite follow you, Red," said he gently. "Except that you're very tired. I'm afraid that I've been extremely thoughtless, dragging you along as I've done. I forgot that your legs are not as long as mine."

"It ain't a matter of legs," said I. "An antelope, it ain't got long legs, and neither has a mountain goat. But they travel, you bet."

"Yes, that's true," said he, not seeing that there was

anything personal in what I said. "Even a fast horse, I've noticed, seems often to be built low—closer to the ground than others. But we'll rest here, Red, just as long as you like. And you can set the pace from now on."

Well, I didn't rest long. After all, it was downhill all the way, and we coasted into Pottsville, as you might say, and got to a hotel along about dusk.

The dummy says goodby to me at the door of the hotel as I turned in. He'd see me in the morning, he said.

I was stumped. I was too tired to have any lies handy. And I didn't dare offer him any charity. Darn his proud heart!

Then I said: "Look here, Slope. You stay here with me, will you? And you can pay me back. You can whittle the margin off of one of your shares of stock and pay me back."

He thought it over, but it took some more persuading. I managed to show him, now that he was so near his own property, even a bank would give him a loan, and it was all right to accept the money he would need.

So he found out what the price would be and he sat down, and he wrote out a note, saying that he, Edward Dugan, on such and such a day, had received three dollars and twenty-five cents from—

"You haven't told me your real name, Red?" said he.

I looked at the smile on his face, the kindness and the trust in his eyes. I had decided a long time ago that I would keep my real name hid, but now I got it out of my pocket, unwrapped it, and showed it to the air for a minute.

"My real name is Charles Lafarge," said I.

I half closed my eyes. I could see in a long line the places where Charles Lafarge was wanted, and the faces of some of them that wanted him. But here I'd gone and spit out the truth.

Slope thanked me.

"I know," said he, "that you wish to use a nom de guerre, so to speak. Of course, the knowledge of the truth is private, between us."

That was enough for me. I knew, somehow, that dyna-

35

mite and picks and shovels could never dig that name out of Slope. He was that kind. Better than a tool-proof bank safe.

Anyway, I got my note, duly signed, and it said that in thirty days from date, without grace, Edward Dugan would pay me back that three dollars and a quarter.

I still got that note, signature and all. I got it under glass, so the rain can't spoil it.

I get kind of dim in the head, remembering my way through dinner that night, and getting to bed afterward. I remember something about a couple of blokes in the dining room uncorking two bottles of Colt's champagne. After the popping was over, things went right on as usual, with a Chinaman sopping up some of the red that had spilled on the floor.

But I was too sleepy to pay much attention even to a killing, and when the town woke up right after dark and begun to whoop and howl, it didn't matter much.

Matter of fact, I got upstairs over the bend of Slope's arm. He peeled me and shoved me into bed. The next thing that I knew, clear and real, there was a knocking at the door, Slope was opening it, and I sat up in the pink of the early morning light.

The door opened, and I slid half way back under the covers again. The bloke looked like a bull, and he was.

"Are you Edward Dugan?" says he.

"Yes, I am," says Slope.

"I wancha, brother," says the bull.

"Do you?" says Slope, politely surprised.

"I been looking out for you," says the bull. "I'm Detective Frank M. Sidney. Retained for a gent that wants you as soon as you come to town."

"Well, well," says Slope, in the calmest way that you please. "Am I under arrest?"

It surprised me. I knew that he had plenty of nerve, all right. But it give me the shakes even to think about a cop, let alone see one face to face. It made stripes and bars dance in front of my face.

"You ain't under arrest, brother; not yet," says the

bull. "But there's a gent that wants to see you, and wants to see you bad. So come along."

"I am here with a friend," replied Slope.

He waves a hand toward me and goes on:

"Perhaps the gentleman will come to call on us here?"

The bull gives me a squint, with another at the tear in Slope's coat. There was almost more tear than coat, matter of fact. Then he says: "This here bloke that I'm talking about, he wears the same hind name that you've got. He's Ronald Dugan, but he's a swell. You better go see him in his own joint."

"Ronald!" says Slope with a happy smile.

He turns to me.

"Think of that, Red! Ronald is here!"

I sat right up and nodded.

"Then there's something in the air," said I. "All right, Buddy," I went on to the bull. "We'll look up young Dugan after breakfast. You tell him that."

"Yes, we'll see him after breakfast," says Slope.

The bull gives an eye to me. "Do I know you, kid?" said he.

"No," said I. "You ain't had that much luck."

"Oughtn't I to know your mug?" says he.

"You ain't moved in circles that high," says I with a chill beginning in the pit of my stomach.

He took a step closer to me and looked me over again. Then he nodded. "I'll do some remembering," says he.

"Remember your way out while you're about it," says I.

He squinted his eyes and nodded again as he turned to leave.

"This other Dugan lives in the Imperial," says he over his shoulder as he slams the door behind him.

"There was something discourteous in the manner of that man," remarks Slope. "I can't exactly say what. His general air, perhaps. Wouldn't you say so, Red?"

I didn't say. I was thinking what a fool I had been to give that bull so much tongue. And I wondered how far and wide he could remember.

CHAPTER 7

We got breakfast inside of us, and then went over to the Imperial. I had a better look at Pottsville on the way.

It was some town, you take it from me. It had been built in a day, as the saying goes, and it looked as though the day had been Saturday, when the carpenters only work half time, and careless, at that. It was only throwed together. A mule could've kicked his way right through the heart of it. A bull could've charged through Pottsville and thought it was just a brush tangle.

It was mighty interesting, though. There were jewelry shops, shining bright, and, shouldering 'em, would be blacksmith hang-outs; then a tent, then a hotel made of tin cans and hope, and close by a lean-to with a miner cooking a meal on a shake-down of a stove, with a piece of canvas rolled up in front.

The crowd in the street was the kind of a crowd that wouldn't pay much attention to Slope's coat. There was everything from Injuns in blankets to gamblers in long-tailed coats. There were freight teams going up and down the street, with the mules nodding slow and earnest in their collars, and there were cow-punchers just in off the range to look things over and lose their money before they started home. There were prospectors just starting out to sight a fortune between the ears of a burro. There were bums and yeggs and crooks and honest men. There were sun-baked Southwesterners and tenderfeet with red, peeled noses, footsore cowboys, and workers of all kinds with tired hands.

Besides, there was excitement in the air. It was the feeling that something was about to bust wide open and show you the insides of things.

I was glad, in spite of the bull that had looked in on us, that I was in Pottsville. It was like being in on a big job that's kind of betwixt and between right and wrong, jail and a happy home, if you know what I mean.

Then we got to the Imperial. It was the best in Pottsville. It was three stories high, and it was the kind of a hotel that always had scaffolding up somewhere, painting or repairing, or a new wing being added. It had a big lobby with columns in it. The columns were built of wood, painted to look like marble.

It was a gay place. It looked expensive, and it was expensive, too. And the most expensive-looking thing about it was a young gent that got up out of a plush chair and came over with a smile to shake hands.

I looked at him pretty careful, because I guessed that this was dear Ronald, that had such a good heart.

He had a good suit of clothes, anyway. He was all in brown, and he had a blue tie to set off his blue eyes, with brown shoes on his slim feet. He looked as cool and easy and slick and silky—as a snake, say. His hair, it was parted so fine that you could see the broad white line of the part all the way to the back of his head, and his hair was dark with the gloss that had been used to make it lie down and be good. You couldn't imagine it saying no night or day. I remember that he had on a double-breasted coat, and you can always tell a real slick dresser by his double-breasted coat. The most of 'em, they look kind of like a right idea that has gone wrong, and they look like too much stomach and not enough chest, and they is always wrinkles here and there. But there wasn't no wrinkle in Mr. Ronald Dugan, that had the fine heart. No sir, he was smooth all over.

He was about the most beautiful man that I ever seen. I mean, beautiful. He had a dark skin, with bloom in his cheeks like nobody's business, and his eyes, they was big and soft and wonderful. When he smiled it was like turning on an electric light. I mean, his teeth was so many and so white.

I stood around and admired him. You could tell that he wanted to shake hands, because he put his out before he more'n got out of his chair, and he kept it out all the way across the room.

"My dear Ned! My dear Ned!" he keeps on saying as he comes over.

He turned on his smile, too. I never seen such a resting place for a punch as that smile of his.

Old Slope, he busts right up and grabs Ronald's hand; and Ronald, he cries out with a sort of a squeak.

"Ah, I've hurt you again!" says Slope very concerned.

Ronald bites his lip and tries the fingers of his smashed hand one by one, and his eyes turn into a glitter and a glare. But right away he switches on his electricity and smiles all over the place.

"It's so good to see you, Ronald," says Slope, "that I forgot about my grip."

"And it's so good to see you," says Ronald, "that I'd lose the hand and not mind a bit. Where have you been all this time, my dear fellow?"

"I've been walking across the country," says Slope. "I want you to meet a great friend of mine. Everyone calls him Red. So I'll introduce him by that name. It's a Western custom, it appears. Ronald, I want to present Red. Red, this is my brother, Ronald."

I went up and shook hands with him. After I finished, he slipped his fingers out of mine and took a look down to see whether I'd got them dirty, I guess. His smile, it sort of sickened out at the corners. I mean, it went out and left the wrinkles.

"Oh," says I, "I'm glad to meet Ned's favorite brother."

Ronald, the big-hearted, he seemed to get an idea out of that remark. It slid slow and sure into him, like a hatpin, say. And he pulled his eyes off the tear in Slope's coat, and he handed me a look that went in at the right temple and came out behind the left ear. However, I didn't drop. I just winked at him.

It was a mean thing to do, and it was a mighty foolish thing to do. There ain't any use in letting anybody see, right off the bat, that you despise 'em and see through 'em. It ain't Christian, for one thing; but, a lot more important than that, it ain't good policy. It's better to put a good face on everything. If you can't put a good face on something, be blind in one eye or wear dark glasses.

Anyway, something sort of passed between me and the warm-blooded Dugan in that second. After that we always felt just one way about each other, only more so as time went on.

Ronald gets his glance back on Slope finally, and he says: "I've been waiting out here for days and days, terribly worried, wondering what could have happened!"

"What happened was mostly to several pairs of shoes," says Slope, with an affectionate hand still on Ronald's shoulder. "I came along at a good, steady pace, but this is quite a broad country of ours, Ronald. It's a good many days across when one is on foot."

"True, true!" says Ronald hastily. "I'll never cease regretting that I was so short of funds at the time that—"

"Oh, my dear fellow; my dear Ronald," says Slope. "Don't speak of it again. Your kind will was more than money to me. I've thought of it many times since."

"Have you?" says Ronald, turning on his smile more than ever.

"Yes," says Slope, smiling right back, as honest and as stupid as ever I saw.

"And now," says Ronald, "I have some good news for you."

"Have you?" says jolly old Slope, brightening a lot.

"About your mining stock!" said Ronald brilliantly.

"Good!" says Slope.

"Yes, very good news indeed," says big-hearted Ronald. "You thought that it was only worth about a thousand or fifteen hundred dollars when you left home. Isn't that correct?"

"That's it," said Slope. "And now?"

"Well, old fellow, you've never been much of a business head, have you?" says Ronald affectionately.

"Not much of a head at anything, I'm afraid," says Slope. "But particularly not much of a head for business. What happened?"

"There was another letter from Mr. Christian after you left home, and I knew that you wouldn't mind if I opened it for you."

"Of course, I wouldn't mind," said Slope cheerfully.

41

I begun to prickle all over, and I cleared my throat loudly. Brother Ronald gave me a look that would've set fire to wet wood. He got back only about half his smile as he hurriedly went on to the dummy:

"The proposal was renewed," says he, "in that letter which I opened, so I threw myself into the breach in your absense."

"Good old Ronald!" says Slope, his eyes shining like a pair of candles.

"Well, I wanted to do what I could," says modest Ronald. "I wrote a careful letter, and opened up a correspondence very briskly with the result, finally, that I made Christian increase the offer very liberally."

"Good man!" says Slope.

"To what, do you think?" says Ronald.

"Perhaps double?" says Slope hopefully.

"To five—thousand—dollars!" said Ronald the beautiful.

Now, during the last part of this talk I was getting more and more cold in the pit of the stomach, because I began to guess that I would have to step in and do something. It was clear that Bonanza Chris wanted the Christabel bad. He was offering to raise his price. He had offered —well, enough to pay the dummy five thousand and to interest Brother Ronald. And if big-hearted Ronald wasn't getting a slice of the fat, I'd eat sawdust without wearing green glasses.

Ronald, the arranger, that's what he looked like to me. And now he was saying, while he patted the thick arm of Slope: "It's all arranged up to the last step. We have only to go over to the office of Mr. Christian, and there you sign your name—once! And five thousand dollars is yours!"

CHAPTER 8

Of course, I tagged along, but Brother Ronald was not pleased. "Mr. Christian is a very busy man," he ventured, "and we can't impose on him by bringing young persons along to waste his time." I wanted to bang Ronald on the beak. I saw Slope nod. He was always agreeing with everybody.

"It wouldn't be wasting his time," I put in. "I'm an old friend of his and he'll be glad to see me. He told me to drop in on him at his office any time I came this way."

I got Brother Ronald's eye all to myself for a second and I winked at him again.

"Why, Red, I'm surprised that you haven't told me this before," said Slope.

"I don't believe a word of it," declared big-hearted Ronald.

He emphasized and drawled his words, going up and down the scale, like a woman does when she's mad.

"You don't have to believe, Ronald," said I. "I was saving it as a surprise for Slope, in case he found it hard to crash the gate."

Ronald got kind of purple and says: "This little rascal has no manners. I am *Mr.* Dugan, Red."

"Your kind of mister stops on the other side of the Rockies, Ronald," I told him.

Ronald was near the exploding point, but Slope laughed a little.

"I dare say," explained the dummy, "that he means you are slightly overdressed for this part of the world. Red is an odd boy, but he has a great little heart in him, Ronald. Don't be annoyed. Let's get on together."

43

He drew his brother along with him, with Ronald lagging a bit, and me handing him the wink and the glad eye from behind. He wanted to eat me, but I was betting that I could give him a powerful case of indigestion.

We got along to the office of Bonanza Chris. It was a lucky time, too, because just as we pulled in under a row of windows painted: "Henry Christian, promoter, legal adviser, et cetera," out the door comes a pair of gents leading a woman between them. She was a range woman, good and brown and bony, and she was so mad, she was crying.

"You stay out, sister," says one of the bouncers. And he gives her a shove.

It was a wrong move, when there was a Slope around.

He took that rough by the scruff of the neck and slammed him against the wall so hard that he sat down right where he hit.

"You mustn't manhandle a lady," says Slope.

The other bouncer had out his rod, by this time, and Slope remarks to him: "Don't point that thing at me, please!"

Believe it or not, the thug sneaked his gat back inside of his clothes and faded through the doorway.

"I wish that you'd broken their necks for 'em," says the woman, "and the neck of Bonanza Chris right afterward. Oh, the ripe, prime fool I was to trust him. Lies, lies, lies! That's all he's made of! He's robbed me of every penny. And here I am, still making a fool of myself—yapping in the street like a mongrel pup! But I'll bring back them that can talk to the big fat-faced crook!"

And she went off down the street with a stride that meant business. I liked that woman. I liked her look, her stride and the way she doubled up her fists. I liked having her pop out of the place that way, too, because it was so handy for Slope. He rubbed his chin with his fist, a way that he had, and looked after her.

"She seems quite excited about Mr. Christian, Ronald," says he.

"Of course," says Ronald, "you understand that every client of a promoter expects to get rich overnight. They

44

lose their tempers if miracles aren't worked for them."

I got a good hearty laugh out of my system, so hearty that even Slope took notice.

"What's the matter, Red?" he asked.

"I was only laughing," said I, "to think of anybody trusting a four-flusher and yegg like that fellow Bonanza Chris. What money he's made has never got outside of his own wallet. He's taken scalps all over the range. He's famous. If he's offering you five thousand for your mine, it's worth five hundred thousand, most likely."

I'd put my guess on the table, and I wanted to see what happened to it.

Big-hearted Ronald saw to that hand, however. "It seems to me that Red has picked up a great deal of idle scandal," he observed. "We know, Ned, what happened to the rest of your mining stock. Now you have a chance to make a good lump sum through a sale. If Mr. Christian was dishonest, he would simply have swallowed this stock, along with the rest. He has explained everything to my satisfaction. A great many ventures he was backing fell through. Things like that will happen. Father's money—your share of it—was unluckily invested in the wrong places."

"Yes," says Slope, "that sounds very possible and plausible. And five thousand dollars, after all, is a great deal more than fifteen hundred. Isn't it?"

"Of course, it is," said Ronald. "When I think of the great fortunes that have been rolled up out of a much smaller beginning than five thousand dollars—"

He was working Slope through the door, by this time, and I saw that I would have to shut up for a while and see what happened. So we climbed the steps, and came to the offices of Bonanza Chris.

There was no trouble getting in. We walked through the door that wore the right label, and found Bonanza walking up and down with his thumbs in his vest pockets, whistling. He was a great big soft, fat, pink man. He looked like Turkish towels and bath salts. He smelled kind of sweet and soapy.

There was acres of his face, from the high brow to the

45

folds that hung down onto his red-and-yellow necktie, so that there was most usually a mist on the rock that he wore in his stick pin. All that acres of face was mowed clean. I took to wondering how he could've shaved into the smile wrinkles, and how he must haul and pull that big wad of pink putty around to get a safe shot with his razor.

He wore striped trousers and boots shined up so bright that they looked like a reflection in still water. He had on a checkered vest, with a gold cable strung across his stomach in a double loop. His handkerchief, it stuck out of his top pocket, and the way he was standing, you could see the top of his leather cigar case in his inside pocket.

Take him all in all, I never seen a man that looked more like money. I could see the ghosts of whole herds of prime beef, lambs, deer, and shoals of shining fish that had swum as far as Bonanza Chris, and disappeared forever. I could see kegs of foaming beer, and heaps of cold bottles that was all gone to make that flabby face and pink skin. The funny thing was that his eyes was bright, like the eyes of a kid.

Ronald introduces his brother, and Bonanza Chris goes and takes one of Slope's hard fists in both his hands, stands right up close to him, stomach to chest, so to speak, looks bang into his eyes, and says: "My dear Mr. Dugan, I know the bad fortune you've had through your mining investments. Mother Earth is a hard task-mistress. We try to win her smiles, and she is apt to show us nothing but the hardness of her elbows! But now it's in my power to do something for you. I am going to take over your interests in the Christabel at a handsome profit to you. I have a dreamlike hope that perhaps, some day, something will come out of that wretched hole in the ground. Besides, I want to make some amends to you. Your father has lost heavily. His losses are in my mind night and day. What I now offer is not a great deal. But it is a beginning. It is a great deal better, I dare trust, than nothing at all!

"And now, if you have brought your stock certificate with you, I have prepared the document for the legal transfer. I have the cash on hand, and it is simply a matter of your sitting down at that table and signing your name once."

One of his fat hands come up behind Slope's shoulder, and pushed him gently toward the table.

It was the slickest flow of mush that I'd ever listened to. I didn't wonder that a dummy like old Slope was taken right in. He started for the table with a grin like a hypnotized kid, and over his shoulder, the fat man gives one long, deep look at Ronald, the big-hearted.

Oh, I understood, all right. I coughed. I coughed pretty hard, too. The tears came into my eyes, I coughed so loud. Ronald, he shot a whiplash glance at me.

"By the way," said he, with a mean snarl in his voice, "this young fellow, who has the name of Red and none other, so far as I know, says that he knows you very well."

"Ah, does he? Does he?" says Bonanza. "Do you know me, son?"

"Don't you remember me, Chris?" I asked.

I wondered how good I could make my bluff with that crook.

"I can't say that I do," said Bonanza.

"I told you so, Ned," said Ronald. "This youngster has simply been lying his way around the face of the clock."

"Ah, ah," says Bonanza, shaking his head, "at his age? At his age?"

Sadly, but not unkindly, he waged his fat forefinger at me. Then I pulled my bluff from the hip, so to speak, and let it fly.

"Why, Chris," said I, "you forget that time the posse was giving you the run up there in Montana and you stopped at Uncle Al's ranch, with your hoss clean petered out, and I helped you to catch a new nag in the corral. Don't you remember me now?"

I'll never forget the thoughtful look that Chris gave me. Then he nodded, slowly. "The time that the scoundrels who stood against all law and order were trying to run me

47

out of the country—I remember you, perfectly, now," said he.

And he held out his hand!

CHAPTER 9

It sort of choked big-hearted Ronald to see me pumping the hand of the fat crook. And I had a chance to wink at Mr. Christian. He winked right back, too, just a flicker of an eyelid, and kept on smiling and beaming down at me.

"You've grown, son," says he, "since that day. That's why I didn't know you."

"Yes," said I, "I've growed up a bit, too."

"I promised you five dollars the next time we met, and there, son," says he, "is the money."

With that he forks out the fiver. And the shine of it looked pretty good to me, too. But what mostly flabbergasted me was the slick way he had of offering me hush money—pulling me off the trail. He didn't know that I knew anything about him, much, or that I could hurt or stop his game in any way, but just the same he was taking no chances.

I looked at that five-spot and I wanted it bad. I had to rub my hand on my trousers to get the itch off the end of the fingers. But I wouldn't make myself one of Bonanza's men for that price. So I said: "You've got me mixed up, Bonanza. It must've been some other fellow that helped you out of some other scrape."

A few acres of his smile slid off with a rush, while he slowly slipped the money back in his vest pocket.

Old Slope was saying: "There's the champion of the

world, Mr. Christian, in helping people out. He's done more for me than you could possibly guess."

Christian didn't turn to him; he kept his eye on me. He measured me, and he plumbed me.

"Yes," he said, "I've not the slightest doubt that the boy can be useful when the right humor strikes him!"

I saw around the corners of that remark to what he was really driving at.

Then he got his flabby paw on Slope's shoulder and pushed him down into a chair. Slope let himself be pushed, and took up the pen that was handed to him, picked his stock certificates out of his inside coat pocket and put them down on the table.

"Well, here we are," says Bonanza Chris, spreading out a paper, putting on his glasses, and looking down over the tops of 'em at the sheet of paper.

All I could see was a big-lettered word, "Whereas," and the letters was put in fancy as you please.

Now, I'd seen that word a few times before, and you can take it from me, when anybody opens up with a "whereas," they've got it from the bottom of the deck and the rest of the deck is cold, too. So I gulped and swallowed hard.

Ronald gave me a little attention out of the corner of his soft eye. I guess he wondered what I was gonna do next, and I wondered, too. Because it didn't seem possible to stop old Slope from signing, and I knew dog-gone well, if he did, he was giving away at least ten dollars for one.

Slope had the pen balanced in the air, ready to write, when I said: "Wait a minute, Slope." A little jerk and a wabble ran right through the whole body of Bonanza, when he heard me cut into that game, and Ronald lifted his upper lip just like a dog about to bite.

But Bonanza was slick, that's what he was, and he says, smooth as silk: "Just on this line, Mr. Dugan, and then—"

"All right, Red. In a minute," says Slope.

"I only wanted you to see that everything was squared up before you wrote anything," said I.

49

"Squared up? What is there to square up, Red?" says he. And he gives me his simple, open, trusting smile.

"There's nothing to square up, after all," said Ronald.

"What do you mean, Red?" said Slope again.

"I'm afraid," said Christian, "that Red is simply putting in his hand because he doesn't want to stay outside of any picture."

"I'll tell you what I mean, Slope," said I. "Before you go to signing something, you ought to look things over. This Christabel, it was worth nothing, then it was worth fifteen hundred, and now it's worth five thousand, plus Ronald's cut, and Ronald's expenses out here and back to the East, again."

That whelp of a Ronald, he lost all his color at one swipe.

"Expenses? Expenses?" says Christian, blankly, but genially, too.

But I saw one of his soft hands double into a fist all white behind the little finger.

"There are no expenses," said Ronald, "of course."

"I don't know what you mean, Red," says Slope.

"I'll explain," said I, jumping in the dark. "But first, I want you to look your big-hearted brother in the eye and ask him why Mr. Christian sent him a check?"

That was enough to make Slope look with a frown at Ronald, and he didn't need to ask the question. I had put it for him, and I had put it straight. Somehow, I'd managed to hit the mark in the dark though, as a matter of fact, it wasn't hard to guess that Christian must have sent Ronald traveling expenses and something over, to show him that his heart was in the right place.

Anyway, that shot of mine went right through Ronald's nerve centers. He had to grab onto the edge of the table and lean on it, with his arms shaking.

I was pretty nearly sorry for him. I never saw a fancy man turn so suddenly into a worthless, whipped, shaking cur as Ronald did just then.

Slope didn't know what I was driving at exactly. But even Slope, trusting as he was, couldn't help seeing that

Ronald, somehow, had been caught between the pantry and the back stairs with the pumpkin pie in his hand.

"What is it, Ronald?" he asked. "I don't understand!"

Of course, he didn't understand, but he was beginning to smell a rat, I could guess.

Ronald pulls himself together with a jerk. He flies into a passion, like any fool of a girl might've done. He stamps, and his voice rises and squeaks, as he answers:

"I know what it means! It means that this worthless rat has dared to accuse me of underhand practice—me—your own brother. I've come out here across the continent in your own interests and now—"

"Hush, Ronald," said Slope. "I know that you're doing it for my benefit. Of course, I know that!"

"It hardly appears that you do," goes on Ronald. "Or you wouldn't allow the brat to remain here, after he has insulted me."

"I've half a mind to wash my hands of the whole business," says big Bonanza. "It's only because you interested me in your brother's unlucky case, Mr. Dugan."

"Oh, I know that you all mean the best in the world by me," says the dummy.

Bonanza took this for a lead, and he followed with his whole hand. "For one thing," said he, "I can't allow a scoundrelly whippersnapper like this to stay in my offices after he's insulted such a gentleman as Ronald Dugan."

With that, he makes a pass to catch me, and I let him take a good hold. I wanted him to have hold of me, because it fitted in with my next hand. He wasn't hurting me a bit, but I let out a howl as though he was breaking me in two.

It did what I wanted. It fetched Slope out of his chair with a bound. The pen was heaved into a corner, the table staggered as though it were on the deck of a heeling ship, and then there was Slope touching the shoulder of Bonanza.

"Don't touch him," says Slope.

His tone made Bonanza back clear across the room. I stood back against the wall, closed my eyes, and grabbed the place where Bonanza had got hold of me.

It was a pretty good play, and it got old Slope hotter than a fire.

"If Red is thrown out, I'm thrown out with him," says he. "And if anyone touches him again, I'll touch back!"

He had hold of the back of a chair, as he said that, sort of steadying himself, he was so angry. And I saw Bonanza red with anger, sweating hot, too.

Just then the crosspiece on the top of that chair crunched under the grip of Slope, like a chicken bone in the teeth of a hound. The sound of it and the sight of what had happened changed Bonanza's attitude a lot. It gave him a glimpse into some of the facts about Slope, and what he saw, did his innards a whole lot of good.

"Stuff and nonsense," he remarks, "I didn't mean to hurt Red. I'm sure I didn't, although a man never can quite know his own strength when he's excited. It simply irritated me beyond any expression to hear such language as he had used about your brother, to your face, Mr. Edward Dugan."

That was a good twist for him, of course. The more he talked up, the more I saw that this deal he was trying to put through was a big one, in his eyes. It meant money. It meant a lot of money.

"I don't want to have anybody insulted," says Slope.

He reached out and gathered me in alongside of him. Then he holds me out there at arm's length, wrinkles up his brows and stares at me from under 'em. Good old Slope! He was fairly beat.

"Now, somebody tell me what it's all about!" says he.

"I can tell you," said Ronald. "It simply means that Red is a slanderous young scoundrel."

"Is he?" says Slope, looking terribly pained. "Come on, tell me, are you, Red?"

"Ask him who I slandered," said I, quickly.

"Whom did he slander, Ronald?" says Slope.

"He slandered me!" says Ronald promptly.

"Ask him what I said about him?" said I.

"Well," said Ronald, getting pale and pink all at once, "the fact is that he dared to intimate that I was accepting a concealed profit of some sort, whereas you know that I would never make a profit at your expense and—"

Slope looked at me, as his brother wound up in a hopeless gesture of disdain at the whole tawdry business.

"Slope," I said, "if the deal was straight, your brother never would have come. He only needed to tell Christian that you were coming here, and Christian could have met you and offered you the five thousand himself. Isn't that clear and straight?"

CHAPTER 10

I was putting the thing as simply as I could for fear that Slope would miss the idea. He was still trying to absorb it, when Bonanza cuts in: "I begin to lose all interest in the affair. It's not a matter of any moment to me. It was simply a really kind concern in your welfare."

Slope looked at all three of us, in turn. Then I laughed, a good, hearty laugh, and I said: "Listen to him, Slope. He says he'll wash his hands of the business, but sooner than let you get out of the room without signing that slip of paper over there, he'll shed blood. He'll do more. He'll shed money, bales of it. Because Christabel is one of the hottest prospect holes that was ever sunk in Potts Valley, or I'm a liar!"

"A liar, I fear, is what you are!" says Bonanza, his big, loose lips beginning to pinch together with hate and malice.

"Raise your price," said I, "because that's your only way out. You've hired Ronald—you've paid his expenses out here and back. You've promised him a split in the profits and now you'll have to spend a little more."

"Ridiculous nonsense!" says Christian. "But, Mr. Dugan," he goes on, "to cut short this absurd and disgusting scene—"

"Yes," says Slope, "it certainly is disgusting!" And he shook his honest head.

"To cut it short and save my valuable time," says the thug, "I will actually pay you, for your immediate signature and the stock certificates, ten thousand dollars cash! You can have thirty seconds to consider it in!"

With that he smacked his fat hands together.

I laughed again, while Slope started for the pen and the fallen paper, because that sounded like a whole heap of money to him, of course.

But my laughter headed him off and I said: "I told you that he'd raise his offer, and you see that he has already!"

Slope stopped dead still.

"He has, in fact, done exactly what you said that he would do, though I can't imagine what possibly could have enabled you to guess!"

"Well," said I, "crooks work along the same lines. There ain't anything new, and I've heard some master yeggs say so! Some green-goods artists, too!"

That was a fact. But I watched Bonanza take that slap in the face as though he hadn't heard it, while he said: "A truce to this chattering, Dugan. Let's get our business done."

"Yes, yes, my dear Ned, of course, let's finish it. Don't make me feel that my trip across the continent has been thrown away," put in Ronald.

The dummy was wavering again, when I hit him pretty hard with: "You can't sign it now, Slope. The thirty seconds are up!"

Old Slope rubbed his fingers through his hair, and Bonanza said one word. It was a short word and there was a lot of air in it. It sounded a good deal like a paper bag when it's exploded with a puff and a bang.

"Great heavens," said Ronald, "are you allowing yourself to be led around by the nose by a spindling brat, a thieving little vagabond who is—"

"Don't say any more," says Slope.

54

Then he did a funny thing. He walked right across the room and stood square in front of me and he looked down on me with his troubled eyes and said: "Red, what is it that you really think?"

So I said: "They've raised the price as I said they would, from five thousand to ten grand. Ten thousand bucks, and the bargaining hasn't really started. They'd go on raising. But can't you see that they're trying to put a deal over? They've got a game on their hands. You're a majority owner of that Christabel stock. It's likely old Bonanza, here, thought that it was no good, at the start, but a little more digging has turned it up as a beauty. I'll bet there's a fortune in it. I ask you to remember one thing more—the sick look of big-hearted Ronald, there, when I pulled the mask off his crooked face a minute ago."

Perhaps nothing else that I said really did penetrate and get home to Slope, but on one peg I had hung something that he could see and remember.

He turned around, looked sadly at Ronald, and shook his head.

"I'm afraid that Red is right, Ronald," he said. "I mean, I'm afraid that I must look into the thing, and take other advice."

Bonanza, having led this mule to water, was so furious because he couldn't make him drink, that he lost his wits entirely and exploded, waving his arms:

"Get out of my office, then, and be damned to you! You blockhead, I'll make Pottsville too hot to hold you. I'll make you jump!"

Slope stared at him for a moment, and then he turned around to me and said: "I suppose that we might as well go, Red. You seem to have been right about everything."

So we walked right out through the door, me stepping fast and on tiptoes, because I felt every second as though I was going to be shot in the back.

As we started down the hall stairs, I heard the voice of Bonanza roaring:

"You're just as big a fool as your brother. You've got no more face than a sixteen-year-old girl. You shivered and shook like a fool in front of a street brat, that knew nothing."

Then the shrill, cutting voice of Ronald came needle sharp and clear in answer:

"As a gambler, you're a joke! You allowed Red to call your cards and you played them one by one, exactly as he said that you would!"

We got down the street and Slope was still busy stuffing the stock certificates back into his pockets. I expected him to seem happy and a little angry, too. But he was only saddened.

"It's all right, Slope," said I. "That brother of yours is spoiled meat. Yeah, he's pretty high; he's kind of rank. But you're out of touch with him now and I hope that you'll stay out. I guess you can see now how much he wanted to help you before and why he didn't even fork over railroad fare for you!"

Slope's face puckered up as though he'd been hit. Then he said: "Red, don't you think we had better not talk about Ronald any more?"

It stopped me, you can bet. I felt sick and ashamed. He was so simple, old Slope, but with all his gentleness he had dignity, too, and it was like the dignity—well, not of a king, but of a priest, that believes in something so big and grand that he don't waste no time despising ordinary, ornery folks like you and me.

I didn't make no back chat for a considerable time. Then I hear Slope sigh and stifle the sound of his sigh, too. At last he says: "Red, I'm going to stroll around and find a job of some sort and perhaps you would like to go with me?"

That was like him—go to work and grub and slave and then have his pockets picked at the end of every week, I suppose.

I told him the oldest and the stalest joke in the world.

"You know, Slope," said I, "about the surest way of making a million dollars?"

"What's that?" says he as ready and pat as an end man at a minstrel show.

"Work a million days," I quoted, "for a dollar a day, and don't spend a darn cent."

He though about that for a while. Then he said: "But, of course, one would have to spend money for living expenses."

Then the point of that old, worn-out, busted, hamstrung joke got home to him, and he laughed good and hard. "You're an entertaining fellow, Red," said he.

It kind of soured me, I must admit. It was kind of too simple, even to hear from Slope. "Well," I said, "the way for you to make money, and lots of it, here in Potts Valley, is not to work a lick with your hands."

"No?" said he, believing as a child. "How should I work then?"

"With your head," says I. "And listen to me. I've been luck to you, haven't I?"

"You have, Red," said he. "You've been grand luck, too!"

"Will you let me do something more?" I went on.

"Of course, I shall," said he.

"Well, then, let me do the planning for the two of us, for a little while."

He nodded. "You're a very clever fellow, Red," said he.

It makes me kind of sad. He was so humble that he could have put on a top hat and walked under a snake without tickling his stomach.

So I said: "It ain't that I'm smart. It's only that Potts Valley is full of crooks. And I ain't an expert at walking a ruled line, myself. So I sort of understand what's going on inside of their heads. You see?"

"I hope I see," says he, pretty blank again.

"But," said I, "what we need to do is to get hold of one honest man, and that's hard to find in a mining camp, believe me. I've been in 'em before."

"Of course, honest men are useful always," says he, "but what is our pressing need of one just now?"

"To be a safe-deposit box," says I.

"Ah," says he.

"Oh, Slope," I broke out, getting a little peeved and sore, "don't you see that big-hearted Ronald and his pal

Bonanza Chris are going to try to get thost stock certificates out of you, even if they have to brain you or hire a pair of gunmen to shoot you up?"

"Do you think that Bonanza would do that?" asked he, very shocked.

I saw that he had left out Ronald's name. But he didn't protest at the mention of him in that connection, which made me guess that I had put a crimp in that kind brother for good and all. It was sort of encouraging to think that I had made that much progress.

"I think Bonanza would cut your throat sooner than carve a beefsteak," said I. "And believe me, I'm right. He'd cut mine, too, and from now on I'm working to save both our hides!"

CHAPTER 11

In about one minute after this I seen our shadow, right enough. It was a picture of the bull that had come over and found Slope at the hotel and promised to look me up later on. Only he wasn't hurrying now. He was just keeping his eye open. It takes a mighty bad conscience or a mighty good eye in the back of the head to spot a shadow that knows what he's about.

This one knew the game pretty well. Sometimes he was stepping into a cigar store and coming out with a cigarette burning in his face, or else he'd be stopping to look into a shop window, or standing on a street corner like he was waiting to meet somebody. Another time he'd be stepping out brisk and fast, like he was hurrying to an appointment, and I spotted him a couple of times swinging right up behind us and going around a corner like he didn't know that we was on the same planet.

A good shadow, he turns himself into about twenty people, so's you won't notice him in the crowd. He wears his hat at different angles; sometimes he slouches; sometimes he stands straight; sometimes he has both hands in his pockets, sometimes only one; sometimes his coat is open, sometimes only on button is fastened.

But I'd seen shadows work before, and nobody was ever looking out for one of the sneaks harder than I was looking at that time.

I didn't say anything to Slope, because he would've turned around and asked the shadow if he was really following us, to which the shadow would've replied that he'd never seen his face before and wished that he wasn't having that pleasure right then.

No, I didn't tell Slope, but I steered him into a store, and there I got an envelope.

It wasn't no common envelope, mind you. I made so much fuss that I was sure that the clerk would remember me for a long time; and, when he offered me two kinds, I wanted still another with a linen lining. When I couldn't get that, I shook my head and said that I didn't suspect that the two samples he showed me would do, but finally I took one of them.

We walked out of that store, and on the way out, I slipped a little wad of paper I'd picked up off the counter into the envelope.

Then as we came out onto the street, I passed the envelope, all gummed, to Slope and asked him to put it in his pocket. He did, saying: "What is it, Red? I don't mean to be prying, but I wonder why you put that blank paper into such a good envelope."

"It's a trap to catch suckers," said I, grimly.

He shook his gentle, dumb head and didn't answer. Then we come by a bank that looked like a real bank, and it had the sign out that I was seeking. Safe-deposit boxes!

I asked Slope, when we got inside that bank, to ask for a box, and I said that I would pay the rent for a week. And I told him to ask for the finest strong box that they had; which he done what I said, and the clerk, he looked kind of scornful down his nose at Slope's ragged coat with the tear in it, but finally he charged him a dollar a day for seven whole days. I passed him the envelope with the blank paper in it to put away for Slope, and with Slope's name on the receipt. Then we walked out of the bank again.

"I follow you in a haze," said Slope. "I really don't know what this is all about."

"Your haze ain't nothing to the haze of the gent that's working up our trail," said I. "He's gonna get into the mud up to the hips, Slope, and I think that maybe we're gonna get a couple of peaceful days."

He shook his head again. Just then I saw the shadow turn into the bank behind us, and that made me so happy that I started in to laugh right out loud.

"Did you see something, Red?" asked Slope.

"I seen a sucker rising for a hook," I answered, and that was all the explaining that I done.

Yeah, I itched a lot to tell Slope. I was proud of what I'd done. I wanted to shout the news out to everybody. But I figgered that it wouldn't do any good to tell him and get his temperature up before I knew which way he would bust. So I just mystified him some more, and I said: "Now we don't have to go sneakin' out to the Christabel to take samples out of her, or run any risks like that. We can tell how rich she is in another way."

"How is that, Red?" said Slope.

"If the week runs out and nothing happens to that Trimble & Parker Bank, the Christabel is just a little thing—a little fifty or a hundred-thousand-dollar job, d'ye see? But if the safe in the Trimble & Parker joint should happen to be blowed up inside of the next couple of days, then we know dog-gone well that the Christabel is a beauty headed toward the million-dollar line, as sure as they can tell by the ground they've broke already."

Says Slope: "Red, aren't you amusing yourself a little at my expense?" I laughed again, but I grabbed his thick arm and squeezed it. I dunno how or why, but somehow I liked that dummy better every day.

"I ain't laughin' at you, Slope," I answered, "but I'm

laughing with you at a lot of hard-boiled suckers that ain't half as tough as they think they are."

Just then we passed a saloon, and the cool smell and the odor of whisky and beer in the air, sweet and sour, came out and fanned my face. It felt a lot better to me than any dog-gone breeze off a meadow in May that the song writers are always gettin' heated up about. So I said: "Let's go in and grab us a couple of mugs of beer, eh?"

He stopped and looked at me. "How old are you, Red?" said he. I told him.

"And you drink?" said he.

"Aw, go on, brother," said I. "Look at Germany. Look how much beer they drink. Beer don't do nobody any harm."

He didn't argue, but he just went in with me, and we found the long barroom pretty full. A lot of people go bust in mining camps, but never no saloon keepers. I had to slide in between two gents, and I waits for my chance and ask for two schooners of beer.

"Only one, Red," says Slope.

That brought down my temperature a lot.

I got one big mug and backed out of the line and the pair of us got seats at a table in a corner. That was all right. But I said to Slope, as I sipped at the beer: "Don't you drink beer, Slope?"

He looked straight back at me with a wrinkle of pain between his eyes.

"I don't want to hurt your feelings, Red," said he, "but I can't drink with a fellow of your age."

I wanted that beer and I wanted it bad. The cold, sour sting of it was hitting the right place. But somehow the look of Red and the gentle sound of his voice took the head off that beer, so to speak. It got flat on me. I couldn't taste it no more.

I got to thinking what a queer fellow Slope was and wondering how such a dummy could have such strength, not in his hands only, mind you, but in his brain, too.

What other man in the world could've spoiled my beer for me? There I'd sat down to have a good drink and congratulate myself on the smart thing that I'd just pulled, and now all of the glory was gone flat and dark in a splash.

He didn't press the point. He began to talk quietly about something else, I forget what. And just then there came a hullabaloo in the back room, and the chairs in there, they went over with a bang and a crash. Voices begun to roar out.

Two bouncers with a business look in their eyes went into that back room. I mean to say, they started to go in, but a jet of people pouring out hit 'em and washed 'em backward.

The folks come out of that room all bent over and sprinting hard, with a look on their faces like they wanted terrible bad to get somewhere else.

They was the vanguard. There was more action behind 'em. Three or four more gents came out, trying to squeeze through the doorway all in one bust.

They was kind of damaged, too. One of 'em only had the half of his coat on his back, another had a red eye that was swelling out fast and looked like water under the skin. Then there was one that wabbled as he run.

Then comes a man with a sort of run and a jump. As he gets clear of the door, he whirls about with a leveled gun in his hand and the old murder look in his eye. I'd seen that look before, and I started to slide for the floor, but just then a fist and an arm shot out through the doorway and the fist cracked the gun packer under the chin and hoisted him.

Nobody cared where he landed, I guess. We just watched the gun and seen it shoot a nice little round hole in the ceiling.

Then in come the gent behind the long arm. He wasn't so terrible big, neither. He was just six foot something and made lean—not the weak kind of lean, but the kind where all the muscles, they are wires, and all the bones are iron. There was a look about this fellow as if you couldn't hurt him with a sledge hammer. There wasn't much to his head to hit, for one thing. It was mostly nose and jaw, and a pair of big, flapping ears to keep the sun from burning his shoulders, and he had a scalp lock of pale hair that stuck straight up without no waxing.

I never seen such a man!

He was pretty well lit, and he was enjoying himself a lot. He said that he was a two-legged Gila monster and that he was ready to bite. He also said that he was an ornery buzzard that lived on jawbones; that he was a chinook blowin' and that he aimed to thaw out Pottsville and make a dog-gone marshland out of the spot where it had stood, because such a lot of thugs and crooks he never had seen in his life, and the next time they tried to rob him with a brake on the roulette wheel, he wouldn't stop at busting the machine and taking the cash out of the tiller, but he'd wreck the dog-gone joint.

He wanted a fight and he wanted it bad, he said, and he invited any two of the boys to step up and accommodate him, because he was just ready to whoop.

He got this far, when one of the bouncers slid up behind him and took a two-hand hold on a length of rubber hose with a weight in the end of it, and socked "Blondy" right on the bean.

He fell down, joint by joint, and piled himself up on the floor.

CHAPTER 12

Now that he was down, the fellows that had been trying to make themselves small in the corners of the room, they all came out with a rush, like dogs for a wolf when it's down, but before they got to Blondy, Slope jumped out of his chair and stood over him.

He held up his hand to warn the men back, but they wouldn't stop. They'd tasted too many of Blondy's fists;

and they wanted to get at the cash that he'd taken out of the crooked roulette game, too, I suppose.

So they came straight on, and the first man, he pulled a gun and reached for Slope's head with the barrel of his Colt. Slope picked that gun right out of the air with one hand and with the other he pushed the fellow away and drove him clean through the crowd.

Somebody else had tackled Slope knee-high. He picked up that yegg and threw him in the face of the rest.

Then they all backed up. They seen that they had followed a mountain lion right into the den of a grizzly bear, and they didn't like the look of things.

It was a funny thing about Slope. Ordinarily, he wasn't so big that you'd pick him out. But when he got into action he stood a foot higher and a yard wider, at least.

Well, Slope picked the big fellow off the floor, and just then Blondy revived and he hung there over Slope's arm and grinned up into his face.

"Brother, was it you that slipped me the knock-out pill?" says he.

"It was not I," said Slope. "Shall we get out of this place?"

The other one, he got onto his feet, and steadied his legs till they sagged no more at the knees.

He said it was a good idea to get out of that dump, and afterward, when the bees were no longer buzzing in his brain, he'd come back and mash the house flat.

So they went out together, and I followed along behind. Looking right and left, as the big fellows passed, I seen a dozen hands start to fetch their guns out, and then stop a bit, to think, and before they finished thinking, we was out in the open street.

"We'd better have something to eat," says the tall boy, a lot soberer. "I ain't been taking to solids for about a week, and I feel kinder empty. Say, you come along and feed with me. How come that mob didn't tear me to bits after I hit the floor? Did you keep 'em off me, brother?"

"Why, not at all," says Slope.

But I busted in: "He just threw a couple of them in the

faces of the rest and they got kinder discouraged. That's all he done."

The stranger, he grinned at me and then nodded.

"My moniker is Blondy," says he. "How does the lettering go on your front piece, brother?"

"Red," said my partner, "calls me Slope."

"Slope and Red, come and feed with me," says Blondy, "and if you don't want to eat, you set back and watch a real man put away some food. I gotta buy you something. I got two handfuls of the long green out of that till at the roulette wheel, and I gotta blow some of it in on something. Here's a restaurant over here. You can be an audience or you can step onto the stage and be part of the show. Either way you wish is all the same to me."

Slope hesitated a little, but I didn't. I got him by the elbow and led him right along, because I seen at a glance that this here Blondy was a native, so to speak, and knew the way around Pottsville pretty near by heart. If he hadn't been a native, I mean, he would've been shot to smithereens back there in the saloon. No, he was somebody that was known, and that was why the saloon bouncers and yeggs didn't salt him away.

I thought that it would be pretty useful to have that sort of man around to tie up to. And to make him and Slope meet level, I said: "You may be hollow, Blondy, but Slope, here, could eat you right under the table. I got five dollars that says that he could."

Blondy let out about seven links of his belt and held out his pants from his stomach.

"You see this here noose?" said he. "That's all gotta be filled! I got a kind of a sad feeling when I think about how bad you're going to be beat on that bet!"

We got inside the restaurant, and Blondy, he didn't wait, but he told me to howl for anything that I wanted, while he ordered two of everything on the bill of fare. When you get venison steak, beef, mutton chops, eggs, boiled, baked and fried potatoes, with five kinds of pie, it's a sort of heap. And the waiters, they turned loose and laughed and shuffled all of that food onto the table.

It was the kind of joke that Slope could appreciate, too,

and he was always chuckling between mouthfuls. And he was still going on steadily with his eating, when Blondy got stuck, somewhere between apple pie and canned apricots.

He pushed his plate away and rolled his eyes as he seen Slope reaching for a second helping of coffee cake!

"I feel just sort of comfortable, now," said Blondy. "No matter how much of a habit eating may be, I guess I've got enough loaded up inside of me to last me for a week. Brother," he went on to Slope, "I used to be reckoned a prime feeder, but I see that I ain't nothing compared with you. I ain't no more than a roustabout in any show where you're the leading man. Brother, where you been keeping yourself all this time?"

"Keeping myself?" said Slope, in his gentle, dumb way.

He looked at me with his brows raised a little, as though asking for an explanation. Blondy looked at me, too, and I managed to keep the Slope side of my face still while I passed a wink to Blondy. That wink wouldn't tell him everything, but it would give him an idea that there was something out of the ordinary sitting at the table with him.

"Blondy is just wondering how two like you and him could've lived so long without bumping into one another," said I. "He didn't think that the world was as big as all of that. I didn't know myself that he took up so little space!"

Blondy roared. He laughed dead easy at almost anything, and I like a man like that.

It's a mighty hard job, when you have to polish up all of your ideas and give a sharp cutting edge and a point to 'em, before they cut through the callus places of some gents and get to the quick.

"The kid is kinder fresh," said he to Slope.

"Fresh?" said Slope. "Red is a great friend of mine," he added, very seriously.

Well, this time Blondy took a long, deep look at Slope, and he seen all that he needed to see. I could see him drop his eyes sudden at the end.

It made me pretty sad. And I wondered how many times fellows had started to talk to Slope dead interested and glad to meet him, and all that, and suddenly found that they were walking off into a thick fog.

Yes, it was sad, and it put an ache in me, and I hoped for a time when Slope would do something so great, so brave and grand that the whole world would know how fine he was and rate him high, no matter how slow his brain might be.

I hooked into the conversation, finally, to take the lead out of the seconds. They were soaking up coffee, by this time.

"Blondy," said I, "besides owing me five bucks, what else do you know about Pottsville?"

"I know it from the forelock to the spurs," said he. "I've roped it, rode it, and broke it. And it's broke me. Up to today, it had a lead in the game with me. Today I got part of my own back, thanks to Slope's handy way of throwing around growed men. What d'you want tuh know about Pottsville, anyway?"

"I want to know a couple of things," said I.

"Before you make any investments, eh?" says Blondy, with his grin.

"Yeah," I broke in, "I just been looking around, and it appears to me like a fairish kind of dive, only my business agent I ain't so sure about. Which his moniker is Henry Christian."

"Bonanza Chris," says Blondy, "he ain't no business agent. He's a business undertaker. He buries everybody that comes his way. I gotta say that he does it handsome. After he's put you under the ground, he'll put up a headboard for you, son."

"You talk like you know him personal," I remarked.

"No," says Blondy, "but I've seen the remains of some that did."

"He has a kind of a persuading manner," I persisted.

"Him? He could talk the eagle off a ten-spot, and when they hear him talk, the dollars never feel happy until they've started rolling his way. He don't use 'soup' or soap, a jimmy or a can opener, or skeleton keys. He don't have to. He just opens front doors and wallets with his chatter."

A good deal of this was over the head of Slope, but the

general run of it was enough to convince him that our first impressions of Bonanzo Chris were correct. I got on to another thing.

"You know of some of the mines?" said I.

"I know 'em mostly all," said he.

"You got them by heart, like you have Mr. Christian?" said I.

"I've worked in a lot of 'em," said he. "I've prospected a lot more, and I've owned a few myself."

"And sold 'em?" said I.

"The good ones I sold cheap," said he, "and the fairish ones I give away, and the bad ones I hung onto till I'd soaked all my money away, breaking ground for nothing."

"That sounds," said I, "like you was a pretty experienced miner."

"I am," says he. "I've been digging all my life."

"Well, then," says I, "can you tell me what there is in a hole in the ground called the Christabel?"

"It's a sweet name for a mine," said Blondy. "Is that why you want to meet it?"

I stared at him a minute, and he looked too ugly to be crooked. So I said: "Partner, Slope wants to find the place because he bought some shares in it a long time ago, and he bought 'em through Mr. Henry Christian."

Blondy laughed.

"Say goodby to that cash, brother," said he.

"Wait a minute," said I. "Bonanza wants to buy them shares back. He wants 'em bad. Ten thousand dollars' worth he wants 'em."

Blondy's jaw dropped with a bang. I seen that I'd registered a pretty good point.

CHAPTER 13

It was pretty exciting, to see Blondy up in the air, like that, because he wasn't the kind that would get off his feed about any little thing.

Finally, he said: "The Christabel is watering at the mouth with gold, if Bonanza offered that much for her. He never pays more'n one cent on a dollar and ninety-nine lies. I tell you, Slope, you're rich if you got that thing in your hands. I'll tell you where to find her, too. I'll look her up right away for you."

Slope thanked him. He suggested that he should walk right out then and there to examine the mine, but Blondy said: "You could get into her all right. They'd be glad to have you in the shaft, but the devil only knows when you'd get out of it, again. For ten thousand dollars, Bonanza would poison the King of England's soup, and the Queen's, too. I'd wait for a dark night and a lucky one, too, if I was you. I'll tell you what. I'll go out there with you, when you start explorin'. I'd like to sit in with a hand against Bonanza, even if I know how he deals 'em off the bottom of the pack."

Slope was glad of that, but he wasn't half as glad as I was. I could see that Blondy was hardy, and I could see that he was pretty straight, too; and his little hawk eyes were as bright and keen as you please. He'd be a handy man to have on your side, no matter how dark the alley.

We got things fixed up right away, and Blondy, he took command.

He said that we'd better separate and then meet again along about evening. Make it dark, and then we'd gather

69

again, on the corner at the right of this restaurant. Slope agreed. He generally agreed with everybody and everything. And so we broke up.

Now I've got to do a thing which is pretty hard to manage, because I have to stop talking about what I seen with my own eyes and put in what happened to each of the three of us before we met again.

My own part I know, and I know it good and hard. The stories from the other two, I heard backward and forward from so many angles that I almost feel as though I was right on deck when hell was popping for them, too.

But it's kinder interesting, because it shows you how long the arm of a crook can be, when he's got money and hired thugs behind him.

Well, to begin with Blondy, because the most part of the trouble hinged on him.

He breezed out of the restaurant first, and he says that he was feeling pretty good, because he saw a flock of trouble ahead of him, and that was just like marrow bones for Blondy. He sauntered down the street with one hand in his coat pocket, a-fingering of the money that he had got off the crooks in the saloon. He was beginning to spend it in his mind, and he'd got as far as a Mexican saddle covered with Mexican silver trimmings, a silver bridle to match, and golden bells on his heels, when a bloke side-stepped up to him and said: "Hello, Blondy!"

Blondy stops and sees a chunk of a man with a patch over one eye, and a smile that stretches one way. "You ain't forgotten me?" says the man.

"I never knew enough of you to forget," says Blondy. "Who are you, Bill?"

"I guess you remember part of me," says the one-eyed gent. "I'm Bill Larkin, from Guadalupe."

"If you're from Guadalupe, I must have known you," said Blondy. "What's the deal for you up here?"

"I'm one of Bonanza Chris's men," said Bill Larkin.

"Why don't you take up plumbing?" said Blondy. "It's a lot cleaner job."

"Maybe it is," says Bill. "I dunno, though. I ain't

70

found it so bad. The boss just sent me out to find you, Blondy."

"You go tell your boss to go to heck," says Blondy.

"I wouldn't want to do that," says Bill. "He wants to see you. Has he got anything agin' you?"

"Not yet, that I know of," answers Blondy.

"All right, then," says Larkin, "there ain't any reason why you shouldn't see him. I'm putting it to you straight. He socks the ones that he's agin'; but he's a good partner for them that work with him."

"I'll be darned if I work with him," said Blondy.

"Don't cross that bridge till you get to it," replied Larkin. "You might go and see the fat reptile just for the fun of it."

"I dunno but that's a good idea," replies Blondy.

For he says to himself that maybe, after all, he'll be able to get something out of the crook that'll be useful for the rest of us. He thinks that maybe big Bonanza will tip his hand a little.

So he goes on: "I don't mind if I take a look at your show, Bill."

He walks down the street with Larkin, talking real friendly, till they come to the office of Bonanza, and up the stairs they go to the front office of the thug, and they have to wait there a minute.

Blondy is tired of waiting and ready to go, when the inside door opens, and a couple of men come out with Bonanza walking behind and between 'em, with his hands on their shoulders, talking low and confidential. This pair of birds is all lighted up with enthusiasm, and when they get to the outer door one of them says: "If the first sink doesn't work, I'm behind another shaft. I'll sink twenty thousand dollars' worth of it on my own capital."

Says Bonanza: "Mr. Craven, you're made of the stuff that turns thousands into millions. There's nothing so well worth taking as a good chance."

With that, he waves the pair of them out of the outer office, and Larkin says: "Bonanza, I've brung along Blondy, which you wanted to see him."

At that, Bonanza darkens up a good deal and pulls

71

out a cigar, bites off the end of it and spits the end on the floor, licks some of the broken tobacco leaf off his lips and spits that on the floor, too. And he lights the cigar on a match that Larkin holds for him, and then he says: "Thanks, Larkin. That's all, just now."

Larkin faded out of the room, and Bonanza says through a smoke cloud: "Will you come in here with me, Blondy?" Blondy walks into the inner office. It looks pretty important. It's got a rug on the floor, which you could see it, Blondy says, fifty miles off better'n the Stars and Stripes, which is some seeing, I gotta say. There was a big, fat-bellied safe in the corner of the room, with high-hat filing cabinets and a roll-top desk, of course, with things shoved into all the cubbyholes.

Mostly, I dunno what business men do with their time, outside of raising a temperature by creaking back and forth in a tip chair. They get down to their offices about nine-thirty or ten, and they knock off at twelve sharp and rush out in the middle of a letter to have a terrible important business lunch with the president of a corporation or something. They wallow back into the office about three and give the door boy a dressing down, fire a stenographer, sit down and look dark, silent and strong till four-thirty.

Then they start uptown and have some cocktails from five to seven. They come home to dinner with a slow, tired walk, and they go and lay down on the sofa and they say to their wife: "Gimme a cold towel to put across my eyes. I've had a terrible hard day! Don't talk to me; just do something. I gotta get out of this business. It's killing me. I'd've give it all up long ago if it wasn't for you and the kids. I'm about wore out. Bring me that cold towel and maybe a hot toddy. I gotta have something to brace me up before dinner."

These "tired business men," mostly, they give me a pain in the neck.

To get on back to old Blondy, he ain't invited to sit down. Bonanza is dark and serious, all right, and he says: "Blondy, don't make a fool of yourself. Keep away from that half-wit."

Frankness was not what Blondy expected from Bonanza, with the cards on the table like this. So he couldn't say nothing, for a minute, he was so surprised, and Bonanza, he went right on and he said: "Now, you're not a tenderfoot. If you were, I could understand. You've been around Potts Valley long enough to know that I've made history here, and what kind of history, too. I've made some men and I've unmade others."

"Yeah, you've done all that," says Blondy, gradually getting the wind back into his sails, but with a lot of shake in the luff, still.

"You want adventure," said Bonanza. "You want to throw in with a young tramp and a half-wit because you think that the Christabel is valuable. And you're right! It *is* valuable. You think that I'm going to try to do the half-wit out of that mine. You're right. I am. You think that you can block me, and there you're a fool. You can't do it. Step on the other side of the line from me, and I blot you out. You understand?"

He didn't shout. He just talked the words out slow and thick around the cigar.

Somehow, what he said sank in on Blondy. Oily smooth talk he would have laughed at, but this stuff was straight from the shoulder.

"Thanks, Bonanza," said he, "for hanging out a red flag for me at the crossing."

"I'll tell you why I'm talking," said Bonanza Chris. "You can't bother me a great deal on the other side, but you can be useful on my side. I want you, and I'll pay you a price. I'll pay you your own price. How much do you want?"

"For what?" said Blondy.

"For double-crossing the half-wit," says Bonanza.

CHAPTER 14

No matter what you may say, and no matter what you may think, I know that it takes a nervy man to talk like Henry Christian was talking then. And I admire his change of pace, too. Look at the line that he had handed out to Slope, I mean to say. Then see the kind of sledge hammer he was using on the hard, steel-lined bean of Blondy.

"I ain't a double-crosser," says Blondy.

"You are," says Bonanza. "We're all double-crossers, at one time or another."

"Show me where I ever double-crossed anybody?" says Blondy, getting sour.

"You walked out on your old man when you were just old enough to begin helping him," said Bonanza. "You borrowed a thousand from Jud Thomas and didn't pay it back, and that's what turned Jud into a road agent. You engaged yourself to marry—"

"Hold on," said Blondy.

"I didn't want to do it," said Bonanza. "But you crowded me, and I haven't got the time to be easy with you. You're not that important to me. I want you; if I can get you, I'll pay high; but I can't pay you with time. Only, don't tell me that everyone is not a double-crosser."

Now, when Blondy looked back over that rough life of his, the explanation of the bad things he had done came into his mind. But he saw the list of the black crimes and it sickened him.

"You sure know a good deal," said he.

"I know everything about the things that concern me," said Bonanza. "And you concern me a little, today. I want your price."

"I've double-crossed in the past," said Blondy, slowly. "But I don't double-cross now. Not a half-wit and a kid."

Bonanza chuckled a little.

"See what a fool you are!" he said. "With the split I can give you, you could make your father comfortable the rest of his days, set Jud up when he gets out of jail next year, and marry that girl. You've always wanted to marry her."

It rather staggered Blondy, when he heard these things all trotted out like ghosts before him, one after the other.

"You're talking about fifty thousand dollars or so," said he.

"I don't try to buy a race horse for the price of a mustang," said Bonanza. "If you go with me, I know that I can trust you. And I'll give you some rotten things to do. But they'll soon be over. That's the best of it."

Now, what came up and socked Blondy in the eye was the picture of that girl that he walked out on; because he was fond of her, and he only wanted a good break and a stake before he went back to her. She wasn't no beauty, but she fitted right into Blondy's heart and filled out all the corners of it.

Besides, the businesslike way in which Bonanza was talking put a new face on the thing. It seemed that every man had to live through certain rotten things. Blondy had done bad things before. One more bad thing, and then he could do some real good. He could turn about and start on the straight road—and with a wife! On the other hand, he hadn't known the dummy and me very long. Already we got dim in his mind. He seemed to see us through the smoke of Bonanza's cigar.

"It makes me kind of sick," said Blondy.

"It'd make anybody sick," said Bonanza.

This sorter left Blondy with nothing to say. If Bonanza had started in persuading him, the game would have been off. Blondy would simply have socked him and walked out.

"I double-cross Slope and he's left flat," said Blondy.

"You're wrong," replied the crook. "I offered him ten thousand. I'll pay him that, too. I'll put it in a wallet and drop it in his pocket—after I've cleaned out the Christabel."

Blondy blinked. Things looked better and better.

"More than ten thousand—what would the fool do with it?" asked Bonanza. "It'd be talked out of his hands in no time. I would have tied him up legally for half that price, except for the red-headed kid."

I don't blush when I put this down.

"The kid seems sorter smart," said Blondy.

"He's mean," said Bonanza, "and meanness and smartness are the same thing, up to a point."

Blondy went back on his tracks a little ways.

"You'd give the dummy ten thousand, would you?" said he.

"I tell you, I would. I mean it. After the Christabel is cleaned out. We'll keep him under observation in the meantime."

"No knocking on the head?"

"Do you think I'm a fool to litter my way with dead men?" asked Bonanza.

"That's right. Murder's a fool's game," said Blondy.

He felt better all over. Bonanza didn't seem such a greasy, slick devil. He just seemed a business man—hard, keen, and all that, but a business man who got things done, one way or another.

"The Christabel must be as rich as the devil," ventured Blondy.

"She is," said the fat man. "She's so rich that I can retire on the loot I get out of her, unless the vein pinches out. That may happen too. But I'm willing to gamble. I've taken chances all my life, and this looks like a good one to me."

He seemed to mean exactly what he said, and Blondy answered: "I've named my price."

"You can have it," said Chris.

"When?"

"Half and half."

"Half in stock and half in promises?" said Blondy. Chris grinned.

"Half in cash before, and half after."

"Half before what?"

"Before you do the job."

"What's the job to be?"

"You're on the inside with Mr. Edward Dugan, alias Slope, the half-wit. You can lead him wherever you please."

"You sound as if you were listening in at the restaurant."

"I have telephone receivers in a good many minds," said Bonanza. "Your job will be to lead the pair into a trap; I'll set the trap, and tell you where and when."

"The kid, too?" said Blondy.

"Yes, the kid, too. I want them both. I may be able to get redhead separately. I'm trying to. If I can't, I want him blanketed with the dummy. He's young, but he's old enough to make a squeal. You see, I've simply got to have him under cover."

"All right," said Blondy.

But he didn't feel so good. He felt that I was pretty young to be socked with the same club that was used on Slope's thick head.

"Now, then," said Bonanza, "you agree?"

"I certainly agree," said Blondy, slowly.

"For fifty thousand?"

"Yes, for fifty thousand."

"I'm going to take half the money out of that safe, over there, and hand it to you," says the crook. "But, first, we'll shake hands on this little deal."

And he stuck out his mitt, and Blondy likewise begun to stick out his.

But just then he noticed the hand of Bonanza, all sort of puffy above the knuckles and glistening with sweat, with the hair growing pretty thick over the first joints of the fingers. And he sickened a little. Suddenly his hand dropped back to his side.

"Are you playing the fool?" says Bonanza, sharp as a whip. "Are you trying to raise your price with me?"

"No," said Blondy. "You almost got me, Bonanza, but thank God, I come to and I'm off and away from you!"

Bonanza didn't argue. He just stepped back and folded his arms, and a bell rang dimly, far away, twice.

Bonanza was teetering slowly back and forth from heels to toes.

"I'll be trotting along," said Blondy, and picked up his hat.

Still, Bonanza said nothing, and then Blondy turned to the door to go out.

It was opened at the same time from the outside, and a man stood there with a double-barreled shotgun across the crook of his arm and behind him there were two more with guns.

But the shotgun was enough, because it was covering Blondy, and he could see that the trigger finger of the fellow was ready. The man was Bill Larkin. And his one eye seemed twice as full of light as it had been before.

"Shall we take him?" asked Larkin. "I told you he wouldn't be no use."

"One minute," said Bonanza.

He went on, to Blondy: "You see how it is. I've got you at every turn. Are you going to have another little think?"

"Thanks," said Blondy.

And I'll bet I can see how the Adam's apple wobbled up and down in his skinny neck as he answered: "No, I'll stay put."

"That's all, then," said Bonanza, and turned to the window. He seen somebody in the street, and started waving a hand in greeting.

"What'll we do with the stiff?" asks Larkin.

"Put him in the back room," said Bonanza.

"Soft?"

"Hard. If he makes a move, slam him. I don't care how hard you slam him, and I don't care where."

"Suppose he has to be planted," asked Larkin.

"You talk like a fool," answered the fat man. "I give you the deck, and you ask me what sort of a hand you should deal yourself. Make it five aces and be damned, for all of me."

And then Larkin laughed a little, and he looked Blondy over, up and down, as he said: "You'd pretty near forgot me hadn't you, a while back. But I'm gonna freshen up your memory a whole lot, Blondy. Turn around and hold your hands out behind you!"

So Blondy turned, but he turned only halfway around before he shot a fist into Larkin's face and slammed him clean into the wall.

Then he seen the shadow of a clubbed gun coming toward his head, and tried to dodge, but was too late. It got him and darkness settled down over his brain.

CHAPTER 15

Here I take up with me and myself, and a mighty big relief it is to be able to talk about exactly what I seen and heard and done. Which was plenty, as I said before!

Well, when I went out on my own into the street, I felt pretty good, the same as Blondy, but for different reasons. I mean, I felt important, because I was hooked up, hand and glove, with two men, real men. They was both of 'em fighters. And they was both of 'em hard hitters. They seemed honest. I was glad to be in on that kind of a lay. All the while, I knew that I was walking right on the edge of a cliff and that the toe of Bonanza's boot might kick me over it at any time.

Danger, to a kid, don't matter much. It just puts spice in the air. You know how that is.

Well, I went on down the street, and I enjoyed the sights, the sounds and just standing in the sun, even. I was stuffed like a snake, with that breakfast I had eaten.

As I lazied along, half in sun and half in shade, I looked back into other days that hadn't been so fat, like when I walked one winter all the way from Quebec, the far side of the river, to Montreal. And the mosquitos and hell-fire in Mississippi, that was one time when I didn't have a cent and was starving thin. Then there was other times, but none of 'em worse than crossing Shackle Pass—three days of it and a blizzard blowing the whole while.

Now, I was thinking about some of these things and feeling pretty contented. I was as contented as an old horse rubbing against a scratching post in the corral. And there was plenty to look at, always. There was never a dull moment in Pottsville, you can bet.

The most that I seen, to begin with, was a pair of Chinese that run at each other with butcher knives. They was howling and about to chop each other up, but before they started chopping they done a kind of a war dance with their pigtails hopping and flopping, while they yelled out remarks in chink that I would've give a lot to understand. I'll bet that even a mule skinner could've learned something from their flow of talk.

They was about ready to slam each other in earnest, and I was standing on one foot, ready to enjoy everything that happened, when a guy on the next corner picks a Colt out of his pocket and begins shooting, and his bullets smashed into the dust between those Chinese.

Well, sir, it did you good to see the way they dropped their knives and ran in opposite directions, with their hands thrown out in front of them, yelling for help.

The gunman, he begun to laugh so that he could hardly stand, and had to stagger back into the saloon to get another drink and brace himself up for another joke.

But nobody in the street paid much attention.

When there was gold in the ground and the gold fever in the air, it didn't matter how many Chinks carved each other up, or how many whites, either. No, the only thing that counted was each fellow's business. And the devil take the rest.

That's an amusing kind of atmosphere to stir around in, though it's likely to get a bit hard on the nerves, now and then.

Well, I got along, and when the dust of the shooting had settled down, I seen a little crowd gathered and squeezed my way through, and there I seen a thing that would've made you laugh. It was performing canaries!

Would you ever think, unless you seen it, that fool things like canaries, that don't usually do nothing but sit around on perches, with one eye shut and the other half white, and chew a seed now and then, then stop chewing with the husk of the seed still in the tip of the beak, and ruffle up their feathers, open up their throats fit for warbling, and whistle a song for hours on end—I mean to say, would you think that canaries could be taught tricks?

No, you wouldn't. You'd say that their brains was too small. But you'd be wrong, as I was wrong. For there was twelve or thirteen canaries in a cage and the way they carried on, it surely was an amazing sight.

They had with 'em a skinny little runt of a man that looked like consumption plus. He had a pair of sad eyes, and when he spoke, the hollows of his cheeks sunk in deep. His clothes, they was ragged, even judged by Slope's standard. I felt all kind of dressed up and Sunday-like, looking at the runt.

He had a little whistle, and he toots on the whistle, and all of them canaries stand in a line; and they got on little red-and-white silk uniforms, with little guns tied under their wings, like it was "right, shoulder arms." One of them, he has a sword and a cocked hat, and he stands out in front of the rest, and every time the whistle blows he gives a hop and a flirt of his wings.

The second toot of the whistle, the line breaks up into a column of fours, and it marches around the cage, and does obliques, and everything, and those canaries, it was a sight to see 'em hop, when one of 'em got behind the rest.

Pretty soon they bust up into two lines, one on each side of the cage, and there's a little toy gun in front of each line, and one of those canaries at one end, he grabs a string in his claw and pulls the string. It must've been hitched onto a hair trigger, because the blank cartridge goes off with a bang, and all of the other side falls down flat and lies dead.

But him with the cocked hat, he spreads his wings and begins to sing like it was taps over the dead. When he finished, the runt drops a hood over the cage and started passing the hat.

I ain't been able to describe it any too good. But it was a wonderful show, for canaries, I mean. Everybody laughed, and nothing but gold, as far as I seen, dropped into the runt's hat.

I pretty near dropped in the five-spot that I'd won from Blondy, but I changed my mind and give a quarter, instead. After all, they couldn't expect me to play up to the gold that growed-up men was loaded with in Pottsville.

I was beginning to think that the Italian led a pretty soft life, and that it wouldn't be so bad to spend the rest of my life wandering around with nothing heavier than canaries to pack and to have gold pieces showering into your hat, I begun to kinder dream about that sort of life. Then I seen the crowd was breaking up, and the Italian, he was packing up the trundle stand on which he had the birds act.

He gave me a grin and a wink. Then he tapped the cover of the bird cage and said: "You wanta see?"

"Yeah, you bet I do," said I.

"I show you something," said he, with another wink at me, a mile wide.

And so I went along with him, pretty curious, because I could guess that those birds had a lot more tricks up their sleeves—wings maybe I'd better say—and that maybe the little man would show me something about how to train a bird.

He led the way, trundling his cart along, and every now and then, he'd turn around, wink and jerk his head at me, to make sure that I was following.

So we come off the street and down a twisting alley that was full of packing cases broke up, half for building shacks and half for firewood. There was tin cans, and all sorts of things in the alley, and the wheels of the cart went over bumps that made the birds all chirp out together in the darkness under their hood.

Well, of course, he wanted to get away from where any crowd would see him, and so I followed along, right brisk, and pretty soon I brush by a doorway, and in the dark of that doorway, like in the hollow of the night, I seen two men, and one of them flipped a blanket around my head as quick as a wink.

He meant business, too. I mean to say, his hand came behind the blanket hard, and clapped me over the mouth so that it knocked me pretty near silly.

I begun to kick. And a voice said far away, outside of the blanket: "Stay still, you fool, or I'll knock you over your red head!"

So I did what I was told. If you've had a few knocks over the head, you know they ain't no good.

I was carried along for a good ways, and the man that was carrying me said that I ought to be put out cold and left in somebody's garbage can, because there wasn't any use packing around a weight like me, but another voice said that Bonanza wouldn't have it that way.

It gave me a sort of shock to hear the name of Bonanza Chris. Of course, I knew pretty well that he must be behind this business, but still there was room for hope, so long as he wasn't actually seen or named.

My hopes went out, then. I didn't even try to struggle. I was just sorter numb.

After a while, I was being carried up steps, and the man that carried me puffed and darned a good lot. After a while, a door opened, and I was dumped down on my feet. Someone said: "Well, here's the lot of 'em!"

Then my hands were tied good and hard behind my back, and the blanket was ripped off over my head, so that I could look around me.

I saw a couple of yeggs. But they didn't matter much. I could see the pretty face of Bill Larkin, for one thing, grinning all lop-sided, and I saw other things that counted more.

For there in one small room with me, lying on the floor close to the wall, and all swathed up in ropes, still as two butchered turkeys, lay Blondy and Slope!

That fairly knocked the bottom out of things for me, you can bet. I felt more than half sick, and I said: "Well, how in the world did you come here?"

They didn't answer. They just looked at me, and then

I could see that they were not only tied, but they were gagged, too. So I let out a yell that cut the roof pretty near off the house. My holler didn't last long, though, because Bill Larkin stepped in and socked me on the chin.

CHAPTER 16

I woke up with a whole xylophone hammering in the back of my head. Things had changed a good deal. There were no guards standing around, and the gags had been taken out of the mouths of Blondy and Slope. There was only one other man in the room, and that was Bonanza himself.

He was sitting on the edge of the table near the window, and he was twisting his thumb into the big gold cable that run across his stomach and untwisting it again. He was smiling, too, as he looked from one of us to the other.

It was no good to try hollering again. If they'd taken the gags out of the mouths of Blondy and Slope, they knew that our yells couldn't get to the street. Even if they did, what did a few yells more or less matter in the street in that town?

"Jiminy, Slope," I said, "how'd they get you, without tearing you to pieces?"

"Why, Red," he answered, "I had that note from you, saying that I should come at once and, therefore, I—"

"Letter? Letter from me?" I yipped. "I didn't send no letter!"

"But it looked exactly like your handwriting," said poor Slope. "Of course it was just a sham. I can understand that, now."

He could understand that—after the mischief was done!

But he could be taken in, in the first place, by the oldest trick in the world. I pretty near hated Slope, just then. So I said: "What about you, Blondy?"

"Oh, only a sock on the head," said he. "What about yourself?"

"An old Italian, a flock of trained canaries and two saps waiting in a doorway framed me," said I. "I'm gonna go and ask to get into a home for the feeble-minded. My brains seem to've leaked out, some way or other!"

"Have you finished telling your stories, fellows?" said Bonanza.

We all three just looked at him, and he looked back, from face to face. He was pretty pleased, and he showed it.

"You see how things come out," said he, "when you stand up against intelligence, money, and hired hands. As a matter of fact, I rate the three of you a little higher than this. I thought it might have taken me at least a half day to get you all. But not at all!

"In fact, this is the easiest little dodge that I've worked in a long time. No real trouble, and everyone collected under one hospitable roof. I hope you'll enjoy yourselves, gents, because you'll be staying here for some time."

I got up to my feet and stretched myself a little. Then I walked to the second window. The shade was down. Only, I could look down through the crack that showed under it, and the distance that my eye dropped to the ground made me feel sicker than ever. We were cooped up for fair.

"Stand away from the window and sit down on the floor again," said big Bonanza.

"Oh, all right," said I.

"Mind you, I made no allowance because you're quite young," he went on. "And you've caused me trouble enough already, and if you trouble me again, I'll teach you a lesson you won't forget."

I knew he meant it. I sat down so fast that I nearly drove a nail through my spine. It was sticking right out from the wall, and I give a jump and a grunt—I didn't dare to holler!

"Hurt yourself, eh?" says Bonanza. "That's all right, too. You're not hurt the way you may be before the finish of this party, son."

He turned to the others.

"Did you hurt yourself badly, Red?" Slope asked.

"No, I'm all right," said I, and then I broke out, because the meanness was all boiling up in me. "You've got the edge on me now, Bonanza, but you're going to choke on me before you've swallowed me down."

"I won't try to swallow you, son," says Bonanza. "I need cheap meat for dog feed."

He laughed a good deal, very pleased with himself.

He broke off his laughter to say to Slope:

"This morning the boy had a bright idea, didn't he?"

"Idea?" says Slope, blankly.

"Dog-gone," groaned Bonanza, "can't you understand anything? I say the kid had a bright idea and put your stock certificates in a safe-deposit vault in the bank. Am I right?"

Slope cleared his throat, but he said nothing.

I could tell what was sticking in his crop.

"Answer me, you flat-head," said Bonanza. "I know anyway, but I'd like to hear it from you. You put the stock certificates in the bank, didn't you?"

Slope shrugged his shoulders.

Then I got a little queer touch of hope, that Bonanza was so sure about that faked envelope that maybe he hadn't even searched through Slope's rags—maybe the real stuff was still resting in Slope's coat pocket!

This made me jump, and that dog-gone nail, it ripped my wrist open. It was a painful cut, and I felt the blood run hot on my skin. But there was no good calling attention to the way I had hurt myself. Bonanza would only have laughed.

Then, while he went on talking, I got another idea that seemed like a beauty to me. I began on it right away.

Bonanza was saying: "Now, Mr. Edward Dugan, you're about to taste the results of absolute folly. You were offered a fair price and more than a fair price for your property. You were offered it by a man whose

86

power, if you had cared to inquire about me in Pottsville, is enough to give better men than you pause. But you preferred to be bullheaded. Am I right?"

"Yes, Mr. Christian," said Slope, "You're right."

"You've struck a bad snag," said Bonanza. "Now you refuse to answer my questions, which makes matters worse for you. The fact is, I don't need to have your reply. I know that the envelope was deposited, and I know what it must have contained."

He grinned again, triumphantly.

I saw Slope look down at the floor, and for my part I had to frown and cough to keep back a grin of my own. I mean, Bonanza looked so fat, and confident, so happy and full of himself!

Well, he went right on talking, free and large and easy.

"As the matter stands, you'll get nothing except your freedom, but that I'm willing to offer you in return for a little note, written and signed, addressed to your friends, the bankers, and asking them to deliver to bearer the envelope that you just deposited. Are you ready to do that?"

Slope sighed and looked, strange to say, at me.

"Don't you do it, Slope," said I.

I saw the eyes of Slope widen and widen; he was pretty well flabbergasted because I advised him to hold onto the pad of blank paper in an envelope.

"The brat is a fool," said Bonanza. "He seems to forget that I have all three of you in the hollow of my hand. But I've stood a great deal from him, and now I'm going to show him that—"

He got just that far as he started across the room toward me with his fists tight. I wondered if he really was only bluffing, but then I seen in his eye that he meant it; he was going to lay me out, even if I wasn't his size. I felt like yelling, but just then Slope put in hoarsely: "Don't do it, Mr. Christian. Don't hurt him!"

Bonanza took one more step and towered over me. I thought even then that he would treat himself to a kick in my face, at the least. But he changed his mind, because he heard a creaking sound, and he turned around and saw Slope straining at his ropes, with his face terribly furrowed and contorted, and his shoulders swollen with the effort.

I suppose that he had seen a good many men in a silent fury before, but he was staggered by the look of Slope, just then. I mean, he actually went a step back to the wall, and he called out in a shaken voice: "Well?"

Slope stopped heaving at the ropes, but his chest was still working slow and deep as he said: "I'll sign anything that you write for me, but turn Red loose. He's too young to punish."

The mouth of Bonanza worked so as to produce a smile.

"I'll turn you all loose, my friend," said he, "as soon as you've signed the little slip of paper that I have with me."

"What's the proof that he'll turn us loose after you've signed, Slope?" I asked.

In my mind's eye I could see the frightful face and the black soul of Bonanza, when he opened that envelope from the bank and saw that he had been running down a false scent.

When I asked my question, old Slope said: "To be sure, Mr. Christian, and what is our security that you will do as you promise?"

"What's your security?" said Bonanza. "Well, I'll tell you what your security is. It's simply my word. My sweet word."

He began to walk up and down the room in a cold passion, and every time he passed me he slowed up and looked at me as though he was already tasting me as I went down his throat in small bits. I never saw a man look so mean.

"You're going to take my word, because you can't help yourself," he went on. "You're no better off now than a lot of black slaves in the old days. You're not even so well off. I could cut the throats of the three of you and slide your bodies into a hole in the ground and nobody would ever miss you, and nobody would ever look for you.

That's why I'm so free with you—because I know that you're a set of vagabonds—because you don't count. You're trash. And I can afford to throw you away."

"Mr. Christian," said Slope, "this is being contemptible!"

I was rather surprised. It seemed that there was some things, after all, that Slope could see for himself. Or was Bonanza holding out a light that the whole world could see by?

"In the meantime," said Christian, "tell me if you're ready to do as I ask?"

I never saw such as face Slope's such scorn and contempt, such disgust and deep anger.

But he said: "I'll write my name down for you. But if you touch Red before, or afterward, I'll manage to free myself. And I'll kill you, Mr. Christian, with these hands of mine!"

CHAPTER 17

Once, a long time ago, I was going through the south side of my town, across the river, long after dark. I'd been fishing down the creek and, as I come up toward the bridge, I went by a shack, and I heard a man's voice crying out in a terrible way:

"I'm gonna kill you. I'm tastin' the death of you now. I'm gonna kill you. I'm gonna dig these here thumbs of mine into the holler of your throat, because you ain't no good, and you ain't worth living!"

He stopped a minute, where his voice had gone up to a scream, and I heard the sobbing of a woman, soft and quiet and hopeless. That was an awful moment but compared with the quiet way of Slope when he told Bonanza that he'd kill the crook if he touched me, it was nothing at all. It put the chills and the wriggles into Bonanza, all right.

"There's murder in you, is there?" said he, and he forced out a funny little laugh.

"Well," he continued, "I told you before that I'd turn you all loose as soon as you've done the necessary things, and I'm a man of my word.

"I'll help you to stand up and sit at the table."

"I can stand up, I think," said Slope.

Tied as he was, roped hand and foot, he stood up. Then he hopped, both feet together, to the table and sat down in a chair.

The telling of it don't sound much; but it was like watching a wrapped and buried mummy, so to speak, stand up and move. Bonanza's eyes fairly bulged out of his head.

But he shoved a paper in front of Slope and put a pen into his tied hand, and Slope managed to wriggle his fingers until he had written out a signature that satisfied the fat man.

The instant it was made, Bonanza snatched the sheet of paper away from him, and he went back, with rapid steps, toward the door, still facing Slope, and he begun to laugh in a way it did me no good to see. His nostrils, they flared out and sunk in as he laughed. It wasn't pretty, if you ask me!

Then he opened the door, fumbling behind him, and walked out.

"We're stung, boys," says Blondy.

"We're what?" asked Slope politely, from his chair.

"We're in the soup. We're nailed up. We're boxed and labeled and shipped," said Blondy, "if that makes it any clearer."

"I'm afraid," said Slope, polite and careful, "that I haven't mastered all of the Westernisms."

"Westernisms be darned," said Blondy, getting peeved. "Ain't I talking good American?"

Slope looked hurt and a little afraid. "I simply haven't heard them before," said he.

"Blondy means that Bonanza doesn't intend to turn us loose," I said.

"That's a suspicion that I was beginning to have myself," says Slope. "There was something distinctly unpleasant about his face as he went through that doorway."

"You bet your shouting it was distinctly unpleasant," says Blondy. "It was all sour."

Then he turned his head to me: "Whacha say, Red?" he asked.

"I ain't saying anything," says I.

"Whacha doing then?" asked he.

"Cultivating my disposition, dummy," says I.

He scowled, and then he grinned a little.

"The kid's got some spirit left in him," says he. "I dunno but what he's got an idea, too."

"Ah, yes," said Slope. "Red is full of ideas. I thought for a moment, Red, that the fellow intended to strike you."

"He was going to bust me all over the map," said I, "until he heard the teacher's voice."

"Teacher's voice?" says Slope.

"Oh, darn it," breaks in Blondy, "don't you understand anything?"

Slope lifted that lion's head and looked at him, and Blondy went on hastily: "I don't mean to step on your toes. Only, the kid was saying that Bonanza Chris intended to break him open, except that you spoke out. And you spoke good and loud, brother, and I'm proud of you!"

"There is something irritating about Mr. Christian," remarks the dummy. "I don't think that his standards are very high."

"He doesn't think his standards are very high," I points out to Blondy.

"It's a harsh thing to say," answers Blondy.

"Yes, I suppose that is harsh," says Slope. "Perhaps I should have said that he merely appeared rather—"

"Oh, leave it be," replies Blondy.

And he groaned.

In the meantime, I had been working away at that idea which I had. It had been forced on me, a couple of

91

times, all by itself. I mean the nail that had jabbed into me twice. A nail that had a good, long, sharp point like that was something that ought not to be wasted, and ever since I got that idea, I had been using every minute worrying at the rope that tied my hands behind my back, rubbing it up and down against the point. When Christian got out of the room, I worked faster and harder and didn't care what noise I made. I only tried to keep rubbing the rope at the same place, and now I could hear the little strands and the threads ripping and snapping.

But it was a miserably long business. How I longed to have my eyes on what I was doing! But I had to work with my eyes in the dark, and just tell myself to be patient, and all that. Easy to say, and mighty hard to do!

All this time I could feel the steps that Bonanza's messenger must be making to the bank. I could see him turn in at the door and present the note to the clerk. After comparing the two signatures, the clerk would get that envelope.

I tell you what, I made that journey step by step, and I didn't hurry it, because I counted five for every step of the way there, and back. And, all the time, I was picking at that rope, until my arms got numb to the shoulders.

Then I heard Slope, saying: "I seem to hear something, like a rat gnawing."

Blondy had tumbled before this, and he says, short and sharp: "It's the kid working at his ropes. Shut up and hold your breath!"

"Working at his ropes?" asked Slope, and inched his way around in the chair, and looked hard at me, with his eyes wide open.

Yes, he could understand that, and what it meant. Three of us were about worse than dead, unless we got loose before the messenger came back from the bank. There was a sudden give to the ropes. I almost fainted.

"Are you loose?" whispers Blondy.

"Have you managed it?" inquires Slope.

I tried. No, my hands were still held fast, and I worked in deeper on the frayed spot—worked like mad. There seemed to be only a single strand holding me, but it held like iron. Then, all at once, it snapped, I felt the cords unravel a bit at the wrists, and in three shakes my hands were free and in front of me!

I jumped for the door like a flash.

Blondy gasped: "Are you going to leave us, kid?"

"He won't do that," observed Slope, calm and resigned, and I sorter blessed him for having that faith in me.

Well, I got to the door and I turned the key softly in the latch, and then I hauled up a chair and put the back of it under the knob. Next, I jumped for Slope.

At the same time, I heard a voice, clear and strong, in the next room, saying: "You've been long enough about it!"

"That there clerk," said the voice of Larkin, in reply, "he couldn't trust me, till he compared the signature twice over, and wondered why there was a kind of a wabble in the writing. Then he showed it to somebody higher up in the bank, and that fellow, he showed it to somebody else still higher. That was the way of it, but at last they handed it over and here it is."

All that while, I was working at the knot that held Slope's hands, but it was tied hard as iron.

"Knife?" I asked Blondy.

"No, darn it!" said he. "Try this knot."

I jumped to him and tried his knot. But it was the same deal! Those knots were sweated as hard and as close as a knot in wood!

So I jumped back to Slope again, because it seemed to me, straight and decent as Blondy was, a hundred of him wouldn't make one of old Slope. Still the infernal rope wouldn't give, and then I heard Bonanza roar out: "Blank paper!"

"Hey, hold on!" says Larkin.

"You dirty runt," yells Bonanza, "I'm going to flay you alive. Give me back what you took out of here!"

"I didn't take nothing. I didn't take a thing."

"You lie!"

"Look!" says Larkin. "The seal wasn't broke when it come to you."

"By thunder, it wasn't," says Bonanza, so low that I

could hardly hear him. "They sold me. The kid did it. The dummy would never had the brains. Now you come with me, Larkin. I'm going to show them what it means to trifle with me!"

CHAPTER 18

Of course, what I heard, the other two in the same room with me could hear also. And they never turned a hair. I never saw such nerve.

Just then, I could thank God, because the first turns of the knot slipped suddenly loose in my fingers. But the shaking of my hands jerked my grip away from the other turnings and windings and the knot!

At the door, came the pair of them, and I heard the knob turn, and then the voice of Bonanza muttering: "That's strange. It couldn't have locked itself!"

He shook the door. "By the Eternal," said he, not loudly, "they've locked the door from the inside. One of them, at least, is loose. Or else, Slope managed to do it with his bound hands. What fool tied his hands in front of him? Larkin, run like lightning to the back entrance. Call some of the boys!"

I heard Larkin running fast, and then the heavy shoulder of Bonanza was heaved against the door.

It was only a sheet of flimsy pine, warped already, and now it split from head to foot at the first shock.

I heard the big man grunt. Then, he gave the door his shoulder again, and this time he walked right in on us. And still I hadn't that knot untied!

Well, there was Slope, facing the door, and there was Blondy over against the wall and me, crouched low and small behind Slope, working on like a drowning rat, still fighting for the last chance, but kinder knowing that it was all no good, because Bonanza had the advantage of being a complete crook, and he had all the cleverness and he had the luck, too.

He says: "And, so, Mr. Dugan, you thought that you could pull the wool over my eyes?"

Of course, Slope said nothing. Perhaps he didn't even understand the expression that had been used.

"Yes," said Bonanza, "you thought that you could pull the wool over my eyes. A good little trick, which I suppose that the brat invented for you. But it won't do. I walk through such little hamperings, just as I walk through the door which you cleverly managed to lock. It was due to Larkin's idiocy that your hands were tied in front of you."

"Yes, that appears to have been an oversight," says Slope.

The beast came out in Bonanza's voice: "I'll oversight you, you half-wit!" says he.

"That's unfair, I think," says Slope. "I'm not quick. But I believe that my understanding is sound."

The fat man roars. "You darned pudding head, where did you put those certificates?"

"But why should you be told?" asked Slope.

I was so amazed by this answer that I almost stopped working at the knot.

Every minute, I was wondering how it was that Bonanza didn't see me. Even though Slope pushed his hands as far as he could to the side, still it seemed certain that my shoulder and my head, at least, must be in view. Still Bonanza went on as though he saw nothing.

When he came in and spotted Slope and Blondy in place, just as he had seen them, I suppose that he forgot to remember me. He just took it for granted thcat everything was all right in the room.

"Why should I be told?" repeated Bonanza Chris. "Why should your throat remain intact?"

"Even if you had the certificates, you would still wish to murder us?" asks Slope.

"I would. You fool, what importance are you to me the minute that I have them?"

"You promised to set us free the instant that I signed my name," said Slope.

"And wouldn't I've been a fool if I had? You lied to me, Dugan. It was a dirty, sneaking lie, but I found out. I brush through the little clouds that creatures like you try to throw up before my eyes."

Now, at that instant, the knot gave suddenly, easily, in the tips of my fingers, and a sort of mistiness came over my eyes and my whole brain, because I knew that now everything would be all right with us.

The knot gave, just as Bonanza said: "It wasn't your device. You haven't the wits for that. It was the red-headed brat, and he— Where the devil is he? Where the devil—"

He started running around the chair, and I heard the swish of the rope as it came free from Slope's big wrists.

Just as I saw the furious and half-frightened face of Bonanza come into view, Slope reached out and gathered him in, and he squashed him, I tell you, in that giant grip of his!

I got up, shaking and staggering.

There was no noise from Mr. Henry Christian; he was just blowing bubbles when I picked the gold knife out of his vest pocket and took the watch and chain along that were hitched onto it. I opened a blade of that knife and in a jiffy I had old Slope free from head to foot.

I was turning to Blondy, then, when Larkin crashed in at the back door of the room.

I remembered then, like a fool, that I hadn't locked that door when I had the chance. But anyway, I didn't feel that the game was done, when Larkin flung the door open and rushed in on us.

And there was Slope, rising, and holding Bonanza Chris between himself and Larkin's gun.

There were plenty of others behind Larkin, and a bad-looking lot they were, the worst that I ever saw!

"What in the devil is loose?" asked Larkin.

"Keep away," says Slope, "or I'll throw Bonanza

through the window and then try my luck with your guns. Keep away!" And he lifted Bonanza lightly and stepped back toward the window.

I was already down behind Blondy, and he was as free as the day after two cuts from my knife. Bonanza croaked like a dying man: "Larkin, keep back, or I'm a dead man. Don't try to edge in, you fool. Keep back! He's killing me with his hands!"

There was a sort of a catch in his voice. It wasn't pain or fear. It was plain rage. Anyway, Larkin backed up. He kept pointing his gun at Blondy and me, and then at his boss and Slope. But he didn't know what to do. He could only choke.

"What'll happen? I got five men here with guns. We can eat 'em," he said.

"What good will it be to me, if you eat them while I lie on the ground below that window with my head smashed in," said Bonanza.

"Yeah, there's something in that," says Larkin.

I kinder laughed. I was a little hysterical, perhaps.

"Dugan, I've got to bargain with you," remarks Bonanza.

"How can I bargain with you?" says Slope. "It appears to me that your promises are absolutely worthless."

Bonanza turned his head toward me, and his face convulsed in an ugly way as he met my eyes.

"You, Red, tell him what to do!" he directed.

It pleased me a good deal that Bonanza had to call me in. I stood up, and big Blondy stood up with me, and then we crossed the room together.

I said: "You know, Slope, old-timer, that you can heave Fatty out the window, but then they'll blow us off the face of the earth. Make a deal. We walk Bonanza down to the street, and then we turn him loose. And his gun packers, they can see that we deliver him and sound. Once we're in the open, it's an even break."

"Ah, I understand," said Slope. "Is that satisfactory to you, Blondy?"

"I'd like to carve a steak or two off this porker," says Blondy, "but I guess that the kid has hit the nail on the head. We've got to use Bonanza to pay for an out. That's all there is to it."

"You hear it?" said Bonanza. "Larkin, keep the rest of the fellows in hand, will you? This inhuman devil has the strength of an ape in his hands!"

"It's kinder funny. I dunno how this happened!" replies Larkin.

"You raving idiot," yells Bonanza. "I'll show you how funny it is in a few minutes."

We walked out of the room and through the office to the stairs. Then he said: "Now, gentlemen," and it was funny to hear him try to put his manners on, again, "now gentlemen, it appears to me that we have met and parted as equal antagonists. You can see that you are free to go to the bottom of the stairs. And I'll remain here."

"That's all right," says Blondy.

"No, it's not. He doesn't want the folks in the street to see him in our hands," said I, "with his necktie higher than his ear. It won't be so good for his reputation. He won't seem such a great boss as he was before. So let's take him down and let the sun have a peek at him, Blondy."

Blondy began to laugh.

"You're right," said he. "I'm feeling better and better. And only five minutes ago, the grave mold was collecting all over me!"

So down we went to the street, with Larkin and his gun crew following along behind us, but we stood on the sidewalk, which was pretty high off the street level, just here, being built of boards, we all side-stepped from the corner of the entrance.

There was twenty or thirty people in sight just then. And all of them seemed to see what was happening at the same instant. They stood and gaped.

"Say, fellows, won't you let me get back inside!" whined Bonanza.

And Blondy yelled: "Pottsville, here's a little keepsake for you! With our compliments!"

And he took a step forward and kicked Bonanza with all the might of his long leg.

Well, Bonanza seemed to rise and float. He landed on his face and the dust puffed out on each side of him. He lay still!

CHAPTER 19

You take a crew of miners, lumberjacks or cow-punchers and a joke don't have to be terribly refined to tickle 'em. And this tickled that lot in the street. I guess some of them had been trimmed by Chris, one time or another. Anyway, they must've been a little tired of his fine front.

Now, when they seen him get to his feet, all smeared up where the dust had stuck to the sweat of his face and white where it covered his clothes, they leaped back and roared, and they kept on roaring. I seen one of Larkin's hired hands with a gun begin to shake and quiver all over too, though he just managed to keep his face straight. Well, it was a thing to make you laugh, all right, and I laughed with the rest.

A lot of the men in the street, they gathered around and wanted to know what the show was about and Blondy, he surprised me by making a little speech.

He said: "Fellows, it's the little matter of a mine called the Christabel that Mr. Fat-face Christian, alias Bonanza Chris went and sold to my friend Slope Dugan here. And then he found out that that hole in the ground was a beauty, and so he's just been trying to buy that mine back with a gun. That's all!"

It raised a good-sized growl out of the crowd.

"What's to be done about it?" asked one man, loudly. And Dugan answered: "There ain't anything to be done about it. There ain't any sheriff, or even a common cop out here. There's only a mob."

"Mobs have put crooks down before this!" yells somebody.

"Not this mob," said Blondy, snarling mad. "Bonanza Chris and his gang of yeggs have been running things too long. They know your measure. There was a time when Western towns could make their own laws and execute 'em, too. But this ain't that kind of a town. It's the kind that lies down and lets anybody come along and kick it in the face. Here, fellows, come along."

And he sorter took charge of me and Slope and marched us away.

We went through that mob, and it was an angry lot of men. Those on the outside was newcomers, asking what it was all about, and those on the inside was humming like wasps. They didn't know whether they wanted the most to lynch Bonanza Chris or Blondy. But Bonanza, they knew, had his gunmen always around him; and Blondy looked kinder discouragingly big. So we got through, all right.

Says Slope: "I don't know that I should have spoken in quite that manner to them, Blondy."

"Maybe, you don't," said Blondy. "But all I'm cussing myself about is that I didn't get in a few more hot shots that I've thought up since I left off talking to 'em!"

Then he says: "You fellows think that the day's only beginning, but it ain't. It's wore along to pretty nigh in the middle of the afternoon, though not hardly anything has happened yet. But if you got an appetite worked up, we might as well go and feed."

Hungry? You bet we were hungry. Five minutes in the hands of Bonanza's fancy workers, that was enough of an appetizer to make it seem a week since you tasted food.

"Unfortunately," said Slope, "I haven't any money."

Blondy looked at me.

"He hasn't any money!" says he.

"It's too bad," said I.

"But since we're talkin' about money," says Blondy, "how much do I owe you for manhandling Bonanza and saving all our hides?"

"Owe me?" said Slope. "Why, nothing, of course! We're all for one and one for all, I take it."

"We are," said Blondy, "and is my wallet any better than your fighting hands, when it comes down to that?"

Slope sighed.

"The point I should like to make," said he, "is that charity—I mean to say, that to accept—"

He stumbled and stopped. He was sweating. He looked more worked up than he had been when he was lashed hand and foot in Bonanza's back room.

"Are we all together?" Blondy asks him.

"I trust that we are all one," says Slope, solemnly. "I owe you both so much that—"

"Aw, shut up!" says Blondy. "All you owe me is the kick that I gave to Bonanza. The rest of the time, I've only been shooting off my face and gumming up the cards. But if we're all together then voting goes in this crowd. And me and Red vote that you eat on my funds till you take your ten million out of the ground."

I took Slope's arm and gave it a squeeze.

"Don't you go and hurt Blondy," said I.

"I wouldn't dream of that," said Slope, and to Blondy: "Thank you very much. I'm delighted."

"Quit talking like a book," says Blondy, "and watch me feed my face. I ain't had a square meal for a month!"

And he took us straight back to the same restaurant where we had been before. At the entrance, Slope backs up a little.

"Doesn't it occur to you," said he, "that the waiter, or the proprietor, perhaps, may be intimate with Bonanza? At least, a great deal that we said in that place seems to have been reported."

"You said something there, son," said Blondy. "And that's one reason that I wanta go back there."

So we walked on in, and the waiter came and asked what we would have.

Now, I hadn't noticed him before, because I'd been so

hungry, but I could see, now, that he was a rat all right. He was shifting from one foot to the other, asking what the gents would have, putting the knives and forks straight, and pouring out water from a carafe, all the time.

Blondy said: "The first thing we'll have is a little information."

"Know the name of every hole in the ground in Potts Valley," says the hash slinger. "Ask me anything you want to know, gents."

"I want to know," said Blondy, taking hold of him with his eye, "if you write things down for Bonanza, or do you just keep 'em in your big, strong brain?"

The waiter made a little jump back, like a rabbit making a spy hop. But before he could run, Blondy said: "If you try to clear out, I'll have to chase you and catch you and break your rotten neck. You stand there and talk."

Well, that waiter stood and talked, all right.

He was white and sick, with his mouth twitching every way at once. Slope, he leaned his head on his hand, and I seen that his hand covered his eyes. He was kinder sensitive.

"Now, open up, brother," said Blondy, "and give me the latest news on what a skunk is, because I think that you're the newest model and right out of Paris. Cheap, too! What does Bonanza pay you?"

That poor devil couldn't speak a word.

"Tell me what Bonanza paid you for the last batch of dope that you brought him?" says Blondy softly.

The waiter's knees give way, and he caught hold of the back of a chair to hold himself up.

"I didn't mean to harm you none, gents," said he. "I sorter got into the habit of chatting with Bonanza."

"You get little presents from him, now and then, I guess," ventures Blondy.

There was a groan from the waiter. "How much did he give you today?" asked Blondy.

"Ten dollars!" gasped the hash slinger.

Blondy nodded, with his eye on him. "I ain't gonna do anything to you," he said. "That is, not today. But I ad-

102

vise you to kinder keep looking around corners before you step, from now on. You hear me?"

"Yes, sir," says the waiter.

"I'll tell you another thing," says Blondy.

"Yes, sir," says the tame snake.

"Blondy," broke in Slope, "if you don't mind, I don't think that I can very well stand any more of this!"

Blondy give him a look. Then he said: "All right. I'll take my heel off his head. I just wanted to tell him one last thing. Bonanza told us where he got his information!"

"He told you?" says the waiter, through his teeth, and he rolled his eyes. I could guess what vision he was seeing with them, a nice, long sharp knife, to be used in the dark of the night.

"The sneaking, dirty, poison rat!" says the waiter. "He told *you!*"

"Sure he did. I just thought that you didn't know his full name and address," said Blondy. "Now you rustle and bring us the best in the house, and we want a small bill along with it."

We got our food. And it was the best in the house. And we got a lot of attention besides.

All the while, the face of that waiter was like a white stone. And his eyes was only partly on us. It was busy seeing his own thoughts. I didn't feel very good, watching him. I was mighty glad that my name wasn't Henry Christian.

Then Slope, after he'd sat silent through the meal, when he got to his third cup of coffee, says:

"May I say something, Blondy?"

"You may, brother," says Blondy, leaning back in his chair, feeling pretty good.

"It's only this: If I heard everything that passed between us and Christian, what you told the waiter was not strictly accurate."

"Wasn't it?" says Blondy, winking at me. "But now may I tell you something?"

"By all means," says Slope, grave and attentive.

"It's only this: if you see a lot of rats milling around in a pen, you know the best way to get rid of 'em?"

"Drowning, do you mean?" says Slope.

"Drowning is pretty sure, but there's another way that's more fun for you and for the rats. Start 'em fighting, and they'll kill one another off!"

"Ah?" says Slope. "But I don't see how that remark applies exactly, to the case of the waiter and—"

"You'll see later on," says Blondy. "It's just a little riddle of mine, and I'll show you the answer after a while!"

CHAPTER 20

I had wondered why Blondy announced us so loud and bold to the people in Pottsville, the way he had done, but before the meal was over he explained. So long as we were to take a long chance against the thug, Bonanza Chris, it was better to let the people of the place know who we were, why we were there, what we were doing, and what we were afraid of. In that way we became public property, so to speak, and the folks around the town would be more likely to remember us. We were on the map now. If we sank, others would notice. And that, Blondy hoped, would make the game a lot more difficult for Bonanza.

We planned what we would do next.

I tell you, it made me feel pretty important to sit in with a couple of growed up men and have them turn and ask opinions! But you take the real men, the big men, and they don't put on airs. They don't brush a kid out of the way, the way the fakes and the yeggs, and the fools do. Maybe I don't have so many good ideas, but I might have some, here and there, to help out.

However, it was Blondy who sorter took charge of

things and did the planning. He was sharp as a nail, and he went right to the spot with his ideas.

He decided what we ought to do next and that was to go out to the Christabel. He found out where the mine was, simply by calling the waiter and asking.

The rat, he simply said: "The Christabel? Is that what it's all about?"

Then he sketched a little plan on a scrap of paper and showed just where the Christabel was, on the side of the valley, sorter tucked away among the hills, and pretty far from any other claims.

I admired the way the waiter carried on. He was still white, his lips were pressed together, and his look was far away, exactly as though he had a bad toothache. Still, anyone could see, he was thinking about friend Bonanza.

By the time that we got through talking things over, the dusk was coming on, so we left Pottsville and walked a good mile on the far side of the town. Everything looked fine and hopeful, now, with the colored sunlight striking on the mountains, especially since we had added a fourth important member to the party. That was a revolver. Blondy had bought one before we left town.

About that gun, he had a funny talk with old Slope. When we found out what he had done, I was mighty relieved. There ain't anything better than to know that you have a friend along whose words will knock men flat, if things come to a pitch. But Slope didn't see it that way.

"I hope that you won't load that revolver, Blondy," he said.

"Do you?" says Blondy, with a grin that told me that the gun was ready for action right that minute.

"Yes," says Slope. "I hope that you won't. It's never worth while."

"Well, it seems to me that I've heard of cases where a gun with bullets in it has saved the day," answered Blondy.

"But what sort of a day would it save?" said Slope.

"Suppose that you had your back to the wall, with three or four thugs running in at you," says Blondy.

Slope nodded.

"I've been thinking of that very thing," said he. "But I always think that luck will favor a man who trusts to his hands and keeps them clean."

I was sorter annoyed. I decided that I would show Slope how wrong he was, for once in his life, while we walked along that valley at the end of the day.

So I said: "Is that an idea that you've always had, Slope?" He replied that it was.

"Do you think that it always means winning?" said I.

"So long as one has to do with crooks and others of their kind," said Slope. I stared at him.

"Look at Bonanza," said I.

"Yes?" says Slope, always gentle and polite.

"Look at what he's got," said I. "They say that he's got a house that couldn't be beat by the President of the United States and a lot of servants, rugs on his floors, about twenty pairs of shoes, and seven beds, if he wants to have a different bed every night of the week. He drinks his whisky out of a golden flask, I reckon. He dresses the best, he eats the best, and when he goes down the street, everybody says: 'There goes Bonanza Chris, the boss of the town!'"

"I suppose that is all true," says Slope. "But I don't see that twenty pairs of shoes are better than one pair that fits. As for clothes and food, one needs to cover the body and to eat enough to keep one's strength, but—"

"That goes double for you, Slope," said Blondy. "You're the world's champ for what you can carry inside of you."

"Wait a minute, Blondy," said I, "because he's still answering me."

"Go ahead, Slope," says Blondy.

And Slope went on: "It's true that he's well known, but I don't believe that people are fond of him. It's true that everyone in Pottsville knows him. But, when they saw him pick himself out of the dust today, they only laughed."

This speech of Slope's hit me pretty hard. I mean, because it all hung together, and it was all sorter to the point, as you can see for yourself.

"Laughter don't hurt anybody," said I. "Laughter ain't a rock or a bullet, either."

"Don't you think so?" said Slope. "Well, I think I had rather be struck by a bullet than by laughter of a certain kind."

I knew what he meant. I knew the rip and tear of mockery going through a fellow's soul. "You get right down to the point, Slope," said I, "and look at Bonanza. Maybe he's had a fall today, but he'll eat tenderloin steak and salad tonight, and he'll give his cook heck if things ain't just right, too. He'll sleep soft and sound, too. And he'll wake up with a whole lot of schemes for dynamiting the three of us. He'll have fifty pairs of hands ready to work themselves to the bone to do what he says. He don't have to be brave, or good, or nothing. He just has to be smart. But now, you take and look at yourself. You kept your hands clean all right and—"

"Excuse me for interrupting you, Red," said Slope, in his gentle way. "I'm afraid that you're going to take me as an example of the type of man I have been talking about. But I didn't mean to do that."

"Yeah, I bet that you have a lot of sins and black marks chalked up against you!" said I, with a sneer.

He shortened his step so that he almost stopped, and he lifted his poor, dumb, troubled face to the sky, and he said: "Ah, yes, Red! I have done such things that they wake me up at night. I've been cruel and selfish; I've been bitter with envy; but I don't like to think of my faults. I'm afraid to face them, even out here, in the open light of day!"

If poor Slope was "bad," what about the other two of us?

Then, sorter indignant, I remarked: "Well, let's just say that you're a better man than Bonanza Chris, Slope—and—"

"Don't say that," he answered, jerking up his hand, as though to block a punch. "I don't wish to be compared with any other poor devil, Red. I'm better than no one. I'm only worse than I should be."

I moistened my dry lips. I felt kinder wild. I said:

107

"Damn it, Slope, have a little sense, will you? Are you gonna say that Bonanza is in the right in this deal?"

He shook his head.

"I hope that I'm right in this affair of the Christabel," says he.

"Well," I shouted, as I saw my way through to convince him, "listen to this, will you? In the deal of the Christabel, you're in the right. You've had to walk three thousand miles and wear out your feet, but still you ain't got the mine in your hands, and still Bonanza is sitting pretty with a hundred thugs ready to murder us, his hands full of money and his pockets full of cigars. And now you tell me that the fellow with clean hands always has the best of the deal? You try to tell me that!"

I ended up in a sort of fury.

Slope was silent. He was silent for so long that my fury died out, and I began to get cold and say to myself that it wasn't so much for a man to be able to silence poor old Slope. After all, he didn't have many ideas or words to put them in, either.

But, after a while, he lifted his fine head and took off his hat, then stopped dead still, with the wind blowing through his hair. He looked kind of grand, standing there, the poor dummy. And he said:

"Well, Red, it's true that Bonanza Chris has a great many things to make him comfortable, and a great many tools are ready to his hands, but still I feel that he lacks what I have."

"Go on," said I. "You tell me what you got? Three quarters of a coat and one pair of shoes!"

It was a smart answer, and I was pretty proud of it, but Slope shook his big head. He reached out those terrible hands of his and laid one softly on my shoulder and the other on Blondy.

"Well, Bonanza has neither of you for a friend. And what has he that is half so fine?" he said.

CHAPTER 21

Maybe you've noticed, as you went along through life, that the folks that you can't talk to and argue with, are the ones that get all kind of lifted up, now and then. That's the trouble with womenfolks. You get to arguing with them and they begin to expand, and their eyes get a glory in 'em, and they lift up their heads and walk right along through the clouds, no matter how their feet are stumbling.

Slope was kinder that way. He was as gentle as a girl, but you couldn't no more argue with him than you could with a girl. I felt sneaking and small and terrible low, to think that Slope should pride himself on having a sneak thief like me for a friend! But you can't hate a man for liking you more than he ought to.

Blondy says, short and hard: "It's time to turn around and go back down the valley, I guess."

So we turned around.

We hoped that we had laid a false line for the Bonanza hounds to run on, and now we doubled back through the night and went down the valley.

It wasn't so easy to get past Pottsville.

I mean, all of the paths and the trails were pointing in toward that town, like it was a place that was worth getting to, and we had to strike across unbroken country, stub our toes, bark our shins, and scratch ourselves on shrubbery. Lemme tell you this, shrubbery out West has a point to it, always, and it scratches like a cat, if you don't keep clear. I've seen a puncher in brand new heavy leather chaps ride out of a morning and come back with his chaps torn clean through in a couple of places. And we wished that we had on iron chaps before we ever come to where we wanted to come.

At last Blondy, that had eyes like a cat in the dark, got down on his hands and studied the skyline. Then he said that we had walked too far, and that just over to our right were the two hills with the cleft between, that the waiter had marked down for us.

Now that I studied them carefully, the way the lines were etched in dim and broken among the stars, I seen that Blondy was right, and we walked up toward the little pass between the summits. There, in the double dark of the pass, where you couldn't hardly see your own thoughts, we stopped and talked things over, softly, with the wind seeming, all the time, to be stealing up on us and listening.

"What shall we do now, Slope?" said Blondy.

"Why, walk straight ahead, of course," said Slope, "and see what we can find."

"And suppose," said Blondy, "that Mr. Bonanza Chris, he don't aim to have people stumbling around the Christabel either night or day, but has some hired shotguns watching the place. What then? Rifles and revolvers ain't much good in the dark, but a shotgun kind of lights up its own way, I've heard tell. It feels its way to the mark."

I broke in: "We ought to scout out the dump and the hole of the Christabel, I think."

"Sure we ought," says Blondy.

"Very well," says Slope. "I'm sure that you both know a great deal better than I do what is best. But just a moment, please. I have another idea that troubles me. I should have thought of it before."

"I know," said Blondy. "You think that stalking around is sort of trespassing on the night, maybe, and ain't hardly right?"

"No," says Slope, judicially. "I wasn't thinking of that, though there may be a great deal in the idea. But I was thinking that both you and Red may be taking your lives in your hands. And for what? After all, I haven't even offered you a share in the mine, supposing that it should come to be of any value. I hope, of course, that your time

110

won't be wasted. And now I want to offer to each of you, a third of the——"

Blondy broke in, his voice heavy, and with a panting sound in it.

"You remember what you said a while ago, Slope, about finding a pair of friends. Well, we've found you. Suppose that is shotguns over there in the black of the night? Well, a man don't want to take his life in his hands for hard cash or even the hope of it, but he will for a friend. Let's leave it that way."

"Blondy, I hardly know what to say. I'm terribly touched," answers Slope.

"Don't you tell us nothing," said Blondy. "We're wasting time, Slope, the thing for you to do is to wait here and hold the base of supplies. And the kid and me will go ahead and scout out the mine."

"But," says Slope, "I really must have a chance to——"

"Stay still, here," said Blondy. "You make too much noise when you walk. This ain't a fight; it's a scouting trip. Red's a cat and, though I got a white skin, I'm Injun by nature."

He took me by the arm and we went off, with old Slope murmuring behind us.

"Can you beat him?" I whispered to Blondy.

He give my arm a grip.

"Nobody could beat him," he answered.

Pretty soon, we got into the hollow where the mine was, according to the waiter. There was a grove of poplars and there was a dim streak of tarnished silver, that was running water. Between the grove and the stream, we ought to find the mine.

Blondy said that he would go straight on. I was to skirt around closer to the edge of the trees. If I didn't find the dump there, I was to cut back to the edge of the trees. If I didn't find the dump there, I was to cut back to the edge of the water, and there I'd find Blondy, somewhere, and we'd lay out a new course and new ground to cover.

It seemed a good idea, and I said all right, in a whisper. Just then I wouldn't have trusted my voice to speak out loud. I was scared to death, scouting along there in the dark, because I knew that what Blondy had said was right. A shotgun can see in the dark better'n a cat. I've had more'n one load of rock salt in the seat of my pants, and buckshot is a lot deeper medicine, any way you look at it.

Well, I sneaked off a little ways, and then I dropped on one knee and tried to listen, but I couldn't hear anything but the little rushing of the stream outside me and the jumping of my heart. I rested on one hand, and my elbow bent and shook, as though I'd been lifting heavy weights the whole day.

Then I decided that I wasn't cut out for this sort of work. I was only a kid, I felt, and the strain was too much for me. I'd just linger around, and then cut clean around the trees and come down to the water's edge and find old Blondy and tell him that I hadn't located nothing.

But, next thing, I thought of Slope, waiting off there in the dark, troubling himself because his two friends were in danger on his account, and somehow that lifted me a whole lot. I was able to get up and go on. When I stopped, a few yards later, I had hold of myself again. Still, it was most ghostly work.

The high mist, that had almost covered the stars, and made them burn dim and small, was brushed aside by the rising of the wind, and let through enough light to help a body to see.

Mind you, it made everything more ticklish, too. If you can see, you can be seen.

Well, I remembered what I had known all my life, and what moves fast is quickly seen, what moves slow is hard to find, and what moves slow, pausing now and then, is the hardest of all to see.

I got down on my hands and knees, and I felt every rock and stone and twig, so that my knees could follow after and find the same spots, and light on them right.

Thus, I worked along for what seemed to me a long time. Then I looked up, and it seemed to me that I seen the poplar grove standing just exactly as far as it had been when I parted from Blondy and started the scouting expedition.

"I'm a cheap skate and a quitter," said I to myself. "Blondy will scout out the whole mountain range before I even get to going!"

With that, I stood right up and stepped ahead, not near so careful as I had been before. I walked right on, as I was saying. Suddenly, out of the ground at my feet, as it seemed to me, a voice says plain and deep and clear: "Who's there?"

I stood still. It wasn't Blondy's voice, and I stood as still as a rock, and I wished that I was a rock, too. I could only thank God for one thing—that I was a kid, and that growed-up men ain't likely to be so hard on a kid like my age was then.

Then I seen—before me, half rising to his feet, a man getting up, and the sleek gleam of the starlight ran down the twin barrels of a shotgun. I could just make the thing out, and it was right under my nose.

Just where I had got my confidence was the point where I ought to've gone ahead like a hunting snake.

"I'm here," said another voice a little distance off, that wasn't Blondy's neither. "Whacha want?"

The nearer man, who had spoken first, seemed to turn a little. I slipped to the ground like a wet rag and lay still.

And I heard the first man saying: "Not you. I seen something right here beside me, 'Lefty'!"

CHAPTER 22

He stood clean up and stepped right out straight for me. Bigger than a giant, he looked, coming with his head among the stars, and straight for me. He was right at me.

I tensed myself, and I decided that I'd give myself a swift roll, in the hope that he'd stumble and fall down when his toe struck me.

Stumble he did, but it just happened before he got to me. I heard him catch his breath, and then he stepped high, right over the flat of my body! Yeah, I was making myself pretty flat, you can bet. But I never had no better luck than that.

He went on a stride or two. I closed my eyes a second, but I had to look out again.

"Find anything, Socks?" said Lefty.

"I don't seem to find nothing," said "Socks," his words rumbling. "That's a funny thing, too. It was something that I could pretty near reach out and touch."

I heard the steps of Lefty as he approached a little closer.

"You know how it is," he said. "Sometimes when you turn your head sudden, you seem to see a shadow, or a lighter spot, move in the dark."

"Yeah, I know how it is," said Socks to himself, still thoughtful.

"You just imagined something," said Lefty.

I loved hearing him say that. He was one of those gents that always have ideas about everything.

"I didn't imagine nothing," said Socks, getting a little angry. "I seen something come right up and stand here; dog-gone if I didn't!"

He turned back to me and walked in a circle around me. He kicked his boots at the stones. One of 'em rolled and hit me on the mouth hard. But you bet I didn't yip. I was gagged by something stronger than a handkerchief.

"I'll get the lantern, if you think there's anything," says Lefty.

"Yes, there was something, all right," says Socks.

"I'll get the lantern, then."

"Yeah, you go and fetch it."

I could feel myself turn green. I didn't need no light to tell what color I was, because only that color could explain just the way that I felt.

I could hear the footsteps of Lefty as he walked away; Socks stood right over me.

"It's damn funny," I heard him say.

Then he made a cigarette. He was standing so close, I heard the paper rustle in his fingers, and the tobacco grains dropped onto my face.

When he lighted a match I looked straight up at him, and saw a face as black as murder, covered with a short, curling beard. His shirt was open at the throat, and I seen the light glint on the hair of his big, arching chest. He was a man with a pair of shoulders, too, was Socks.

He lighted his cigarette, and he held the match up and squinted. But I knew that he wouldn't see me unless he bent his head more. I thought what a fearless kind of man he was to light a match when he'd heard something prowling around. He might just be holding a match for somebody to shoot him by.

Pretty soon the flame burned his fingers, and he threw the spark of the match away and darned a little. After that I heard him spitting loose tobacco grains off his tongue and lips, and the sweet, sharp smell of the tobacco loaded the air.

Then I heard Lefty returning, and the screech of the lantern as he pushed the chimney up.

"Aw, wait a minute," said Socks. "Maybe it wasn't nothing much. Maybe it was only a wolf, or something that'll sneak up close in the dark."

"Yeah," said Lefty, "maybe it was that. I remember once waking up and finding the tracks of a lobo within three feet of the edge of my blankets. It certainly gave me a chill."

"Where was you sleeping?" asked Socks, turning around.

"Out in the snow. It was up in Montana. I was dog-gone glad when he gave me his back!" said Lefty.

"They don't sleep out in the snow, even in Montana," said Socks.

"Don't they?" asked Lefty, sharp and hard.

"No, they don't," growled Socks.

"Well, I was sleeping out in the snow," said Lefty, hard and sharper still.

"Aw, shut up, you and your snow," said Socks. "I'm gonna watch the spot where I thought I seen that shadow." And he sat down, facing toward me again.

I didn't feel none too good, at that. I didn't dare to move, and now I could feel the stones driving into my ribs, and my legs, and the pit of my stomach.

But I couldn't move, for there he sat, with the gleam of the shotgun right across his knees.

"Speaking of snow—" insisted Lefty.

"I ain't speaking of it," said Socks.

"Speaking of snow," said Lefty, his voice rising a little, with a fighting whine in it, "I was sayin' a while back, that once I was sleepin' out in the snow in Montana."

"Well, go back and sleep there ag'in," says Socks.

"Speakin' of snow, and sleepin' out," said Lefty, in the same mean kind of a voice, "it kinder appeared to me that you didn't believe what I was sayin'."

"Is it likely that a gent would sleep out in the snow?" asked Socks.

"I said that I was sleepin' out."

"You've said a lot of other things, too."

"I was sleepin' out in the snow," said Lefty, and I hear the rustle of him as he stands up, "and I wanta know the look of the puncher or yegg that says that I didn't sleep out!"

"You know the look of me," said Socks.

And he didn't even turn around. He was considerable of a man, was Socks. "You got a look that might be changed some," said Lefty.

"Might it?"

"Yeah. Nature didn't carve you perfect, according to my way of looking at things."

"Nature didn't give me a sour map like yours, if that's what you mean," replied Socks.

"But speakin' of sleepin' in the snow, I didn't say that it was nights, but a night," pursued Lefty.

"Oh, darn you and your nights," said Socks. "How come it, anyway?"

116

"You didn't have the brains to ask me that before, eh?" said Lefty. "Didn't think that there might be no reason why a gent should have to sleep out in the snow?"

"Sure, I can think of reasons," said Socks.

"Like what?"

"Well, like a little gun play, out of a friendly game of cards, or something like that."

"Sometimes your ideas are dog-gone near to human," observes Lefty.

"Yeah, brother," said Socks, "but you want to remember something."

"And just what've I gotta remember?"

"That you're in the United States of America, where every man has got a right to his own opinion."

"Yeah, that's right, too," said Lefty.

"They said that you was hard to get along with, but I don't mind you, Lefty."

"Who said that I was hard to get along with?" said Lefty.

Socks laughed. He was a man.

"What's that down there?" says Lefty softly.

"Where?"

"Down by the water. I seen something on it."

"What was it?" asked Socks.

"The shadow of a tall man, stalkin'!"

CHAPTER 23

I only needed to lift my head and I could see the shadow clearly enough. The stars brightened up a good deal, and down below us, where the narrow, tarnished surface of the creek spread out into a small pool, I could see the silhouette of Blondy, tall and lean, bending forward, picking his feet up carefully, and putting them down like a cat.

Poor Blondy! I almost laughed out loud, watching him. He looked like a clown, a bad clown. He looked like a fool, too. But you can bet that I didn't let myself go—not with that pair of neat-handed murderers so close to me! Then I thought of the danger that Blondy was in, and it fair made me sick.

I could hear them talking together. They were cool, those two. You can tell a real horse breaker by the way he looks at a wild horse before he tackles it. You could tell the sort of men-killers this pair was by the way they talked over Blondy.

Says Lefty: "I tell you what; I'll just take that pump gun. It ain't so sudden, but it keeps on lasting."

"I'm keeping the double-barrel," says Socks. "And you'd better have that other one here. Two loads of buckshot, one after the other, do a whole lot to take the spirit out of a man and the hide off his back."

"Yeah? I'll take the pump gun, just the same," says Lefty.

"Come on, then," replies Socks, speaking low, "and lemme see if you work as loud as you talk."

"Don't you worry about me none," whispers Lefty. "Just remember that a gent is likely to overshoot a lot at night."

"Thanks for nothin'," said Socks. "You're left-handed, so you come on my left, and we'll cross him up."

"Ain't you gonna give him a chance? Ain't you gonna sing out?" said Lefty.

Up to that point I'd thought that Lefty was really the lowest down and the meanest of the pair, but now Socks says: "He looks like a crook and he walks like a crook. Likely he's one of the three that we got word about. Though from what old man Bonanza says to me, I reckoned that he mostly wanted the head blowed off the kid."

"I'm best pleased," says Lefty, "to have a man to handle. Well, come along and we'll blow him to heck!"

And off they went.

The breath was fair out of me. When I pushed myself up on my knees, I was fighting to make my lungs work. I never had pure fear choke me the way that it did then. I was waiting every second to hear the roar of their guns, and I was wondering what I could do.

Run after them? They'd hear me coming, and turn around in time to blow me where they wanted to blow Blondy.

Sneak around soft to the side? There wasn't time to get to Blondy that way. He'd be dead long before.

What should I do, then? Well, I didn't know, but I did the first natural thing that came into my mind. I mean that I crawled straight ahead to between the rocks where the pair of them had been confabbing about sleeping in the snow, and such silly stuff, and there I found what I was after—the second double-barreled shotgun that Socks had been talking about.

Well, it was a beauty. It was one of them high-priced shotguns that look as big as a cannon and are as light as a feather. I hoisted it, and it come good and free and easy to my shoulder. I was so happy to have it that I thought of shooting it off after the thugs.

But I saw in a second that I'd never reach them that way. They were already a good bit too far off. They were only ghosts of men now, sneaking away through the dark.

Then I touched my toe against the lantern, and it jingled softly, and seemed to me like a voice was calling to me to look down at it.

At the same time I got my idea.

I dropped to my knees again, put the gun down, slid out some matches and lighted one, holding it tight between my hands. I could do that and hardly let out a flicker of light. An Irishman had taught me how to light a pipe in the wind!

The lantern chimney was already raised, so all I needed to do was to touch the match to the wick, and the wick was rich with oil, so that the flame ran suddenly right across it, and threw up its head high, and began to smoke.

I jammed the chimney down, and the holders screamed

119

against the wire runners. But that didn't matter. As well begin with a screech of iron on iron and follow up with the sort of a screech that I intended to make.

Then I jumped up, and I got onto one of the stones, which I aimed to make me seem a whole lot taller—taller than a tall man, even—and I let out a whistle like a steam engine between a pair of my fingers. I yelled, making my voice hoarse to sound·like the voice of a man.

"Come on in! Come in! They're down by the creek Cut 'em off! Shoot, and don't give no challenges! Yeah! We got the mine! Who-o-opee!"

Sounds like a fool speech, don't it, now especially, since I've wrote it out all in full?

Well, maybe it was a fool speech, but I made it sound some that night, I tell you.

I figured that I was being pretty bold and desperate, to stand up there and hold a light for such as Lefty and Socks to shoot by!

A few whirls of that lantern, and I thought that it was enough.

I dropped off that stone, glad to be alive, and I picked up the shotgun and fired off the barrel in the general direction that Socks and Lefty had gone in.

After that I was too plumb scared to move. But I heard Blondy up and give a howl like a wildcat on the side of me toward the creek. On the other side, down the valley, I heard the voice of Slope.

And that was a voice. I mean to say, that roar of his hit the rocks and banged back and forth like hammer strokes from cliff to cliff, and the whole dog-gone hollow, it seemed full of voices shouting.

It was a mighty comfort, you can believe me, to know that that voice belonged to a friend.

Still, I didn't feel any too good, for I remembered that I had shot off both barrels of the shotgun, and the only thing left to me was the gold knife hitched onto the gold chain that belonged to Bonanza Chris, and that I had "forgotten" to give back to him.

Well, I got that knife out, and I laid low, and I was so dog-gone scared that I didn't even have the sense to put out the lantern. And that was how Blondy found me!

It makes me grind my teeth when I think about it. For there I had been playing pretty smart, and pretty bold, too, I thought. And I got into a blue funk and I queered everything, and lay down on the ground like a fool and left that lantern burning right there beside me.

When I heard the step of a man, I got up sudden to my knees, my heart all ice and fire, because I knew that I was a trapped rat, and I held the knife ready to strike, and I felt my face muscles drawing hard.

Then I heard Blondy laugh, and the knife, it just dropped out of my hand. He reached down and picked me up by the scruff of my neck, and he held me out at arm's length and turned me around.

He wasn't no Slope, but he was about three of any other man.

"Did they hurt you, kid?" he said. "Is that why you were lying down there by the lantern?"

All the fear was out of me. I was only full of hot shame, and I tried to hunt through my brain for ideas and excuses, but my brain went right back on me, and all that I could do was to blurt out:

"I was just kind of taking a rest, Blondy!"

Blondy, he roared with laughing, and I'll never forget his look as he held me out with one hand, and the long barrel of his Colt hung down from the other hand in the lantern light.

I reckon that he was about the meanest-looking picture that you ever saw in this world. He kept on a-laughing till I hated him.

"Leave me stand down on the ground again and I'll bite your hand off," says I to him, and I meant it.

He dropped me, but he kept on roaring.

"There's a couple of gunmen somewhere around here, and they'll come back and shoot the laugh out of you," I said to him.

"Well, son," he answers, still laughing, "they won't come back in a hurry. I seen two shadows legging it down the valley; separating, too, like they didn't want to be seen together. They won't be hurrying back, even on

121

your account, kid. That was certainly a caterwauling that you put up!"

"It saved your mangy hide for you," said I, with my face still hot. "The two of 'em seen you stalkin' like a fool along down there, with the water showing you up clear and strong. They were hunting you through the dark, and they would've got you with buckshot, too," says I.

He reached out and give my head a pat that I ducked away from.

"Didn't I see how close they got?" says he. "Yeah, I understand all about it, and it was a dog-gone bright idea for scaring those polecats away from the mine. And I won't tell Slope how tired you got, if you're a good kid and keep your sassy tongue inside of your mouth for a while! But who's this cavalry charge comin' on foot?"

I looked and seen a big man running fast, and carrying a big load, so it was a wonder that he could run at all, and he swept into the circle of the lantern light. It was Slope!

CHAPTER 24

Yes, it was Slope, and when he come up he threw down the load that he was carrying, and it fell flop on the ground and laid there, still, face up. It was Socks!

But Slope didn't pay no attention to him. He just grabbed me.

"Are you badly hurt, Red?" says he.

"No," says I. "I ain't hurt at all. Why?"

He squatted in front of me on his heels, and he kept hold of me with both hands, the way that fool grown-ups do with kids now and then. You would thought I was a baby or something.

"I heard you cry out, Red," said he. "I know that you're hurt. Don't be too brave. Tell me where you were hurt!"

It made me mad. "Darn it, Slope! Will you cut out the nursery talk? I wasn't hurt at all; I was just sounding the horn to make a pair of thugs here think that the whole valley was full of gents, and they must've thought that it was, by the way that they legged it. I ain't hurt at all."

By degrees I was able to convince him, and the pain went out of his face. He smiled, and I got to feeling a little different, mad as I was for being treated like a fool kid.

He stood up, and he said: "Thank God!" in a voice that I remember like it was only five minutes ago.

Blondy was saying: "Where did you pick up this pretty little thing?" We all turned around and looked at Socks. He was coming to, and he was beginning to sit up, but every time he moved he groaned.

Slope looked worried. "I've acted very hastily," he said. "I had heard Red cry out. Then, as I ran toward the sound of his voice and the light, I met this man in the dark. So I picked him up and took his shotgun away from him and brought him along. I thought that in case he had manhandled Red—in short, I was angry—I hope that he's not badly hurt. I must have thrown him down too hard!"

He was all commiseration and worry. I never seen such a man like a lump of putty because he'd knocked down a gorilla like Socks.

Blondy, he gives the hairy chest and the bulging shoulders of Socks a look, and then he looks at Slope.

"Yeah," said he, "you threw him down pretty careless, all right. But you done something else to that grizzly bear. You must've picked him up a lot more careless than you put him down!"

There wasn't no pity in Blondy, though. He says to me: "You think this was one of Bonanza's guards here that went a-gunning for me?"

"I don't think. I know," says I. "This was the one that wanted to shoot you without giving no warning."

"Did he?" says Blondy.

And he rammed the toe of his boot into the ribs of Socks.

"Sit up, yegg," says he.

"Don't do that, Blondy!" barks Slope, real sharp and nasty.

The kick seemed to pull Socks together all at once. And he pushed himself up with his hands. There he sat, with his back against a rock. First with one hand he felt his ribs, and then with the other he felt of the back of his neck and his eyes rolled. He seemed a good deal surprised to find himself all of one piece.

"Did a landslide hit you, brother?" inquires Blondy.

Socks says nothing at all. He just looked murder from under his black brows. He wasn't pretty, is all I'll say about him.

"Stand up!" says Blondy.

Socks got to his feet. He had to haul himself pretty hard to make the grade.

Then he says to Blondy, slowly and heavy: "Was you the one that tackled me?"

"No," said Blondy. "It was the kid over here," and he pointed out Slope.

"I hope I didn't hurt you," says Slope, real eager and humble.

Socks blinked. "You hope you didn't hurt me?" he repeated. He gaped at Slope.

"He seems to doubt you, Slope," says Blondy.

"You come on me suddent," says Socks, "or I'd've brained you. You kinder took me by surprise, or I'd've slammed you where you need slamming, you puzzle-faced blockhead, you!"

Slope didn't talk back. Instead, he looked hurt, almost alarmed, and looked at me for help.

"He ain't had enough," said I. "He feels kinder big and manly still. Well, Socks, it looks to me like you ain't being taken by surprise now. So why don't you take a pass or two at Slope?"

He turned around and give me a long, hard look. I never seen a meaner look. "That's Slope, is it?" said he. "And that lengthy gent is Blondy, I guess, and you're the brat, eh?"

"Yeah, I'm the brat, beautiful," said I.

He stuck out his jaw, and his black beard bristled. He didn't seem to feel no fear of what might happen to him.

He said: "How'd you come to know my name, eh? You sneaking redhead!"

I laughed in his face. It was a chance for me to shine, and you can just bet that I shone, all right.

"Why," said I, "I didn't happen to stand up and introduce myself, but I was the shadow that you thought you saw, and you had to turn around and talk to Lefty about it."

"Darn," says he, slow and deep and bitter. "You was hanging around here somewhere after that?"

"Yeah, right over there," said I, pointing. "When you stood and rolled your cigarette, the tobacco crumbs dropped in my face."

He couldn't speak. He could only just stand there and growl deep in his throat, like a beast. So I let him have both barrels, hard and straight.

"It was me that laid here," said I, "and heard the fool talk about sleepin' out in the snow; and it was me that heard you and Lefty plan to murder Blondy there. It was you that wanted to kill him without warning, you dirty, cold-blooded hound! It was me that lighted the lantern and swung it and hollered. I called in the gang and shot off the gun you'd left behind you."

He twisted and he writhed. He ground his teeth, and I saw the flash of them through his beard.

Said Slope: "This is getting pretty horrible. Blondy, will you tie his hands, or secure him in some way: He seems dangerous."

"I'll show you I'm dangerous," says Socks. "I'm gonna wreck the whole lot of you!"

Blondy came up and stood close to him.

"You're going to be a dead man in half an hour," said

125

he. "Don't bother us by shooting off your face or your half hour is up right now!"

Socks, he listened. And Blondy tied his hands behind him with a length of twine, and then we started for the Christabel at last.

I've pretty near forgot the mine. But there it was, standing behind us the whole time, and only a lot of other excitement kept me from mentioning the dump that slid down the hillside, and the ragged open mouth of the shaft. Now the three of us started for the mine, driving Mr. Socks before us.

CHAPTER 25

It wasn't much of a shucks to look at, that mine. Which I mean to say there was the same raw, rough look about that hole in the ground, the same sort of a feeling that it was about old enough for scorpions and spiders and snakes, and such, to've made their homes in it.

The lantern light filled it and seemed to overflow it.

The shaft, it was sunk on a level, then it goes down a step, then it makes a right turn and dives a pace or two. It straightens out after that, and that hole in the ground, it ends up with great big piles of broken ground. Rock, a tenderfoot would've called it, slanting away from the finish, like a final blast, a dog-gone big blast, too, had been turned loose, and nobody had cared to cart out the rock and see what was what.

"Is there anything worth seeing?" asked Slope, trying to keep the disappointment out of his voice.

"No, there ain't a darn thing. It's just a hole in the mud," says Big Socks, "if you want to know the truth about it. There ain't a thing worth having in it. And you three have been a set of fools from the start."

"Bonanza Chris would spend fifty thousand to keep nothing at all, would he?" said Blondy. "He'd hire a pair of high-priced throat cutters like you for nothing, would he?"

Once more Socks could do nothing but growl fiercely.

When he couldn't think of nothing to say nor nothing else to do, he'd keep looking at me, and I tell you his eyes were phosphorus; green phosphorus, at that, shining through the shadows.

I studied along the walls of the shaft, but I couldn't make out anything that looked like the lead had caused somebody to sink the hole in the ground. But, then, I wasn't no expert. I only knew where to look when somebody pointed things out to me.

Blondy, he seemed to know a lot. And he went back to the mouth of the cave, looking over every inch of one wall of the shaft; and then he turned around and looked over the other side on the return trip. But we wound up again standing in front of that slide of big rocks, and no particular satisfaction in the mind of anybody, lemme tell you.

Slope and me, we both looked at Blondy and waited for him to speak, but Blondy keeps his mouth shut and his jaw muscles sticking out as though he was hanging onto a rope with his teeth, looking over the edge of a cliff.

He looked pretty hard and pretty thoughtful.

Then he went back to the mouth of the shaft, walking bent way over, and stepping out long and sharp.

At the mouth of the shaft he sat down, and the rest of us, we sat down too; all except Socks.

Nobody said a word. It was plain that Blondy was the one to do the talking. Only Socks, he began to chuckle, soft and deep. It was plain that he enjoyed things a whole lot.

"Brother, if you keep on laughing. I've gotta remind you," said Blondy suddenly, "that in another fifteen minutes you'll have a wider mouth to laugh with than you

127

ever had before, but I don't think you'll be seein' the point of any jokes."

A funny little embarrassed laugh come out of Slope, and he says: "One would almost think, Blondy, that you actually intended to harm a helpless prisoner, who—"

"Aw, shut yer face!" said Blondy.

I saw the silhouette of Slope straighten up with a jerk. He said nothing. But I knew that he was badly hurt.

We went through another period of silence.

I could see through the whole thing. We'd just been following a wrong trail all the while. It was blank. All our dangers and all our hopes were nothing.

Then Blondy said in a sudden growl: "Looka here. Ain't anybody got a word to say? Ain't there any ideas outside of mine—which is that this dog-gone mine is a bust?"

Well, I laid back and turned the thing over in my mind, dead easy and slow, like you do something that don't mean anything to you, but it's all a mess, done up and gone and used.

When I say I turned it over, I mean that in a flash I seen everything up to the time we walked into that mine. From that point forward, my memory ambled ahead dead slow, and I was looking at every step we made, smelling the underground and the damp choke of the air, noticing the way that the light of the lantern had glinted on the rocks, and all of that. I was remembering, too, how many hopes had jumped up in my heart, how I was always sorter seeing the shine of gold and getting my fingers crooked to pick up whole chunks of it. But always, when we came closer, the bright places had turned into the flat sheen of rocks! And so, in the finish, three times we had wound up with the pile of rocks at the end of the shaft. And I seen those rocks again, almost one by one, and shook my head.

There wasn't nothing showing in those rocks. There wasn't even a gleam of color. And them that had set off the shot must've simply shook their heads the way that I shook mine.

It was like, that pile of rocks, the stones that lie at the

bottom of a landslide, that've been shook up and jostled about, so that they all lie there together, about of a size, regular and even, almost like a wall that's been built, or laid up for the cementing.

Now, the minute that comparison come to me, I had a thought that socked me between the eyes, and I sat up with a gasp.

"What's the matter, kid?" says Blondy. "Chokin' on something?"

I begun to laugh, kinder wild and high. And I kept on laughin', because the more that I laughed, the more the light begun to shine inside of me and show me an idea.

"Go on and choke, then," says Blondy. "I'm tired of laughin' jackasses tonight."

"No," said Slope, always kind. "There's something in Red's mind."

"There's a lot of air in his mind!" says Blondy, very mean.

"Yeah, and that's right, too," answered Socks.

"Shut yer face!" says Blondy to Socks. "Heave up your idea to the surface and let's have a look at it, kid."

I answered him then: "Look at that bunch of rocks in there, at the end of the shaft."

Says Blondy: "I've looked at 'em three times, and they can be darned. There ain't a sign of color to any of 'em."

"Sure, there ain't," said I.

"Is that why you laugh?" he asks me.

"Think of another thing," says I. "You've seen the look of ground after it's been broke by a shot. Some of the chunks are big and some of 'em are small. Some are roundish, and some are all splintered. Ain't I right?"

"Well, what if you are?" says he.

"Look at them stones in there again," says I as my idea grew on me, "and you'll see that they're all about of a size, and that size is a handy one for carrying!"

Slope didn't say anything. I heard Socks mutter something under his breath and knew he was cursing me. But it was music to me.

Blondy, he just rose up, and he says, slow and solemn:

"The kid has turned on the lights." And he grabbed the lantern and sprinted into the shaft.

Slope would've run after him, but I reminded him of Socks, and so he took him by the shoulder and pushed him ahead. Socks told him again that he would eat his heart and enjoy it one of these days, and Slope, like somebody that was afraid, was saying that he was sorry that he had hurt him, and that it was all a mistake. Every time he apologized, Socks got nastier.

That was the difficulty about Slope. Unless you knew him and refreshed your mind by studying him every day, he was likely to deceive you a good bit. He was mild, and there was no mistake about it. But he was like a good blade. It bends to a point, and then it springs back and rips your hand open!

You couldn't press old Slope too far, as Russia found out, like I told in the beginning.

So they went down the shaft ahead of me, and Slope says over his shoulder: "I don't know why Blondy is so excited."

"Because you're a half-wit!" says Socks kindly.

I was pretty near glad to hear him say it. Here I'd gone and hit it, and Slope didn't know what it was all about.

Well, he was a trial, was old Slope, for sure! I said: "My idea is that with their last shot the boys ripped open something so good that they was afraid to show it to the world, for fear the world would get dizzy, or something, and so they turned around and went to the crook they knew the best, Bonanza, and they told him what they'd uncovered. And that's what you did, Socks, and Bonanza was the one that you went to."

"You lie!" says Socks.

"I don't lie, because he told me so," says I.

"The dirty, sneaking hound. He gave everything away, and we could all three've been rich!" says Socks.

He kind've stopped himself at the end and started swearing again, because he saw that he'd fallen into a simple trap.

"Slope," I called out, "we're gonna lay bare the face of a million dollars tonight!"

"You're a comforting fellow to have along, Red," says he solemnly. "I don't know what we'd do without you."

Then we came on the sight of Blondy at work like a madman, tearing away the big chunks of stone and throwing them behind him.

Slope and me, we didn't ask any question. We just fell to work and started doing the same thing. A sort of blindness came over me, and all that I saw was tons and oceans of gold, and fine horses, and fine guns, and big, shining palaces, all mine! I didn't have any claim, though, on what might come out of that mine!

As we worked along, pretty soon the heap of stones, it got thinner, and the top of them fell down and showed where the explosion had ripped and tore the face of the rock, but still there was nothing but ragged rock to be seen.

The heart went out of us. We stopped, Blondy and me.

"It's a bust. It was a bright idea of yours, kid," says Blondy, "but the right idea went wrong, the way that bright ideas often do!"

Well, we stood there and hung our hands, but Slope, he went on working away, not having heard what was said.

He was heaving the rocks away. He loved the work, because it gave him a chance to exercise all of his big, cushiony muscles. He fairly made things fly, I tell you.

All at once Blondy jumped forward with a sort of a groan, and he hit Slope on the shoulder and told him to stop, told him that he was a fool, and in the way. Then he dropped on his knees on the rocks that were remaining, and started to claw at the stone.

Then he stood up and turned around to us, and he was shaking and wavering from head to foot, like a crazy man.

He laughed out wild and loud, and I stared at his awful face, and then I looked down to see what his hands were filled with.

He had ripped the ends of his fingers on the stone, and

131

the blood was fairly dripping down, but I seen that his hands were filled with rock so old and worked on that it was black, like the blackness of rot, and in the middle of that pool of shadow there was a glint—a yellow glint!

A howl came up in my throat and made the shaft ring. I snatched one handful of the stuff and rubbed it out, and there was gold—not grains, but long, twisting wires of it—the richest stuff that I ever looked at, and here and there I'd seen fine ore, rich ore, believe me.

But this here gold, bedded in that rock, was like fruit that's so ripe that it falls to the ground. You didn't need to be any expert to see that millions, maybe, were there, and all one needed was a scoop shovel to dig it out and throw it in the lap of the world!

CHAPTER 26

There we stood, Blondy and I, grinning and laughing at each other like fiends, and, strange to say, it was old Slope who brought us back to our senses with a jump.

"Socks seems to have left us!" he remarked.

Well, he had, too! With that rush of gold fever sending our temperatures uphill, we had paid no attention to him, and, like a wise man, he had got out of our way.

We all ran out to the mouth of the tunnel and stood there, blinking at the stars like owls at the sun, but the stars were not talking to us just then.

Socks was clean gone, and before long we might be having trouble.

But Blondy said: "After all, they can't manage to get to Pottsville for quite a spell. In the meantime, we can pocket some of this ore, take it in to the assayer's, and see what kind of tune it sings per ton. But you won't need any capital to develop this, old son. You can come here yourself with a pick and shovel and dig out a thousand dollars the first day. After that you can hire a gang and open her up in earnest. I never seen gold like this; it's thicker than wheat at ten sacks to the acre!"

I felt the same way. Thinking about the treasure, it seemed to feed me like bread.

We went back inside again and took up a pick that lay on the floor of the shaft, and pretty soon we had all our pockets filled. It was dead easy. One smash of the pick and twenty pounds of rotten, black rock, loaded with wire gold, fell to the ground. Blondy said that he could wash twenty pounds of gold a day with his hands from that vein!

We were all pretty happy, as you can believe, when the top dropped out of everything and the bottom came up with a slam and hit us on the chins, so the speak.

I mean, there was a crash that knocked us all silly and blotted us out in darkness.

When I come to, the darkness was still around us. I put out my hand, and on one side I felt the rough face of the rock. I tried to stand up, and bumped my head. I felt on the other side, and touched a stone wall there, too.

"I'm buried alive!" said I to myself, and I almost fainted again.

I felt that the air was gone already, that I was choking. I lay flat on my back and gasped. And I hoped that it would end soon.

Even while I lay there, I decided, if I ever got back to the world again, I would never show any mercy to anybody. It didn't pay.

I could see what had happened. Socks had got out of the shaft, and, knowing where to find dynamite and a fuse, maybe back there in the poplars, he had just planted a charge at the mouth of the shaft, a good big one, and crashed the whole thing around our ears.

He was having the last laugh, now, and I could bet that it was a good loud one. I could see his black beast of a head rolling from side to side!

Well, suppose that we had just knocked him over the

head, the way that he would've knocked any one of us.

But we hadn't. No, we'd been nice and gentle, thoughtful and merciful, all of that. The result was that we were all dead men!

I think that it kept me alive. I didn't die of fear, because I got so mad thinking what fools we had been.

All that time, I have to admit, I was thinking only about myself, when I heard something moving among the rocks, and hope came back to me like a rush of light when a door is opened on a dark room.

I yelled out suddenly, and I heard the deep roar of Slope almost in my ear.

"Where are you, Red? Where are you? Where are you?" he kept shouting. Then there was a flicker of real light, and the sound of a match being scratched.

I turned around. I wasn't buried alive at all. Part of the top of the shaft had crashed in, all right. And I'd been knocked down and blocked in on three sides, but at my head I was free. I crawled right out at the feet of Slope, and he took me by the nape of the neck and laughed with joy.

I laughed, too, and tears began to run down my face. I jumped, whooped, and cried all at the same time. I wasn't even ashamed.

Somehow it didn't shame a body to be silly in front of old Slope. It was like he understood that people ain't perfect, and sympathized. Well, that was the way of it.

"Poor Blondy!" said Slope. "I'd almost forgotten him."

"Blondy almost forgot himself," said a voice, and Blondy got up from a dark corner and wobbled toward us. There was a streak of blood running down one side of his face, but he was the same old Blondy. He wasn't hurt bad.

We could thank God that we'd come through without being brained, any of us, because that shot had knocked down big chunks of rock all around us and littered the floor of the shaft, but otherwise it was clear for a good distance toward the mouth.

Blondy sat down on a rock and made himself a cigarette, while I did the same.

"We're done," said I.

"Yes, we're done," said Blondy.

Slope, he shook his head and sighed. Then he laid hold on three or four hundred pounds of rock that lay in a mass before him and heaved it out of the way, and sent it rolling back toward the end of the shaft.

"We're gonna be left to starve here," says I, getting sadder and sadder.

"Yeah, that's about the way of it," says Blondy.

"That Socks, he'll go back and tell Bonanza, and Bonanza will just about laugh himself to death."

"He will," said Blondy. "I wish I'd kicked him with a load of blasting powder, is what I wish!"

Slope said nothing. He picked up another mass of stone and heaved it back. He kept on working, shaking his head, but busy.

"I wonder how Socks got his hands free?" says I.

"How did you get your hands free after that rat Larkin tied you up?" asked Blondy.

"Yeah," I answered, "Socks must've rubbed the cords agin' the sharp edge of a rock. Blondy, how long can folks live without eating or drinking?"

"About three days will do you in, kid," he said bluntly. "I'll last five, maybe. Old Slope, he'll keep the spark in for about a week."

I thought of Slope sitting by our dead bodies, waiting for death. I was kinder glad that I would be the first one to go. It would be simpler.

Then I remembered one time I had crossed a long stretch of desert, after being kicked off a freight train by a hard-toed shack. I'd thought, that time, that I was going to burn up and die before I got to the next station. But to burn, even under that desert sun, was nothing, compared with having to lie there in the thick darkness that sorter stopped up the nostrils like clay.

We had the lantern still burning, but it would soon be out.

"Gotta stop amusin' yourself with them stones, Slope," said Blondy. "This here lantern is burnin' up fast a lot of good air that we'll be needin' later on."

"That's too bad," said Slope. "I'd rather work away than wait to die."

"What's the good of working?" asked Blondy. "We're buried alive. After a coupla weeks, Bonanza will have the mouth of the shaft cleared. Then he'll come in here and pick the stock certificates off your dead body. Afterward he'll send in a report about the sad accident, where three gents that looked like tramps had been buried by a falling rock in the Christabel. Seems to me like there's death in just the sound of that name. I wish that I'd never heard it."

"I've dragged you both into terrible trouble," said Slope sadly, picking up a whole truck load of boulders and rolling them back down the shaft.

"Look here!" I barked at Blondy as he picked up the lantern to blow it out. "We ain't dead till we give up. Slope's right, maybe. He's cleared out about six feet of this here rock, and there ain't more'n thirty or forty feet waiting in front of us!"

"Eh?" said Blondy.

He got up, stared, and then he started to work.

He was a strong man, as I told you before, and he certainly began to heave things around like a derrick.

But even he could not handle the stone masses that Slope managed to shift. There was no limit to Slope. He was just like a man made out of rubber. The more there was to lift, the more he stretched himself, until it seemed like he would drive his legs right down through that solid rock unless his grip managed to budge what he'd laid hold of.

He kept heaving up the keystones of the rubbish, and Blondy, he pulled away the smaller rocks, and I kept running back and forth with the little fellows—just like twenty and thirty-pound toys!

That was all right, too. It didn't bust my back. Nothing hurts you when you're sorter fighting for your life. Everything was easy for me. Time stood still. And we worked like mad until finally Blondy sat down with a jolt and a grunt.

He was petered out, and no wonder, for we'd cleared

out about thirty feet of that shaft, I want to tell you, and we'd done it without ever stopping for breath.

We looked around us, and we grinned at one another.

"Look here," said I. "When Socks takes the good news back to Pottsville, won't old Bonanza suspect this very thing—that we'll dig ourselves out? Won't he rush men out here to watch the mouth of the mine, and won't Lefty and that other pet, Socks, be the watchers, with shotguns? You bet they will. When we dig ourselves out of here, we'll just be waltzing into the mouths of guns!"

Said Blondy: "You shut yer face or I'll shut it for you. You think too much. We gotta be three fools and keep hoping. Hope is the thing that turns the corner every time!"

CHAPTER 27

Well, to cut a long story short, the lantern went out, and then Blondy said that we might as well all lie down and sleep, because there was still going to be work ahead of us when we woke up. So down we lay, and I heard Blondy humming as he found a good place for stretching out. He was certainly a cheerful kind of man to have along when the pinches were bad!

I don't know how long I slept. I know that I dropped into it like a stone from a cliff into black water; I hit sleep so hard that I splashed.

It must've been hours later when I heard Blondy singing out: "All right, fellows. We've had our five winks, and here's Old Lady Daylight come to show us the way home!"

Sure enough, right there before us, glimmering through

the chinks among the stones, I seen the gleam of the day, and the welcomest thing I ever seen was that sight.

We pitched in again, and I watched their big backs swelling and heaving and straining with the work. They were almost like strangers, except that Blondy spoke now and then, while Slope just pegged away, saying nothing, and working for ten. He had hardly spoken since the explosion, but I saw that that simple, patient way of his was what had saved us. Blondy and me, and people like us, we would've given up the job until hunger and weakness made us start it, and then it would've have been too late. It was Slope that showed us the way out with his hands, not with chatter!

In about an hour we got out a stone that let the daylight flood full in, and we rapidly widened the hole. We could see across some trees and into the blue of the sky, where there was a cloud blowing. I've heard people talk about the beauty of ships under sail in a blue sea, but I never seen nothing half so good as that cloud was. It was news from home; if you've got a home to get news from!

It wasn't all blue sky and sunshine, though. Pretty soon something else came through, and it was the voice of Socks on the hillside above us, and he was saying: "All right, fellows! Whenever you're ready to stick up your hands and march out, you can come. You're welcome to come, too!"

He laughed, with a chuckle like the grunting of a pig when it finds an extra good apple in the heap of spoiled ones.

The three of us didn't answer Socks. We sat down, Blondy and me did, while Slope, he finished moving back the rocks until the entrance to the cave was clear.

We could look out now, and down the hillside to the left, but to the right, and above us, the ground rose up sharp, and there was Socks and his men with guns. We could hear 'em talking.

"What'll we do?" says I to Blondy.

"I give it up," says Blondy. "We better leave it to the teacher."

It sounded like the right answer. It made me more

138

than a little bit sick, but that was all right, too. I couldn't help wondering at Blondy, making his little joke, at a time like that!

Slope didn't stop working, even with the entrance to the shaft cleared. No; instead of stopping, he began to pile up the rocks, one on top of the other, making a low wall that angled out from the entrance to the right. He picked out nothing but good big stones that could stand a shock, and he fitted them together real careful, like a stone mason picking out chunks for his wall, to build it all even.

I kinder thought that Slope had lost his brains, and I seen that Blondy was staring at him, too.

But then I heard the snarling voice of Lefty, that said: "Stop 'em from buildin' that wall."

"What good can a wall do 'em?" says Socks. "They're cooked, that's what they are!"

"They ain't cooked if they can build that wall and shoot at us through the chinks of it, you fool!" yells Lefty. "They've got us cooked up here on a bare hillside!"

Well, I seen the idea, then.

They couldn't tackle us from the left. Blondy's revolver covered that part of the hillside, all right. And now the wall was three feet high, and gradually stealing out farther and farther, and Slope was picking up the stones real careful, and laying them on the top without showing his head or even his hands!

Well, we seen then, Blondy and me! It was a simple-enough idea, maybe, though I never would've thought of it in a thousand days. I wonder if it ever could've come to Slope, either, except that his way was to get busy with his hands, in a pinch, and then trust to getting hunches that would tell him what to do. I suppose that is the best way, because if only you can make some sort of a start, no matter how small, there's usually a way of getting a conclusion tacked on at the end!

Well, if that wall went on and was built long enough and high enough, pretty soon it would make a safe shelter from the hillside, and then, through chinks among the stones, fire could be opened with the revolver.

Blondy ran right out on his hands and knees, sort of like a spider, and he said to Slope:

"You've got the idea. But I've got the gun. Now you go back and roll down stones to me, and I'll carry on the wall and watch for a chance to shoot."

After that we worked on that scheme.

Then it seemed better to roll down a whole mass of stones at once, and we did that, the slope of the ground making the job easy. We sent down tons and tons of them, as they laid easy to the hand, and then we left the mouth of the shaft and began to work to build up the wall in a semicircle. That semicircle would be like a shield in front of us.

They didn't leave us alone. From the time that we sent the big mass of the stones down the hillside, they began to shoot. And their bullets, they hit the stones and shook them, but never toppled one off. Now and then they opened up with shotguns, and it sounded like the crash of a wave when the load of buckshot came roaring against the face of the wall. They were just hoping against hope that maybe one of the shots would find a way through a crack and sink into one of us, but they had no luck at all.

All this time Lefty was cursing like a wild man, but Socks, he didn't curse at all. I could guess that he was just choked up with hate and meanness.

Pretty soon Blondy got his chance, and leveled his revolver through a crack, took a good aim, and fired. The recoil jerked the gun back from the wall. We didn't have to ask if he'd hit a mark, because we heard a sharp, short yell, like a dog yips when it's kicked. Then we heard more darning and footfalls scampering.

"They won't bother us for a while. We can cut for Pottsville, fellows, I guess," says Blondy, grinning clean to his ears. He stood up, a lot higher than the wall, to show that it was safe.

Even so, I got up by inches, but then I could see, when my eyes were above the top of the wall, that the hillside above us was clear.

It looked simpler than ever, the idea of building that

wall in front of the cave, but I know that simple things like that are what make the world spin around!

That was the way of things, and how we got out of the Christabel a whole, long night after we got into her. Death never came no closer to three folks than it came to us during that night, believe me.

We kept a sharp eye around us as we started back for Pottsville. It was likely that one of the thugs might've gone back to report the news, and that the others would lay around and try to pick us off as we went along, but we didn't sight any trouble all the way into town.

It certainly felt good to me when I saw houses all round me, and people walking and talking, free and cheerful. I'd been feeling bullets in my back all the way to Pottsville. Now I felt safe again.

We turned a corner into the main street and almost stumbled over Bonanza Chris. He stopped and we stopped.

I held myself sorter tight, waiting for Slope or for Blondy to murder him, and he must've expected the same thing, because all the color was knocked at one wallop out of his face. But he got his voice to running again in short order. It would've taken an earthquake to stop that smooth tongue of his.

"Well, fellows," he said, "I'm glad to see you all again. I really am glad. Three dead men was a high price to pay, even for the Christabel. Now that you've been inside of her and taken a look at the kernel, you can understand why I was so anxious to have that nut all to myself!"

That was an amazing speech. I thought so then, and I think so now, because by kinder admitting everything that was bad about himself, he came out into the open and seemed to make the whole business a big game in which we had just won a trick.

"I dunno why I'm not splitting your black heart open with a club, Bonanza," Blondy said.

"Good fellows never take advantage of an unarmed man," said Bonanza, though he backed up a little. But already he had talked the color back into his face, and already the smile was back on his lips. I never saw such a man.

141

"Well," said Blondy, "you've made a pretty good little play, Bonanza, but you're beat from the word go."

"Yes, I'm beaten," said Bonanza. "But you have to admit that I haven't had a fair chance. The game wasn't even. Mr. Dugan had the certificates, and my hands were tied without them. You'll agree that I tried hard to get them away from him. If this is a gamble, I've stacked the cards against you fellows a dozen times, but I couldn't beat the cards that you were holding."

Blondy began to laugh at that.

"No hard feelings, fellows," said Bonanza, and held out his hand.

Then a funny thing happened, for Slope said, not loud, but quick: "Don't touch him, Blondy."

He even brushed me and Blondy aside, and he says, quiet and soft, looking into the face of Bonanza: "I hope that we don't meet one another often again, face to face. It's not safe for either of us, Mr. Christian."

CHAPTER 28

Chris, as though he had been shot through the stomach, doubled up a bit and hit it off down the street as fast as he could walk.

Slope stood there and looked after him, cold and calm, but with a terrible light in his eyes that I never had seen before. It made me seem a baby, and Blondy a little child, to see that look in the face of old Slope.

Finally he got to going again, but said not a word about Bonanza, even when Blondy cut in with: "Whatever he may say, the old sneak still has it in for us, and he'll cut our throats if he has half a chance."

142

That was a good invitation for Slope to speak up, but he didn't.

Then Blondy went on: "The only good, safe way is to raise a stack of money, right away quick, and send down about ten men to work and ten men to stand on guard, if we have to. Then we can run up a shack, and everything will be hunky dory!"

"But where could we raise money?" said Slope.

"I'll show you," said Blondy. "I'd kind of enjoy showing you." And he turned right into the door of the bank where me and Slope had deposited the fake envelope with the blank paper in it.

Blondy went up to the clerk at the paying teller's window, and he says: "I'd like to see the president."

The clerk grinned. "Yeah, I'll bet you would," said he.

Blondy grinned back at the clerk. "Tell the president that some red-hot business is waiting for him, will you?" says he. "Me and the other two gentlemen want to talk to him."

I don't know why, but something in the way he spoke made the clerk frown, and then it made him nod slowly, like he was keeping time with a bell which was ringing somewhere.

"All right," said he. "You can see him, because he don't happen to be busy this very minute."

He took us around and knocked at a door and showed us through into an office where a man sat all by himself, with his hands folded on top of his desk, looking straight before him.

It was a minute before that look faded out of his eyes and he was able to see us. And I knew what the color of his dream had been, all brilliant yellow and shining. The same hunger was gripping the heart of him that had gripped my heart the evening before in the shaft of the Christabel. Gold was what he was dreaming about, and gold was what he was seeing.

When he was able to see us, he said briskly: "Well, gentlemen?"

Blondy spoke up: "Introducing you to Mr. Edward Dugan, that wants a loan from you."

"Ah?" says the president of the bank, not moving a muscle or stirring to get up. "And for what purpose does Mr. Edward Dugan wish to borrow money?"

"To develop a mine," said Blondy.

"Ah, he wants to develop a mine, does he?" says the other. "There are a few thousand other people in Pottsville and near it who want to find a mine and develop it."

"Mr. Dugan has the mine," said Blondy. "He just wants the hard cash to start things rolling."

"Ah, is that all?" says the president. "How much does he want?"

"He don't need a lot," replied Blondy. "He could waste a few days and dig his capital out of the ground, too, but he's in a hurry, and he wouldn't mind making a fifty-thousand dollar loan from your bank to open things up fast."

"Wouldn't he?" asks the president.

"No, he wouldn't," says Blondy.

"I suppose that I'm to take a day off and inspect the property, eh?" said the president.

"No, we brought the property along for you to inspect right here," says Blondy.

With that he pulled out a handful of that decayed, black rock and dumped it right on the smooth, polished, shining surface of the president's desk.

I saw the banker jump, resenting the impertinence. His eyes were blazing, and he was ready to have us thrown out, but then he got a good look at that ore, and he sat down again with a sudden jar that shook the room. He picked up some of that rock dust and drifted it through his fingers, and another kind of a blaze came into the eyes of that banker, you can bet!

He sat there for quite a while, and I seen that he was not fingering just this here pile of ore, but his own hopes for the future.

Slope, he was shifting about from one foot to the other, and he didn't understand at all why old Blondy had asked for so much coin, or why the president was taking so long about it, except to find a polite way of throwing us out of his office.

Finally Slope, he said: "I beg your pardon, sir. Fifty thousand dollars—I'm sure that my friend was only joking—because we really don't need to—"

"Fifty thousand?" said the president, short and sharp. "Fifty thousand? Oh, darn fifty thousand. You can have a hundred thousand if you want it. I'll have to take a look at the thing to see that it's really there. That's all."

He looked up from his dreams about himself, and he said: "What's the name of this strike?"

"The Christabel," said Slope.

"Christabel? Christabel? I've heard that name before," says the banker. "By the way, you people all sit down. Tell me about it. There must be a romance behind it somewhere. There's always a romance behind millions."

When he said "millions," I nearly hit the floor. I grabbed both sides of the chair that I had dropped down in, and I barely managed to keep myself from sliding off.

"It belonged to Henry Christian," said Slope, "together with some other stock that he sold to my father."

"Bonanza Chris?" exclaimed the banker. "You mean to say that Bonanza sold this mine?"

And then he rolled back in his chair, and he began to laugh. He laughed till he cried. He wiped his tears away, and he laughed again, till he was all doubled up sideways in his chair. Finally he was done laughing, and sorter laid there, helpless and weak, and groaning.

At last he said: "I wouldn't change this news for a Christabel of my own. We always thought that Bonanza was at least clever. This little story will sink the only remaining bit of his reputation." He paused a second. "But perhaps you're friends of Henry Christian, as you call him?"

But Slope replied: "I'm sorry that I cannot discuss him, sir!"

His head went slowly up, like the head of a lion, and the yellow blaze shone again in his eyes. It made me tremble for that fat crook, and it sobered the banker up in a jiffy.

"I understand, I think," said he. "There are reefs and risks enough about a mining camp, but that a man like

145

Bonanza Chris should be permitted to go on with his nefarious practices—well, it's really incredible. Some day, however, public sentiment will turn, and then Bonanza will find it convenient to move on, just as he moved before."

It was fine to hear him talk like that. It sorter showed you, all in a glance, what had made the West the grandest part of the world, in spite of thugs and yeggs and gunmen mixed in. It showed you why mining camps turned into towns, and towns into cities. It made me feel, somehow, that to be honest and straight was the only thing in the world, after all. I didn't feel too good about what I had done and been in the past when I looked into the face of that bank president.

Then he went on to say: "About the money: of course, you can have it. I can do better than that. I can send a real mining engineer to you, who'll properly open up the property and see that nothing is wasted from the start. I can tell you where some unused, half-rusted equipment is lying, to be bought up for a song. In fact, if you've won through in spite of Bonanza Chris, I'll do all I can for you. The world loves success, Mr. Dugan. I congratulate you!"

But Slope raised the flat of his hand to keep the compliment away.

"Congratulate me on having two friends like this," said he, and he introduced us by the only names he knew.

CHAPTER 29

That was a good time. I like to talk about it. I mean, the time before trouble started again, and devilish mean trouble, a lot worse than anything that had happened

146

before. But that spot in between, I like to lay back, sorter, talk it over, think it over, and roll it on top and under my tongue.

Everything went through quicker'n a wink, so fast it make me kinder giddy.

There was the inspection of the mine, when I felt kinder tight and anxious, but it passed quick enough, and I saw that banker—Wendell was his name—get red as beef and white as a fish, all in a minute, when he seen the dark streak of the vein, sliced with the hard cash, yellow as sunshine in the lantern light.

That same afternoon the engineer arrived. He was Tom Parry, and a better gent never stepped. He was a little, busy man, always whistling under his breath, kinder, stepping quick and light around, his eyes glittering and jumping all the time. When you spoke to him, his glance jumped straight at you, and hung onto your eyes and stayed there. You knew in five minutes that he was an honest man. Inside of a week it was plain that he knew his business, too.

He started everything at once—the trucking of machinery down from Pottsville and other mines that were nearer, where veins had pinched out. He said that hand labor was a curse, and that machines were the blood of the age.

Soon donkey engines, they were wheezing and braying, chains were rattling, derricks were groaning, and wagons were raising a dust as they beat down the road to town. Men were gathering, all hand picked by Tom Parry, but the workers were only about half. At any given minute of the day there was sure to be another half made up of folks that had come to stand and look, ask questions.

At the same time, quarters were run up, a building of logs for the head engineer and his bosses; and another long, low bunk house for the men. Everything was policed up careful all the time. While those buildings were being throwed up fast as you please, there was more expert axmen cutting down trees, making a clearing, and building another house down the stream. In that log house there was four rooms, as fine as you ever seen, a kitchen, two bedrooms, and a fourth room for everything else. That was where Slope was to live, because Tom Parry said it would be good to have him handy in case of needing to consult him about anything.

Slope agreed to stay, and then he added: "But you know, Parry, there's no good consulting me. I don't know how to say anything but yes to you."

I guess a flash of temptation came to Parry, then, for I saw him shake his head, sudden, and hard, and then he was his smiling self again.

It was at about this time that Wendell sent for me and Blondy. When we came into his office, he shook hands with us, warm and friendly, like he was welcoming us home from somewhere.

"I have occasion to show you gentlemen," said he, including me with the corner of his eye, "that Mr. Dugan does not forget his friends and his helpers. In fact, he remembers them in the most princely fashion. He spoke to me about this some time ago. And now he has had the documents drawn up with a lawyer's help, and has duly signed the conveyances. Here you are, one for each of you, and each of these little packets represents a one-third interest in the Christabel. As a matter of fact, you two might control the mine over Mr. Dugan's head!"

I was flabbergasted. I couldn't speak. I had been hoping for something, all right. But what I was looking for was a good fat handout, not riches!

Every foot of the vein was opened up—and they were working it every way from Sunday—it got bigger and bigger, fatter and fatter, richer and richer. Then I seen that Blondy didn't seem at all upset by what was being offered to him.

"Are there any copies of these here documents?" says he.

And he picks them up quickly and holds 'em hard.

I was shocked at him.

Mr. Wendell, he looked Blondy over with a stony eye, too.

"No," he replied, "there are no copies. There is no way

148

of altering that agreement, except with your own consent," he added with a smile.

Blondy stood there, looking at the packets for a while. They looked mighty legal, all right, and they had heavy black printing on the outside. On the inside, I could bet, there was something beginning with a "whereas."

Then Blondy lighted a match, though he didn't have any cigarette in his mouth, and by thunder, he touched the match to the bottom of the papers.

I gave a shout and stared at Wendell for help, but he had merely folded his hands on top of his desk and sat there looking on with his eyebrows lifted, the same as a man at a show, where the things that happen in front of his eyes don't have no real meaning, only fun.

Those papers, they burned right up, and a cloud of sooty smoke went up to the ceiling. I seen the charred ash turn black and then gray. It fell to the floor in a shower, and big Blondy, he set his foot on the glowing tagends and ground 'em to bits.

"Thereby," says Wendell, cool and grim, "you make yourself liable to a suit from our friend, Red, to the extent of one third of the value of the Christabel. How much have you in the bank to meet that suit?"

"Aw, don't make any mistake about Red. He's a white man," replied Blondy, and he gave a big sigh.

Then he said: "I was always kinder afraid that Slope would go and do some dog-gone silly thing like this, but I was not goin' to talk to him about it. It might've forced his hand all the harder. By this way of looking at it, he don't hardly deserve to have no mine at all, but Red ought to have most of it, and me the rest." He wiped his forehead. "I'm mighty glad to get this here cleared up," he said.

Then he explained to Wendell: "Money can't talk, between me and Slope. That goes for Red, too. The three of us, kind of—I mean to say, we sorter—"

"I understand perfectly," says Wendell.

He had his head ducked down, his eyes had shrunk to a point, and he looks straight at me and says: "Do you concur?"

"Do I which?" says I.

"Do you agree with your friend here?" he repeats.

"Jiminy," says I, "I always agree with Blondy, except about the way to catch fish. If you stand upstream, the way he does, and then you—"

"He agrees with you," says Wendell, cutting me off about the fish pretty rude. "I begin to think that the golden age is not a dream, after all, but a—"

Then he snapped back his shoulders and gave his head a shake.

"My friends," said he, "of course, one must also consider another thing, which may put you in the wrong."

"And what's that?" asked Blondy, his little forehead turning all wavy with a frown.

"That's the viewpoint of Mr. Dugan. He may be a little hurt when he hears that you have thrown away his offer."

Blondy scratched his chin.

"By thunder," he said, "I didn't think of that. Yeah, he might, too. He's a funny gent. He's touchy, is what he is. You never know when you'll get him wrong."

"He's a noble fellow," says Wendell in a queer, gentle voice. "And I imagine that you two had better think of him at the present moment."

"I dunno what to think," said Blondy.

"And you?" says Wendell, looking at me.

"I ain't been thinking for quite some time," said I. "I'm just flabbergasted."

Mr. Wendell grinned at me, sorter friendly, and said: "Suppose I suggest this. Instead of taking a third apiece, I propose that you take a smaller share, but a handsome one. You deserve it. Mr. Dugan has told me the whole story. A very long, but a very interesting one. It began with a fist fight, and went to a lunch counter, and then to your lumberman millionaire friend."

He looked hard at me. My eyes began to pop. "It continued," he said, "to the affair of the envelope and the blank paper, and a certain matter of cutting bonds and a night in a mine shaft. In fact, I should say that there would certainly be an Edward Dugan with only five

150

thousand dollars in his pocket, at this time, instead of a handsome fortune, except that he found two friends. Looking at matters from his viewpoint entirely, as his friend and financial adviser, I suggest that you take a third between you; that is, one sixth each of the total property."

"Money, it raises hell with friendships," said Blondy, shaking his head. "But maybe you're right. If old Slope, he got on a rampage—it wouldn't be so good."

"No, it would not," said Wendell, nodding his head. "Just what your property is worth I cannot tell at present. I think Mr. Tom Parry feels that only a fool would sell that mine for as much as a million and a half. He thinks that the veins run clear through to China, and east and west to the two oceans. And he's a man who knows his business. So suppose that we take the property on that basis, and you'll see that you have half a million between you, which is two hundred and fifty thousand dollars apiece. That money, well invested in this land of opportunity by a man who knows his business, ought to bring you in a good ten per cent, and I know what I'm talking about. In other words, I'm speaking to you of an assured income for life of from twenty to twenty-five thousand dollars apiece, on the lowest price which Parry would consider for the mine today. Perhaps you really have as much as two, three or five times the amount I've mentioned! But I would certainly regulate my spending on Parry's estimate!"

I took a long, deep breath, closing my eyes. I thought, all at once, of tomato cans in junk heaps, with the labels half tore off and flapping in the wind. I dunno why I thought of tomato cans, except that they're so kinder dreary. I thought of jungle meals, too, mulligans stewed up with swiped chickens and potatoes, and all that, and here I was listening to songs about hard cash!

"Mr. Wendell," says I when I could get my eyes open and my sight unscrewed from the past, that looked at me like a gun, "would you mind talking that down a little for me? Say it so I can understand. I mean to say, a sack of tobacco costs five cents. Now, you was talking about whole dollars, and thousands of 'em, or what was I hearing, anyway?"

He said: "What does a puncher get on the range?"

"Thirty or forty dollars, maybe," said I.

"Well," said he, "every day you get about as much as two punchers get for working a whole year. Does that make it clearer?"

I thought it over. I thought about a puncher when he comes to town flush, when maybe he's got five or six whole gold pieces making music against one another, in his pocket. And I was to get twice that much every day of my life!

"Why, Mr. Wendell," said I, "how could a man go and spend all of that money, would you tell me?"

He only smiled at me. Then his smile gradually darkened and went out like a flame dying on a dry wick.

"This matter of money may be a serious thing for you, Red," he said. "You've done very well for yourself when your pockets were empty, but I think that the time has come when you will need a father more than ever a boy needed one before!"

CHAPTER 30

Just to show you the way that things go, the day the crash began, I was in Pottsville having a bust. I mean, I was blowing a lot of money, more money than I'd ever had in my pockets before. You know how it is—it looks foolish when you see somebody else laying out cash, but there ain't anything more fun than to blow yourself to what you want.

I wanted a lot of things. I could've bought them all

before, but I was saving up so as to be sure that I could have everything that I needed.

I wanted a pair of light revolvers with pearl handles— just .32s, because the man-sized Colt was heavy for me to tote and draw. I wanted a good hunting knife with silver chasing around the handle, and a silver head of Mexican carved work on the butt of it. I wanted good clothes, too; not the clothes that a puncher takes after, but regular city things. I wanted long pants, blue serge, and a handkerchief to stick out of the breast pocket; I wanted brown shoes, not boots, but shoes, so shiny that I could look down and see my face lying twice on the ground before me. I wanted a hat with a soft, narrow brim, and a black band to go around it, a gray hat with a black band. There ain't nothing slicker than that! I wanted smooth, tan gloves, too, and a hair cut, all the way around, not botched off in a tramp jungle by somebody's pocketknife.

Yes, and I wanted a pocketknife, too, with six blades, a corkscrew, a can opener, a pair of scissors, and a nail file hitched on as parts of it. I wouldn't be working the nail file too much, but it would be handy and kinder different to have around. There ain't anything much finer than to be able to sit back and pull out a knife, and open up a little blade and clean your nails, and take a scissors on the same knife and clip them nails all around, and then, when everybody's looking, you open the back of the knife and file them nails off as smooth as a whistle. Then you lean back and slide your knife into your pocket, clear your throat, make yourself a smoke, and act like you didn't realize that everybody was looking at you and admiring.

Well, I got that knife, and that hair cut, the guns, even; and, most important of all, the long pants.

I had often hankered after long pants. I had looked at my skinned knees and wondered how my legs would look when they was dressed up proper. But there ain't any imagining beforehand that can get you used to it.

No, sir; when I stepped into them pants and seen myself in the long mirror in the store, I couldn't believe my eyes. Why, I looked about a hand taller and ten years older right away. I put my hand on one hip and give myself a look, and it was wonderful. I put my hand on the other hip and give myself another look, and that was wonderful, too.

I says to the clerk: "A pretty good fit, ain't they?" That clerk was kinder consumptive, or something, because he was always coughing a good deal, and now he says from behind his hand: "Yes, like they were made to order."

"I think so, too," says I. "Mightn't they kinder be a mite easier around the seat, though?"

He leaned over and give the seams a twitch in front, and then he went around and twitched them behind. He stood off and looked at them pants hard. He was a mighty well-dressed fellow himself. He had on gray trousers and a blue coat; he wore a bow tie, and he was was kinder slim and neat all over. You could tell that he'd been raised by a fine family and must've just gone into the haberdashery business for the experience or something.

"Of course," he says, "every man to his own taste. But for my part, I'd say that those trousers are just about the thing for you."

"Do you think so?" says I.

"I do," says he.

"And so do I," says I, agreeing all the time.

Because it ain't any use going against the opinion of a man that knows his business. And there ain't nothing like a real gentleman to know about clothes. I've noticed it over and over.

Well, when I got fixed up, I didn't feel quite right. I mean, I didn't feel quite like the pictures that you see of young men in magazines, and I says to the clerk that I'll have an overcoat.

He asks: "Isn't it rather a warm day for an overcoat?"

And I says with a kinder easy laugh: "Well, you know how it is. It ain't exactly right to carry gloves, is it, unless you sorter got an overcoat draped over your arm? I don't want nothing heavy, but something kinder light. Price ain't no object with me."

"No," said he, "you've said that before." And he coughed again.

There ain't much you can do for a gent that's dying of consumption like that clerk; only, you can help to make his last days easier and pleasanter in every way. I was terrible sorry for him, and I put ten dollars on the counter where he'd find it after I went away.

I got down the street a ways, and there I found what I wanted most of all, and that was a regular Mexican saddle shop.

I got me a pair of golden spurs with long spoon handles and a pair of little bells on each, the prettiest things that you ever seen. The breast of a humming bird, it ain't no prettier than what those bells were. They was all openwork!

I got me a set of silver conchos to sew up the seam of my trousers when I laid out to buy a riding outfit. And I got a quirt with gold studs around the handle of it, and a green stone in the butt, which, the Mexican he said it was an emerald. I got a bridle that was almost pure gold, too, and you never seen such fine chains. How they jingled and made music. I couldn't hardly wait to see that bridle flash and hear it chiming on the tossing head of a horse! But mostly I got a saddle.

If a king was to go and sit in that saddle he'd forget all about his dog-gone throne, believe me! Then I got a pair of fancy saddle bags that I loaded up with my guns and suchlike things.

I hadn't intended to go no farther about buying, that day, but I knew where horses was to be had, and somehow I up and went there. There was two yards in Pottsville. In one of 'em there was mostly mules and burros, with just a few mustangs and heavy common horses. In the other there was real animals, and that was the yard I went to.

The fellow that owned it was by name of Jenkins, and he was sitting like a crow on the top of the corral fence, chewing at a straw and whistling at the same time. I seen by that that he wasn't no common man. It takes a good deal of talent, and it takes a lot of practice, too, to do a thing like that. If you don't believe me, you just go and try it.

I says that I would like to look over his horses and see if I could get anything to my taste. And he turns around his head and looks me over. And he says: "Yes, sir!" and touches his hat and slides down pronto off of that fence.

It was the first time that anybody had ever tipped his hat to me. It made me feel pretty good, and it made me feel a little sad, too, to think of a fellow being so high that other folks tipped their hats to him. I was sorry for Jenkins. I seen him look a good deal at my gloves and my overcoat. Maybe they done the trick for me.

He says what would I like to see, and I says the best.

"Yes, sir. Certainly," says he.

He gives a whistle, and a shiny Negro comes out from the end of the barn with a currycomb in one hand and a pipe in the other, and he says: "Yas, suh!"

There wasn't any style about that Negro. They don't take nacheral to style.

"Fetch out that cream-colored little gelding, George," says Jenkins.

"Why?" asked George. "For fun?"

"No," says Jenkins. "For this gentleman."

"For this which?" says George.

"Go on and do what I tell you," says Jenkins, really sharp, and frowning.

I was glad to hear him put that ignorant Negro in his place. And I was all the more glad because there was quite a crowd worked up around the corral now, loungers and such, enjoying watching a man buy him a horse. Everybody gets superior and full of information right away, even them that never seen a horse before, hardly.

Then the cream-colored horse, it come out, with the Negro leading it. And there was a horse for you! Its mane was long and tied with ribbons. It had a silver tail that touched the corral dust. And it was just the right size, maybe an inch or two under fifteen hands.

I looked at the gelding in front, and I looked at the gelding from behind. But I didn't let no excitement show in my face. Not me! Finally I says: "What's the price, Jenkins?"

"That hoss is cheap," says he. "It would only stand you up for two hundred and fifty dollars."

I didn't fall down, but I pretty nigh did. Them was the days when you could get a good Mexican bunch of meanness in the way of hossflesh for around thirty or forty dollars. And a right upstanding hoss would cost you around a hundred.

Two hundred and fifty dollars!

I wanted to yell, but then I seen the sun shining on the nice, new yellow gloves, and so I said: "Nothing better than this?"

I heard the crowd gasp a little. And I heard something else, too. It was a freckle-faced kid on the fence that was saying: "The dude kid is all made of money!"

I wanted to go and paste him on the root of his turned-up nose, but there ain't no use starting a fight unless you're dressed sort of cheap, free, and easy. So I didn't pay no attention.

"You want something better, sir?" says Jenkins.

"I'll look at something else," says I with a fine, careless wave of the hand.

I seen he didn't like it. I seen he expected to knock me gally-west with the looks and the price of that hoss.

Then he says, hard and sharp: "George, bring out the chestnut mare!"

CHAPTER 31

I seen that there was a kind of a climax and a crisis coming on by the way that George backed up and took a fresh grip on the lead rope of the cream.

"Mare?" says he. "Chestnut mare, boss? You ain't meaning Kate, is you?"

"Yeah, I mean Catherine the Great," says Jenkins.

The Negro, he gives the boss a look, and he gives me a look, then he leads the gelding back into the barn. I hated to see it go. But I could take it again a little later on. I was only in a fever of fear that somebody else in the barn might sell the gelding to another gent while I was looking at other nags.

Then out come Kate. She come gentle and easy, with her head down a little, and the lead rope sagging between the Negro's hand and her halter. She was one of them deep, dark chestnuts, with a dappling all over the skin, like the shadowy markings of a leopard's hide—just a suggestion of it. And she didn't look like very much to me, at first. I didn't see why there should be such a fuss about bringing her out or calling her Catherine the Great. For she was not all rounded and sleek, like the cream-colored gelding, and her mane and tail, they didn't sweep and flow, but they were just sort of poor and ratty, and nothing to look at. She looked narrow, too, coming head-on, and you could see her hip bones plenty, and her withers. Her neck wasn't arched up, but stuck straight out, lean and homely. Her face was all bones.

Then the Negro, he turned her, and she stood side on toward me, not making no effort to show herself off, but slow and gradual she heaved up her head and pricked up her little ears, and she looked across toward the horizon to ask what was happening on the other side of the world.

By thunder! All at once she looked like she could get there, too, with one jump!

Yes, sir; I said that you could see her hip bones and the withers standing up, but you could see all the rest of her, too—every muscle, laid on in sleek, long-running cords and masses, like water that flows smooth and fast over straight-laid rocks. She wasn't no more than fifteen hands, and she didn't look long and low, neither, but she stood over a mighty lot of ground, and there was plenty of daylight under her, too.

Jenkins, he got over the fence by stepping, it looked like, and he says: "Maybe this here little mare would do for you sir?"

I didn't answer at first: I just looked. There had been a cream-colored gelding, the prettiest ever seen, somewhere in my mind. But he was gone, now. He was just like a dream, and now I'd waked up.

"What's the price?" says I.

"I've marked her down, for one reason or another," says he, "to eight hundred dollars!"

Can you believe me when I say that I wasn't surprised by that whopping price? No, sir! Because money, it didn't seem to have anything to do with that mare. To pay a price for her, take her home and call her your own, it was just foolish. No, it didn't seem right that money should give anybody the right to own such a thing like her!

But I didn't let on. I just said: "The price is all right." Out of the tail of my eye I seen the loafers along the fence sort of sag and droop over against one another. I seen their eyes open up, too, at the idea of a man paying a price like that for a horse. The price of a whole team for one horse, and mentioning it as free and easy as I'd done!

Jenkins was about flattened out, too.

He says: "You say the price is all right?"

"Yes," says I.

He grunted, like I'd nudged him in the stomach with my elbow.

"But," says I, "what about the reasons that you had for marking her down? What's wrong with her?"

"You can see for yourself that there ain't anything wrong with her," says he.

I looked. But I didn't have to look hard. You could sort of look through her, as I said before, and see that she was all right.

"Well," says I, "what made you mark her down?"

He spat the straw out of his mouth.

"It's this way," says he. "She's a wrong size, sort of. She's too small for some; and she's too big for others!"

159

He said it slow;-and he said it sort of solemn. A little snicker went down the fence.

I turned and looked 'em over, to show I scorned a lot of ignorant trash like them, and then I says to Jenkins, calm as you please: "She looks the right size for me. I'll try her."

"Will you?" says Jenkins.

"Yes, I will."

"Very well, sir," says he. "I'll have her saddled."

"Never mind," says I. "I've got my own saddle. If you'll just go and send one of your boys up to the Mexican saddle shop and bring my stuff down here."

"What name, sir?" says Jenkins.

"Just tell them the carved saddle," said I. "That'll be enough."

He was a good deal impressed, it was plain, and he was about to say something, when a terrible coughing fit came over him and cut him short. But he sent George for the saddle. While I was waiting, I leaned my back against the fence and smoked tailor-made cigarettes, which they was a lot too sweet for my taste. It ain't the price of things, always, that makes them good, I found out.

The saddle came, and it made a ripping sensation, I tell you. All that yellow and white blinded you in an instant, but the bridle stopped everything in the way of a sensation.

When the whole outfit was on Catherine the Great, I tell you what, she was a picture. A saddle can't hide a good horse, and no saddle, and no blanket, either, could hide Kate.

She stood like a stone while I climbed on board of her.

"She's reins over the neck?" I asked.

"Ah," says Jenkins, "I reckon that you have been in the West before, sir, seeing you know so much about our ways!"

There was another snicker along that fence. And I looked across and seen grins on every face—grins so wide that you could've chucked an apple down each throat.

Suddenly I guessed that I was about to get an idea of why the price on Kate was marked down. The minute

that the lead rope and halter was taken off of her, I knew
—because, slow and steady, she began to gather under
me, and her back began to arch.

Well, I turned all sick. Because, d'you see, from the
time I was six years old onward, I'd rode everything from
a burro to a steer, and had been throwed off of all of them
more times than it could be told. But chiefly, horses had
shied me off and bucked me off. I'd gone over heads and
over tails. I'd gone through the air in every kind of an
arc, and I'd landed on every part of myself, body and
bones and face.

When you've been throwed off so many times as that,
you may learn something about how to ride and how to
fall—which is just as important—but you also get sick
every time you feel a horse bunch its back under you.
The oldest buckaroos, they feel it, and they turn gray. I
know, because I've seen 'em. You may win the fight, but
you're gonna be hurt while winning.

Well, by the way that Kate gathered herself, I knew
that she was a "champeen" when it came to bucking. I
knew that I was beat. I knew why her price was marked
down so low; but, worst of all, I knew why them grins
was being worn by the loafers that waited to see the show
along the fence.

I begun to doubt Jenkins, too, and the way he touched
his hat and called me "sir." I begun to think that he'd
been aiming to make a show of me right from the first.

Then somebody yelled, sharp and high. It was George,
and when she heard the signal, Kate started to do her
stuff.

CHAPTER 32

She had springs under her, and a pair of wings. She rose right up and gave me a look at the top of the barn, and then she came down and knocked dust out of the ground like a carpet beater out of a rug.

She bucked with her ears pricking, to show that she liked the job and that she would soon let out a few more reefs and really sail, as soon as she was warmed up to her work.

I worked her around the corral, cursing my fine new clothes all the way. There was no stick to them, if you know what I mean. They were like glass when it came to slipping, and so was that brand-new, shining saddle. I was slipping and sliding from the first. I stuck on Kate while she flicked around the corral once, and then she snapped me off as clean as you please.

I came down sitting, with a whang that sent the dust spurting for twenty yards. My head rang with the effect of that thump, and my ears were filled with the roar of those loungers along the fence.

There's nothing like getting what you want and expect. They knew I was coming off, and off I had come in the best style, so they let off all the howls that were packed in their throat, ready for delivery.

As I got up, I realized that things wasn't the way that they had been before. I mean, those clothes of mine had changed. My nose had commenced to bleed, and trickles of red were running down onto my coat. Worse than that, my trousers had split. I knew it, when I got up, by the feel of the cool air and by the yell that went up along the fence. Yeah, I sure was making all of those fellows happy!

162

I seen Jenkins, too. He wasn't laughing, because he wasn't the laughing kind, but a deep, kind of a solemn grin was pushing out the wrinkles around his ears. I could see that he was more pleased inwardly than all of the rest put together, unless it was the freckle-faced kid on the fence. He was standing right up on the top rail, without holding on. He was showing off, that way, yelling, waving his hands, and yipping out things about a darn foreign dude.

I smiled a little to think what I was gonna do to that kid later on. I seen that he was a good bit older than me, and more solider and hefty around the shoulders. But that didn't count. You get a man mad enough and you just multiply his weight by wildcats.

The next I seen that didn't improve my spirits none was Catherine the Great. I went up to her, pretty mad, and pretty sick, too. I had to get on, with all of them howling at me, and it made me weak to think of what she'd do when she got a real good chance at me and was all warmed up. I had got her style, all right, by this time. For one thing, she knew how to come to a stop and turn a dead run into a spin, like a top. She had me beat.

Anyway, I got onto her, and they all yelled and howled and laughed themselves inside out, those loafers along the fence. By Jiminy, it certainly made me crazy!

I took that there emerald-handled quirt, when I had my feet settled into the stirrups, and I whaled into Catherine the Great. She was gonna shed me pretty quick, but I slammed right into her with a good long swing from the left shoulder to the right flank and quarter. And at every wallop a welt stood out on her shining silk coat.

When she felt those licks, she rose up on her hind legs and throwed her dignity to the winds and squealed like a stuck pig. That pleased me a lot. I didn't care, but I changed my mind a little later, because she bolted straight for the fence.

First, I says to myself, she's trying to make me loosen up all holds by that bluff of throwing herself through the fence. I've had horses do that before. But then I seen that she didn't mean to stop, and the way that she had her head stuck out in front of her, it was pretty clear that I might as well haul away at an iron beam as at her mouth.

So I didn't try to haul. I says to myself it's the finish. I could've screamed like a fool girl, but I put the screaming all into that quirt lash and stung her up worse than ever.

She didn't hit that fence, though. No, sir! It rose up higher and higher, till it was over her head. Then she rose up, and she winged across it like nothing at all.

I should have fell off when we landed, I was so surprised at being wafted up into the sky like that, but I didn't fall. That was because she landed on springs and went away on a dead line.

She had both her ears flat back, and I could see the mean red in her eyes and the flare of her nostrils. I could see her eyes bulging and shining, and then I knew all of the horse sense was out of her, and horse fear was there instead.

She was running away!

Now, a fall off a horse on a dead run ain't anything to pick out, but I would rather've fallen off a cloud, so long as I could land alone, than be shed in that corral with those yaps looking on.

So I was kind of glad, and I pitched into her some more with the quirt. Every time I socked her, a shudder ran through her, a shudder of effort, but she didn't run faster, because she was already going full speed, and that full speed of hers was like an express train on a down grade.

Right in the midst of that running she hit some plowed ground where somebody or other was still sticking to farming and letting gold mines go hang.

When I seen that field, I was glad and proud and happy. It was soft ground to fall on, for one thing. Better than that, it was deep ground to run on, and there was plenty of it. There must've been a coupla hundred acres in that layout.

Catherine the Great, she kept on working harder than ever. Every time she made a stride, she drove down pretty near to China, and every time she pulled a hoof up, she throwed a ten-pound clod high above my head. She kept that up for only a few minutes. Then she stopped, dead beat. How she steamed, and how she blew! But she was beat! Yes, luck and plowed ground had kept me in that saddle.

She stood with her head hanging and her ears back, and I seen that that couldn't last. I spoke to her, clucked to her, and jabbed her with my heels, but she didn't budge.

So then I gave her the quirt again, harder than ever. I hated to do it, but there was nothing else in the cards, and the shoulder slash touched the electric button, all right.

She untied herself from her sulk, and one of her ears flickered forward. By jiminy, she began to trot along as nice and easy as you please through that deep ground.

I tried her for guiding, and she was as soft and easy as anything under the rein. Yes, she was right there in my lap!

By thunder, how good I felt! And how proud! I begun to laugh.

I reached off and patted her wet shoulder. She flinched and flickered the sore skin at my touch, but pretty soon she put both of her ears forward.

I seen that she was forgetting. Horses is like little kids. After you spank them, they feel better.

I reckon that it had been a considerable spell since Catherine the Great had been spanked. Mostly, people would be holding on with both hands, the way I'd done during that first fast round in the corral.

And then came the cream. I pulled her around and headed her back for the corral. By jiminy, I wish you could've seen the faces of that crowd along the fence. They sat there like great lumps and gaped. The freckle-faced kid stood still on the top rail of the fence, and he stared, too, like the rest. And nobody laughed.

That did me the most good of all, next to meeting up with Jenkins himself. He stood at the gate of the corral, and I brought the beauty straight up to him. She had begun to pace soft as you please under me. Oh, it was just floating along! I halted her by Jenkins, and I says to him: "She's got some pretty good points. She can jump pretty well. Perhaps I'll take her."

He stared and said: "What's your name, kid, and what stable you been riding for?"

Then a deep voice roared in the crowd: "You dog-goned, ornery horned toad, don't you know that's my partner? Don't you know that that's Red?"

And there was old Blondy over there, laughing big and deep, and enjoying everything to beat the band!

CHAPTER 33

Blondy was all dressed up. He had on a deerskin vest that you could see far away, like a lighthouse, the dapples on it was so bright. He was wearing a bandanna as big as a tablecloth. His Stetson was the biggest one that ever was built, and it sat on top of his little head like a hat on a stick. Under it, you just seen the shine of his eyes, and his big red beak, like the beak of an eagle.

His boots was wore outside of his pants, and those boots had a reason for being outside, because around the top of them there was embroidery that pretty nigh knocked your eye out of your head. And them boots was shined up, so that even the bottom of the wrinkles was as bright as glass. You could tell that he was carrying around the heft of a five-hundred-dollar watch.

I was particularly glad because he'd been there to notice everything, because then he would tell Slope, and Slope would get it again from me. I knew Slope would laugh and smile at me, then pat my shoulder and say that I was great.

Jenkins, he says: "Are you the Red of the Christabel?"

"I reckon I am," says I.

"Dog-gone me, you little rat," says he, "I been sold—by them fool clothes you got on. I thought you was a little tenderfoot dude, is what I though you were. And here you was Red all the time." He laughed, slapped my shoulder, and pretty near dislocated it.

The crowd, it laughed, too, because a crowd is that way. If it can't laugh on one side, it laughs on the other, and it always manages to stay with the gent that's on top! There ain't nothing lower nor meaner than a crowd, I guess. And the bigger the crowd, the meaner it is.

I looked around for the freckle-faced kid, and I seen that he wasn't laughing any. He was dead serious and frowning, looking straight at me.

Well, I wasn't much fit for a fight. I was shaking and trembling from head to foot, and my arms was about pulled out from their sockets from yanking at the reins to steady that wildfire mare. There were sparks still buzzing around inside of my head, I'd hit the ground so hard, and my nose was still bleeding. When I seen the face of that yap, though, I got terrible hot, and I walked up to him.

When I got closer, I was sorry that I ever had started. He looked about twelve or thirteen when I started, but when I come closer I seen that he was nigher onto fourteen. I've been hammered around the world enough to toughen me, but I seen as how he was made thick and solid, like a man, around the shoulders and chest. You would guess that he had done a lot of wood chopping, or else worked in a blacksmith shop. He had a clean, straight eye; and his jaw, it was blunt and square, and made to soak up shocks of all kinds. His arms, they was long, and rounded out at the shoulders, where strength shows first.

Yes, I didn't like my job, and I had to set my teeth on it, to rouse myself up. And I says to myself, when the fight starts, I'll try my old trick of pretending to slip and then coming up under his guard and soaking him on the chin with some uppercuts.

I walked up to him like that, and I said: "You been having a pretty good time out of me, ain't you, you flat-faced, pug-nosed, wall-eyes lump of half-breed Injun, you!"

With that I slapped him in the face and got ready to sock him with the other fist.

But the freckle-face, he reaches out and picks my fist out of the air and stands there, holding my wrist with the grip of a man, easy and calm. I seen the white mark of my fingers on the red of his cheek, and I felt his bright, sharp, steady eyes looking at me.

"I don't blame you for wanting to fight me, Red," says he. "But I'm too big for you, and a lot too old. I didn't know you was one of us. I thought you was a stuck-up dude, and I sure nacherally hate them Eastern foreigners. I'd mostly like to shake hands and be friends."

He'd been acting pretty mean, but when he was touched at the right spot, look what he done, and look what he said!

I kinder laughed, still shaky, and I says: "All right, brother. I reckon that you could tie me in figure eights if you had a notion to. But I had to give you a chance to. You got a terrible loud voice in a pinch! But there's my hand, if you want to be friends. If you don't, I'll fight you right now."

He took my hand, and he give it a good squeeze, and he looks across and grins at me, so's his eyes pretty near disappear.

All at once I says: "I'm gonna see some more of you, brother. You look like a gent to tie to!"

"Thanks, Red," says he.

And I went back to Blondy and Jenkins. On the way I heard somebody saying that that was where Red's bluff had been called, but I didn't mind that. I looked on Freckle-face as a friend.

Jenkins was making a terrible stew about leaving Catherine the Great go, and he said that he never would've dreamed of offering her if he'd thought that she could be rode. Big men and fine breakers had tried her, and all of 'em had been licked.

"What put you onto sailing into her with the quirt, kid?" said he.

"I didn't have no idea," I admitted. "She'd slammed me on the ground, and I was just getting some of my own back before she shed me again. I expected to get in about three licks between forking her and being chucked again."

Jenkins, he sighs.

"That's the way of it," he said. "Kids and strangers, they have all the luck. I been gentling her for three months, and every Sunday I've tried her, and every Sunday she's piled me. But now she's found a master, I'm glad of it. Blondy, make the kid treat her right. She ain't common. She may be thoroughbred, for all I know, but I never seen nothing in a pasture field move like she can move."

He went and rubbed her down all over, while George, he came and swabbed me off in front, where the blood had stopped dripping.

Then I rode back up the main street with Blondy, and him on a great big monster of a horse about seventeen hands high, and Catherine looking and dancing briefly like a dancing firefly beside him.

He said: "You better go and get yourself a new outfit, kid."

"Yeah, I'm going to," said I. "Tell me something, Blondy. Why did Jenkins say that my clothes was a sell? Why did he say that it was a fool outfit? I seen a hundred pictures in magazines that looked just like that."

"Sure, you have," says Blondy. "But they wasn't pictures out of the West. We got our own fashions," says he, and he looks down kind of gradual and approving on his own rig.

Well, it was a good rig, too, as I leave it to anybody, and I seen the hint that Blondy had give me, and I followed it.

Right then and there, him and me, we wandered into that same clothing store, and that same clerk, he comes and waited on us, and he says: "Had a fight?"

"Yeah," said I. "I had a fight with a horse. I want some outfit that will stand a little wear and tear!"

That cough of his came back on him, but he managed

to control it, after a while, though it left him pretty red in the face, and then he took me back where the real togs was—I mean, the kind that you can set on the ground in, and climb a tree, and ride a horse bareback. If there's a stain, it kind of fits into a nacheral pattern. If there's a tear, it's only that much better ventilation.

I picked out everything with Blondy's advice, and I went and got myself a deerskin vest like his, only it had brighter dapplings. Blondy himself admired it a lot, and he said that he would've had it before me, except that it wasn't surveyed to his size.

But one thing that I was mighty particular about was the pants.

There is pants that is, and there is pants that ain't. I was tired of those that ain't. I told the clerk so, and he was pretty serious about it, and he said that the trouble was that a seam was always a seam, just made with thread. Finally he found me a pair of corduroy pants that had a double seat in them, and they was big and baggy, but when I took a fold in the bottom of them they done pretty good. Then we went out, and you got no idea the difference to the way a man feels, the confidence, and everything, when he knows that he's got a double-decked seat under him.

CHAPTER 34

It was just like I expected when we got home. Old Slope, he made a terrible fuss when he heard about the mare. It was late, but he lighted a lantern and went out with me, and I led out Kate, and he looked her over.

He said she was the most horse, for her inches, that he ever had seen, and I reckoned that he was about right. He wanted to know just how I got her, and Blondy told the story first. Then Slope, he made me tell the story all over, after Blondy, and he laid his hand on my shoulder and said that I would make a man one day that the world would hear about.

Altogether, I was having a pretty fine time out of it, laying back and taking things easy. We had some big, deep, comfortable chairs that I certainly liked to lounge around in, and everything would've been perfect if only I'd been able to smoke. But I never could enjoy tobacco much with Slope around. He never says nothing, but he looks at me with a mournful eye every now and then.

Well, we were sitting there like that when there came a bump on the door and Blondy sung out to come in, and in came a man of about forty, tall, straight, gray-headed, with a face mahogany-brown, and eyes shadowed under heavy brows. He looked like a man that would have a pain trying to smile, but he had a deep, gentle voice a little bit like Slope's.

"Are you gents the ones that run the Christabel?" he asked.

Slope got up and asked him to sit down, pushed out a chair for him, and said that we were the men he wanted. And the man said he was glad to sit down, because he'd been walking a long ways.

So he said his name was Joe Milton, and he sat down and took a filling of pipe tobacco from Blondy and lighted up. Then he laid back in his chair and seemed to be thinking through a cloud of tobacco smoke. His gun, it bothered him a little, and he hiked it around more to the front. He asked our pardon real polite for not taking it off, but he said that he had been so long in Mexico, and had had to use it so often on greasers, that he'd got into the habit.

It was pleasant listening to his deep, soft voice. I got hypnotized by it. Then, the next thing I was wide awake, because he was talking about the Christabel.

"I heard a yarn about the Christabel being a mighty big payer. Is that right?" he asked.

"That's right," said Slope. "The engineer says that she's worth between one and a half and two millions, at least."

That was Slope's way—always right out in the open with everything.

This fellow Milton, he opened his eyes and took his pipe out of his mouth.

"Well, that's good news for me," said he, "mighty good news. About the best that I've ever heard!"

He laughed a little, softly, and then Blondy drawls out that he's glad the mine pleases him.

"Yeah," says Milton, "because, one way or another, I reckon that it's half mine!"

We all three looked at one another.

"A half of the Christabel would keep you pretty comfortable the rest of your days, I reckon," says Blondy.

Milton, he nodded and smiled.

"Yes, it would," he said. "A half of two millions?" I'll say it would keep me fine!"

And once more he chuckled, soft and deep.

"I would be kinder interested," said I, "to find out where you bought half of the Christabel?"

He turned on me.

"Where I bought it, son?" said he. "I been shifting around through the mountains all the way from Peru to Alaska all my born days, and I've been and had a hand in a hundred mines, I reckon, in that time. But I never bought a share in a mine yet: Believe me, I've dug my part, lad!"

He said it proudly.

"You dug a half of the Christabel, did you?" said I.

Blondy and Slope watched Milton, and it was kinder amusing. Slope looked alarmed and worried, and Blondy was just sitting back, playing with a big grin, the way that a cat plays with a mouse, if you know what I mean.

"Dug a half?" said Milton. "I dunno what you call a half, but if I didn't prospect this here valley and pick out the Christabel, if I didn't open her up, find color and start the sinking of the shaft, you can call me a liar which I ain't! There's a hundred men that would swear to me opening her up!"

"It was too bad that, after opening her up," says Blondy, "you didn't stay for the gathering of her in."

"It was too bad," says Milton, "but it couldn't be

172

helped. The fact is, when Mary got sick, I had to hoof it to the mountains, and the only way that I could get a bit of money to take along with me was to sell a whole half share to that crooked robber, Bonanza Chris!"

This here news, it jolted me, I must say.

"Bonanza Chris!" said Blondy and Slope at the same time.

I blinked. Things begun to move fast inside of my head. Suppose that Bonanza had faked up the certificates and never had more than a half of the mine to sell from the first? Well, he'd done crookeder things than that by a whole lot.

"Tell me how it happened!" said Slope, leaning forward, dead serious and earnest.

So were we all of us, by that time.

Said Milton: "Why, I told you what happened. I opened her up, and I seen the vein growing. It was getting thicker, and it was getting richer. I come across a regular little pocket of wire gold. There was ten ounces of it! I begun to hope to hit more, and I was going along good, but spending everything for drills and powder and such, when I got the message that my girl was laid up and I had to move. Where was a man to get money from when his girl was sick. I ask you that?"

"Why, from the bank, of course. If you had a good mine started, the bank would've got behind you plenty!" says Blondy.

"Would it?" said Milton. "With only one streak of color every now and then, and mostly nothing but hope that was turning up under my pick? Besides, there wasn't no bank in Pottsville at that time. There wasn't no sign of a bank!"

He shook his head.

"I tried some of my old partners," he said. "But they was always broke. You take old prospectors, and they're either broke on the job or else they're in St. Louis, or Chicago, or New York, or something, spending the boodle that they've made!"

He shook his head again.

"No, sir," he said, "the fact is, everybody that I

173

touched was stony broke, just then, and there was nothing left for me but Bonanza. I didn't know as much about him then as I do now. And we come down and give the Christabel a look, and he says that he don't like the looks of her, but he'll buy her outright for exactly two hundred and fifty dollars."

"So you had to sell out for that?" says Blondy.

"Not for two hundred and fifty grandmothers," says Milton, "would I've sold her out for that. I wanted hard cash on the nail, though, and finally I sold a half share for five hundred to him, and I skinned out and done three hundred miles in five days, and got to my girl in time. She was pretty sick, but I pulled her through, all right."

He warmed up and got to smiling, and it was surprising to see how that face of his loosened up when he talked about his girl. It made a lot of difference to me, too, hearing him talk about her. I felt sorrier and sorrier for him, and more worried at the same time.

"Well," says Blondy, "when you come back, did you ask Bonanza for your half of the mine?"

"Of course, I did," said Milton, "and that crook, he tried to tell me that I had sold out the whole mine to him. As though I would've done such a thing! As though I was such a fool!"

"Did you make a written agreement?" said Blondy. "Did you get a lawyer to draw it up in writing for you and him?"

"Now, what would I've been needing a lawyer for a little thing like that?" said the prospector, frowning at Blondy. "I was in too much of a hurry to get to Mary, anyways, and so I just done what Bonanza suggested, which was to put down my signature on a piece of blank paper, and he filled in the rest of the sale."

"He filled it in for one half of the mine, did he?" said Blondy.

I swallowed a grin that was easy to swallow, because I began to pity that simple fellow, Joe Milton.

In answer to that question, Milton said: "Of course, that's what he filled in. Leastwise, I didn't see him, but that's what he was to write down. I didn't wait to see the thing written out. I was on my hoss and hoofin' it for the hills before he was through with his fool scribbling!"

Yes, sir, there it was out, just as plain as the nose on your face. Poor Milton had been cheated, and it was sickening to think of, when he'd found the mine, opened her up, and then been pulled off the working of her just because his girl was sick!

"Milton, it looks like this to me," said Blondy. "Bonanza cheated you out of half a mine. You get your half back from him if you can!"

Blondy said it cold and hard, but Milton didn't seem to take no offense at that sort of language. He just said: "That's all right, but he ain't got the Christabel no more, and you three have got it. So that's what I rode down here all the way to see you about."

He was simple, all right, but he was pretty much in earnest. What was a body to do with a fellow like that?

Blondy tried. "Look here," he said. "You actually think that we ought to give you half of the mine, do you?"

Milton blinked a couple of times. He didn't raise his voice none, but he looked at Blondy, long and hard and straight, and he says: "Well, sir, it's pretty clear that when I left Pottsville, I had half of the Christabel. I ain't sold or give it away in the meantime. So I've still got half of the Christabel when I come back."

"Don't you see," said Blondy, "that what Bonanza, the dirty crook, put over on you, was to fill out that paper for the sale of the whole mine? Then he sold it again. Mr. Dugan, here, bought it. And we worked for Dugan until he could land the thing, and he gave us each a sixth. That's the way the thing holds now. Your half of the Christabel has disappeared."

Milton, he laughed a little and said: "That's what a lawyer gent tried to tell me up there in Pottsville. I went to him before Bonanza Chris advised me to see what the law could do for me. The lawyer, he said that I didn't have a leg to stand on, so far as the Christabel went. Well, that ain't so. I know, and you know, too, unless you think I'm a liar, that a half of the Christabel, it belongs to me!"

"Then you go back to your lawyer and tell him to do his best for you," says Blondy. "It was Bonanza that cheated you. We didn't. You sue Bonanza, and get what the law will give you, and welcome!"

Milton, he got a good grip on the arms of his chair, pushed himself to his feet, took the pipe out of his mouth, and he says, firm and soft, and kinder noble, it seemed to me: "Gentlemen, the Miltons ain't never been the kind to go hounding around the law courts. We ain't never been the kind to take mortgages and collect 'em. We ain't the kind to fight with served papers and suchlike. The kind of law that can be bought never meant a damn thing to the Miltons. But there was never a one of us that wouldn't die for his rights."

"You're threatening, are you?" says Blondy.

Slope held up a hand. "He doesn't have to threaten," says he. "He shall have the half of the mine that belongs to him!"

CHAPTER 35

That side of it hadn't hit me before. I hadn't thought about Slope's big heart, his fool big heart. I looked across at Blondy to see what lead he would take, but he was flabbergasted.

When Slope had one of his generous streaks on, he simply thrived on opposition. If he wanted to give away his last dollar, and you stood out against him, he's give away his coat, too. So I put in quick.

"You bet he'll have everything that's coming to him, Slope. I want to see him get his right share."

"Good, Red!" said Slope. "I'm very glad to hear you say that."

I passed a big wink to Blondy, and he said:

"I'll tell you what, Milton. I'm for letting you have everything that's coming to you."

I saw a broader smile than ever come over Slope's face. I could see that owning another mine, bigger and better than the Christabel, would not have given him half the pleasure that he had out of feeling that we were willing to act up honest.

Milton looked might relieved, "Well," he said, "when I come in here, I knew what my rights were, and I knew that I had ought to get them. But, knowing what your right are, is a whole lot different from having them in your pocket. I didn't need any teacher to tell me that, you bet. But I see that I've bumped into three gentlemen that are willing to give a stranger a fair chance. And it makes me feel like a fool for having talked a while back about fighting you for my rights."

"Well, you'll get your rights," says Blondy. "We're all three dead set on that. Nacherally, we'll want to investigate and make sure about what them rights are."

"Investigate?" says Joe Milton, frowning a little.

"I've investigated enough to suit me," says Slope. "I know that Milton is an honest man. He wouldn't claim a penny that doesn't belong to him."

"Brother," says Milton, "I think you said a true word there. I don't want to boast, but I think I been rated a little higher for honesty than for smartness all my days."

He laughed a little modestly.

I kinder pricked up my ears, because ordinarily the right kind of a gent, he don't set out and admit the good things that are said about him.

Blondy was right useful just then. He says: "You're satisfied, Slope, and so are Red and me. But what we mean by investigating is to get everything done orderly. We want to make sure, for instance, that there ain't some other gent that'll come along, one of these days, and maybe lay claim onto the other half of the mine. And there would be three of us shot out in the dark, I reckon."

Slope shook his head and put on his puzzled frown. He

admitted that this was right, too. It was wonderful to see how slow and easy Blondy worked up his idea.

He didn't offend Slope an inch of the way.

He went on: "What I mean by investigating is just to go around and find out who knows about Mr. Milton, here, prospecting the Christabel and opening of her up. When we've found that out, which it won't take very long, then I aim to find out when and how he sold the Christabel to Bonanza Chris."

"That's all right," says Milton. He nodded and made a gesture like opening a door for us to walk right on into his house.

"I'd be glad to have you investigate everything about me," he said. "And I reckon that from Buffalo Creek right up to this here digging you find my record pretty straight. Except that there might be a greaser or two that would have something mean to say."

Then says Blondy, a bit hasty and feelingly: "Well, I always aim to leave the Injuns and greasers out of any man's record."

"I always aimed at the same thing when I added a gent up," says Milton, and he and Blondy give each other a real friendly grin.

Yes, we were getting pretty thick with one another, and the more friendly we got, the more I busted out into a sweat. Milton, he says: "Well, fellers, you look around and make your inquiries. It'll be a happy day for my girl Mary when she learns what sort of gents I've run into down here. She ain't gonna believe her ears. She says to me before I start out this evening: "Father, don't go. There'll be shooting, I know, the minute you make your claim!" She'll be all excited when she hears what a straight lot you all are! I'm going back to tell her. And you fellows you can start right in investigating!"

"Thanks," said Blondy.

"Investigating is a useless formality, so far as I'm concerned," says Slope, smiling at Milton like a fool.

"Yeah, but we're two to your one, old fellow," says Blondy.

He didn't point out, you can bet, that two thirds of the

178

mine was old Slope's, and that he could do as he pleased with the rest of us!

"Oh, of course," says Slope, turning to Blondy. "I know that the majority rules in our country!"

"The majority of crooks!" says I, but through my teeth, and to myself.

"I'm going back to the shack," says Milton now. "Over there, by the old Tompkins claim there's a shack that still ain't fallen to pieces. And that's where me and Mary are putting up. You can find your way dead easy to the claim. It ain't a mile off. And any time you're ready to talk more business, just come and give me a look, friends, will you? There ain't any hurry. I want you to make sure that every word I've said is gospel!"

That sounded fair enough.

Almost right from the first, of course, I'd been hoping that this here Milton was just a crook. But I've got to admit that this speech of his cut away a lot of ground from under my hopes. Milton went out, then stopped at the door and turned around to us. His good big jaw was set as he said through his teeth: "Well, fellers, if I'm declared in on this deal, I want to tell you that I hope to make as good a partner, as straight and as clean as you ever had in your life!"

Then he went out quick, before we had a chance to say anything back. A minute later we heard him singing, and through the window I seen him walking in the moonlight, along the trail, then into the trees and the darkness there.

It was all right to hear him sing, but, dog-gone, a minute later somebody begun to sing soft and low right there in the cabin, while I sat with my head between my hands, trying to think.

It was Slope that was singing, of course; just singing to himself, and sitting there with a quiet smile of content on his face, like a cat that's just licked up the cream. But it was Slope that had been licked up by the other cat! That was the little difference.

I felt hot and choking. Right then I pretty near hated Slope, and I felt that I would rather deal with a real out-

and-out crook any day in the year than an honest dummy like Slope, that wanted to give everything away.

I looked at Blondy, and he was purple and crimson from the nose to the ears.

So I guessed that he was about under as much pressure as me, and I said: "I'm gonna go out and get a breath of fresh air."

I'd hardly got outside when along come Blondy, and we step off together till we're out of earshot of the cabin. Then we stop. We don't pause to enjoy the moonshine none, nor the way it glinted and glistened on the pines, nor the blackness of the shadows that it throwed. No, sir! We lay to and begin to do some hard darning.

I had been around a good lot, and I could swear in Canuck and Mexican, I could swear like a mule skinner, a shack, a tramp, a lumberman, and a cow-puncher. But pretty soon, when I was going good, I begun to hear Blondy, and I seen right away that he had a real talent. After a while I just stopped and listened. Finally he eased up and began to pant, like a horse that's run a fast two miles through mean country.

"Well, Blondy, it looks bad," I said.

"No," says Blondy, "it don't look bad. It just looks nacheral, because if he didn't give the mine away today, he'd manage to give it tomorrow."

"Sure," said I. "But I guess that Milton is straight, all right."

"What difference does that make?" says Blondy. "Crooked or straight, Bonanza got the mine away from him. And we got the mine from Bonanza. A darn fat chance Slope would've had of getting it if it hadn't been for you mostly, and me a little bit. But now he's gonna give half of it away. After a while he'll give away another half."

I nodded. It didn't seem to make me feel any better to talk about it out there in the open than it had made me feel inside of the shack. Finally I said: "Well, we'll have a look around and try to punch a hole in Milton's yarn."

"I'd as soon punch a hole in Milton," says Blondy.

"Don't you try, Blondy," said I. "We ain't gonna have

no blood. Besides, that there Milton, he packed a gun around with him like he knew which end to handle it by."

"Speakin' personal," said Blondy, "all I gotta say is that he handled his gun so good that I wonder he's spent much time handling a pick! But that ain't the point. How're we gonna find out the facts?"

"Well," I said, "we can take Slope down and see old Bonanza. If he talks to us at all, I reckon that he ain't gonna admit that he cheated Milton. Not even Bonanza would admit that. He'll swear black is white, and make Slope sure that he honestly bought the whole mine from Milton. Once Slope is convinced, I guess you and me follow in line pretty easy."

"It's a good idea," says Blondy. "It's better. It's a grand idea. We'll take Slope to town tomorrow, and let old Bonanza Chris operate on him. He'll remove his conscience, painless and free."

He laughed: and so did I. We both had a glimmering of hope.

CHAPTER 36

We took Slope down to Pottsville the next day, all right. I was ashamed to take him down the main street, because me and Blondy, we was all dressed up, like I told you before, and I gotta admit that we looked pretty fine. Everybody had to turn around and look when they seen me on Kate and Blondy on his big hoss, just careless, letting the wind blow his coat open to show his fancy vest.

But there was old Slope, and he didn't have no style about him at all. He didn't even have on riding boots, slim, and tapering and high-heeled, like the rest of us had, but he was wearing just plain horsehide boots, like any rough prospector might've been. He was riding on a lump-headed mustang that was always trying to bump its chin on its knees. I dunno where he got it. It probably just belonged to the mine, and he'd picked it up because it was the nearest thing that went on four legs.

He had on a battered felt hat that had been pretty good a few days before, but now it had been trampled on. He didn't wear no coat at all, but just a blue flannel shirt that the sleeves wasn't long enough of it to fit him, so he just rolled them up to the elbows. He had on overalls that was kept up by the lacings behind his hips. There wasn't any style at all about Slope, and the way he got himself up you wouldn't think that he cared a bit about whether people looked at him or didn't look at him.

I was ashamed of him, and angry with him, too. Because there he was, more'n a millionaire, but looking like he might be a hired hand. It surely pulled me and Blondy down to be seen with him. It just lowered us!

When we got to the office of Bonanza, I thought maybe that he wouldn't see us at all, but I was wrong, because we were let right in, and he shooed a whole flock of people out to make room for us. When we came in, he went around and shook hands with all of us, real hearty.

I never seen such a man. You would say that he never had had a cross word with us, and that he really liked all of us a lot!

He was dressed up like usual, looking like money. His big, long-tailed coat was bigger and longer than usual, and his pants, they crinkled behind the knees and on the top of his shoes, sort of rich and careless, like a king might be dressed. He was pinker and plumper and more smiling than ever.

He said: "Now, fellows, this is a real pleasure. Business go hang when old friends come to see me. I never let business interfere with pleasure, you know. Even if we haven't spent many days together, I take it that we've known one another in a way that few other men have done. Am I wrong?"

He laughed at us all around and winked at us all

round, then flicked the ash off his cigar and just let it fall on the bright, rich face of his rug. What difference did a rug make to him? There was plenty more rugs, you'd say, where that little old rug came from.

No, I never seen such a man. The minute that I looked at him I begun to feel right poor. Yet I could guess that he didn't have fifty thousand dollars in the world. Grafters like him, they ain't never rich in anything but ideas, hardly.

He offered us cigars, and he offered us tailor-made cigarettes, which I took one, and slowly sickened because it was so sweet, and because Slope begun to mourn silently over my vices.

Says Blondy: "We've come in to talk to you about a good yarn that we've heard. We were just passing by, and so we thought that maybe you'd like to have a laugh over it, too!"

Bonanza Chris, he got his face all pink and beaming, ready to laugh.

"There's nothing that I love so much as a good one," said he. "Go right ahead, Blondy. And I'll have the best laugh, even if the joke is on me. I'm a democrat when it comes to a joke. The biggest laugh for the biggest number, that's my idea!"

"The idea is this," says Blondy. "A prospector gent by name of Joe Milton, he breezes in and says, can we bother to spare the time to hand over half of the Christabel to him, because he owned it and sold you a half of it. He says he signed his name to a paper, and you made the signature cover the whole mine, and that's how you got hold of it!"

Blondy laughed, and Bonanza laughed a little, too, but only on one side of his face. The other side was dead sober, which I didn't like.

"So Milton's around with his story, is he?" says Bonanza.

"Yeah, he's around, all right," said Blondy.

Slope leaned forward in his chair. "Mr. Christian," he said, "I thought that I should never see you again, for certain reasons, but now I've come to beg you to tell us

183

the truth. Is it correct that you only bought a half of the mine from Mr. Milton?"

Bonanza, he coughed, and then he frowned down at his cigar.

Finally he broke out into a harsh laugh.

"The paper's filed!" he said. "Anybody can see it. There's the signature of Milton at the bottom of the paper, there's the agreement above, in a different hand, to be sure, but it declares that Milton sold his entire claim to the Christabel, and there's his signature under the writing to prove that everything's correct! What more could anybody want?"

"Nothing!" says Blondy hastily.

A little too hastily, in fact, for now Slope gave him a reproachful glance, and I could fairly see Slope's conscience getting up on a high horse, all ready to go on the rampage.

He said: "But, just between us—not that anything could ever be done in the way of the law—"

"No, sir, not a darn thing!" said Bonanza, and slammed a fat fist into a fat palm so hard that he wabbled like loose jelly all over. "Not a thing could be done under the law to break that contract. If you're worrying about that, I'll take a load off your minds. I'll return you good for evil. At least," he went on, seeing that he had talked himself to the end of a rope, "I'll give you a proper break in this matter and tell you the truth: that all the law courts in the world could never pry you loose from the Christabel. If they could," and here he gave us a foxy smile and a wink, "I'd be the man to try the courts!"

He laughed again.

I say once more, there never was a crook like him. If he couldn't coin money out of you with his crookedness, at least he would coin laughter. He didn't seem to care which.

Slope was a bulldog when he got hold of an idea with his eyeteeth. Now he says slow and solemn: "But may we go back a little, Mr. Christian?"

"Go back as far as you like, Mr. Dugan," said Bonanza, a little grim, a little impatient, and giving his cigar an extra flick, though there wasn't any more ash on the end of the coal. "Go back as far as you like, and I'll try to answer you."

"Thank you," said Slope with a great big sigh, like a baby that finally gets the toy that it wants. "Then will you tell me in confidence that will never be broken by——"

"Oh, I know, Dugan," said the crook. "I know that you're honest." He said the last word with a little emphasis, as much as to say that was about all that Slope was.

But innuendoes, and suchlike, they never got through Slope's dull mind. And he says: "I'll only ask you if you actually paid for more than half of the mine?"

At that Bonanza exploded. I didn't blame him. He'd as much as admitted already that he had crooked Milton, and now he was getting a sort of a court confession dragged out of him. And he says: "Darn it, man, if I can make one dollar go as far as two, wouldn't I be a fool if I failed to do it? Besides, in those days I didn't have any idea that the Christabel was such a bonanza. If I'd had any idea, would I've sold it again, at a little advance cost, to your revered father, Mr. Dugan? No, sir, you're darn right I wouldn't."

Slope, he pushed himself up to his feet.

"Thank you very much, sir," says he.

"Oh, yeah?" mutters Bonanza.

"You're welcome—I suppose." He was still hot. I sympathized with him. For Slope had certainly rubbed his nose in the mud right then.

Blondy, he tried to find something else to think about, but Bonanza, he was so mad that he said, short and sharp, that he was a pretty busy man, but that he would be glad to give us more time if there was anything that we definitely wanted from him in a business way.

Well, that got us out of the office and down the stairs. Slope went first, his head high, singing under his breath. I hated him again, real hard. Me and Blondy walked behind.

"What's to be done, Blondy?" said I.

185

"Fight the thing in the law courts!" says he, mean and nasty.

"Then," said I, "old Slope will simply give away the whole half out of his own share."

"Darn Slope!" says he.

"It's too short a way to say it," says I, grinding my teeth. "I would like to take longer. We only got a last hope, and that's to find out if this here Milton really is the gent that found the Christabel."

"It's tolerable plain that he's the man, all right!" says Blondy.

Yes, it was tolerable plain, all right.

But still, it never does no harm to ask questions, so I went to the man in Pottsville that knew everything about everybody. I mean, I went to the oldest blacksmith there; what with sharpening drills and making horseshoes, he caught you both ways and knew everything about you. I leaned in the doorway and says: "Hello, Mike, how's the iron and hell-fire going?"

"Hello, you young splinter off the devil," says Mike. "And how's things with you?"

"Fair to warmer," says I. "Say, you know the name of the prospector that found the Christabel?"

"Sure, I know him," says Mike. "By name of Joe Milton, he was. Sure, I knew Joe."

My heart sank into my boots. I grabbed the last straw. "What sort of a looking gent?"

"About forty. Grayish. Why?"

I turned away and didn't make no answer. It was rude, but I was sick. I knew that nothing could stop Slope from giving away about a million dollars, now!

Maybe it was right and deep justice, but Jiminy, how I hated the idea!

CHAPTER 37

The misery kept on piling up. Slope, he went right over to a lawyer's office, and me and Blondy went after him. Blondy kept right on talking.

He said: "You wanta do what's right, but you oughta take more time, plenty of it. You know the old saying, Slope: 'Look before you leap.' And you're leaping right across a mountain ravine, so to speak!"

"I know," says Slope. "But I must get this done. I see my way."

He was happy, like a child is happy when it's done something good, like decorating the house with evergreens that shed all over the floor and down your back. And the kid stands around with a wide, fool smile, expecting praise. That was the kind of a smile that Slope had on, except that he didn't expect any praise. He never did.

So there we were, sittin' around in the lawyer's office, while he drew up something called a conveyance, which is the way you give a thing away with words that a lawyer doctors up. Mostly the words repeat themselves a lot, and the only thing that I seen clear and bright about that document was that it begun with a "Whereas," done big and flourishing, in the blackest sort of ink. It made my heart stop when I seen that for a beginning; and me and Blondy standing helpless.

Then Blondy, he had an idea, and he sat down and he had a couple more papers drawed up, just the same, and by those papers him and me, we each "conveyed" a half of our shares in the Christabel to Slope, because he'd given away to Mr. Joe Milton two thirds of his own part; that is, a whole half of the whole mine!

Now look at how complicated everything was getting, and the crowd of "Whereases" thick as mosquitoes all around us! It was enough to make a fellow sick, and sick I was. I divided twenty thousand by two. That left me ten thousand, according to the business gents, or maybe more, if the mine turned out richer still. Ten thousand was a heap. It was plenty. It wasn't the money, but the principle of the thing that bothered me a pile. I mean, when you give away something for nothing, it ain't right, and it ain't nacheral.

But rightness or nacheralness didn't bother Slope none. He seen his way clear, and he charged just like a bull. You never seen such a man when he got an idea of what was right. He would've jumped over a cliff and laughed if he'd got it into his dumb head that jumping over the cliff would be any good to anybody.

He was bothered by the idea that we were bearing our share of this here fool gift to Milton. He seemed to think that he ought to share all of the cost of it.

But Blondy said: "No, we're going to do the right thing, the kid and me. It ain't that we want to be dragged into it so fast. We want to take time and think things over. It don't seem right to us to get into such a giddy, dog-gone hurry, giving away about a million dollars. But if you're insisting on doing it, we're gonna bear our share."

Slope nodded. He seen that way of putting it.

And what d'you think that he said? Well, it was this: "I don't like to see your money going, but, after all, it's better to be right than wrong. There's a reward for righteousness somewhere, I'm sure."

I didn't know whether to laugh or cry or just darn, hearing him talk and carry on like that. And he had a kind of a solemn, fool look about him, the way that a woman has when she smiles at her red-faced baby that don't look like nothing at all.

The next thing that he wanted to do real bad was to get to Joe Milton and give him that half of the Christabel. He couldn't resist a bit! So, Blondy, with a look like sour milk, he takes and puts the three "conveyances" into one big envelope, and he shoves that envelope into Slope's pocket. Then the three of us rode back to the mine.

It was my job, when we reached the house, to go over and try to find Milton, and to tell him that good news and hard cash was waiting for him at our shack.

I liked that job. I liked it the way that a cat likes wet feet, but just the same I went, ridin' Catherine the Great.

It kind of took the poison out of things, to sit on the back of Kate, and feel the long, smooth roll of her gallop under me. I liked to watch her sassy head turning a little from side to side and see her ears flexing backward and forward. Jiminy, there was a horse. There is a horse, too, because I can look out and see her now, standing there on the hill in the pasture, with her ears up, and her little ragged mane and tail blowing in the wind like a mist. Not no picture horse, mind you, but a whole crowd of points.

So I felt pretty good as I pulled along toward Milton's layout. I met a gent on the way, and he was steering through the world, sighting his way between the ears of a burro that was loaded to staggering.

This gent, he told me just where to find the old mine. Pretty soon I came along under the pines, with the steps of the mare dead muffled on the thick bed of the needles that the trees had shed, and I come out onto a clearing where there was a crazy lean-to with a curl of smoke drifting lazy out of the top of the crooked chimney. There, in the clearing in front of the house I seen where Mr. Joe Milton was setting in front of a big, smooth-topped stump, and onto the face of that stump he was dealing cards, dead serious.

I pulled up the mare and watched. I never had played no cards to speak of, but I'd seen plenty of games, and never before had I seen a game like that—one man just playing all by himself.

The dealing was the whole part of it. He'd go and deal out five hands, and then he never looked at the hand right in front of him, but he always picked up one that was opposite. I sat there on Kate, and her still as a mouse, while he dealt as much as four or five hands, and always what he picked up and looked at made him shake his

189

head, until finally things seemed to go right. Then he grinned real broad and nodded. He seemed all pleased and warm and happy.

I admired to notice the way that he winked all to himself. I couldn't help thinking would a man practice at cards like that if he had much that was important on his mind, like half the Christabel?

Finally I sung out, and when I yipped, he swings around, and with the move he brings a big Colt out of nowheres; he slips sidelong to the ground and covers me dead certain!

It jumped my heart up into my mouth, believe me!

"Hey, Mr. Milton," I said. "I ain't a robber, and you ain't a train or even a stagecoach, I don't think!"

When he seen that it was me, he got up to his feet and leaned over and dusted himself off. He kinder laughs and says: "Well, sir, I been too long south of the Rio Grande, and got into the bad habit of thinking that everything that happens sudden and unexpected must be dead wrong!"

He straightens up and laughs again.

He had a fine, straight eye, as I was saying before, and now I couldn't help laughing a little along with him.

"You been so long south of the Rio," says I, "that one of these days you're gonna shoot yourself a batch of gents kind of offhand, without thinking."

He nodded, real sober. "I've gotta watch myself," says he.

Then says he: "How long have you been sitting on your horse over there?"

"Me?" says I. "Oh, about ten minutes or so, watching your game of solitaire."

"It's a good game," says he, looking me in the eye. "It's a game that takes learning."

"Yeah. I seen that," says I.

"I'll teach it to you one of these days when I got the time," says he.

"Thanks," says I. "I don't take up cards while my money lasts. When it's all gone, the kind of cards that I learned comes off the bottom of the pack."

He gave me a grin. "You ain't the first that's wanted to learn just the fancy games," says he. "But I'll tell you what, kid. Honesty is the best policy, and it pays you the best in the long run."

"Maybe it does," says I, "but it give you callous spots on the hands and a crook in the back and no sight in your eyes, I've noticed, here and there."

He gave a good laugh at that, and then I told him that Slope wanted to see him bad, and right away.

"What for?" says Milton, sharp, staring at me.

"For nothing but good news," says I.

I seen him sorter relax.

He goes and gets a hobbled mustang that's grazing near by, throws a saddle on it, and climbs into the saddle. Then we start back together.

He admires Kate some, but he tells me she looks too good to be true. His mustang has a lot of foot, he goes on, and he bets me a dollar he can beat me in a race to a blazed pine about a quarter of a mile away.

I looked over his mustang, and it had points, too. It had four legs under it, and four real legs will get a horse there, no matter what the rest of the machine is like.

Of course, I made the bet, and we started when he yelled. For three hundred yards I laid Kate's head on the mustang's hip, and watched Mr. Milton jockey it along. Then I let her out. I didn't even have to tell her what to do. She passed that mustang like nothing at all, and I had to give her head a pull and a jerk to stop her about a hundred yards past the pine with the blaze.

When Milton came up he paid the dollar. He had a thoughtful look.

"She's what she seems to be," says he, "which darn few are in these here days. What did you pay for her?"

"Eight hundred," said I.

"Take your saddle off and I'll give you two hundred for your bargain," says he. "I've seen places where a horse like that was worth more than money!"

I only laughed, and when he seen me laugh and pet her neck, he didn't make no more offers, but he kept looking at her sideways all the way to the house.

CHAPTER 38

It was pretty plain that Milton knew a horse when he seen one. And I says to him: "You been in some tight pinches, maybe, where a set of fast legs under you meant something?"

"Tight pinches?" says he. "I could tell you a few things!"

He laughed, sort of low and to himself, but without no humor in the noise, if you know what I mean by that.

Then he added: "Greasers, they'll give the run when they get the chance. A greaser runs you hard, too."

"I've heard tell," said I.

I looked at Mr. Joe Milton, and I decided, right then and there, that the greasers that give him the run must've been pretty much men, because he wasn't no hombre to chase after careless and free; not a gent like him—not by his looks nor by the way that he had of getting his gun into action.

I admired the look of him, but it made me thoughtful, too. I wondered how it was that a prospector like him was able to learn so much about horses and to spend so much time playing solitaire. Mostly the prospectors I had seen, which they was pretty plenty, had spent their spare time whittling a stick, or smoking a pipe in the sun, yarning in town, or just chipping stones with a hammer.

But Milton, it was plain, was a high cut for a prospector.

Howsomever that might be, he knew enough to like Kate, and so, except for that matter of the Christabel, I liked him, and was feeling pretty good about him by the time we got home. He was an observing man, too, and he admired the way that I rode. He said that I had the right idea, which was more balance than grip. Grip was all right if a gent was following the hounds and hadn't nothing but an English postage stamp to stick on by.

"Have you rode to hounds, Mr. Milton?" says I, hoping for some good stories.

"Rode to hounds!" says he with a laugh. Then his voice changed, and he looked at me. "How would I be riding to hounds in this part of the country?" says he. "No, but I've heard a lot about it from them that have!"

"That's a funny thing," says I, "because I never yet met a real Westerner that ever had rode to the hounds or ever knew anybody that had!"

"You know," says he, "down there in greaser land you meet all kinds, remittance men, and such!"

I nodded. It was true. You never can tell what you'll meet up with south of the Rio Grande. A tramp may be a prince and a prince may be a tramp.

We got home and throwed our reins. When we went inside, Slope come up and shook hands, friendly and long and lingering, with a smile in his eyes.

"I suppose Red has told you that I have arranged the conveyance to you of a half interest in the Christabel?" says he.

"A half interest?" says Milton.

I seen him blink, like a bullet had gone through him. He turned to me.

"No," he says slowly, "Red didn't say nothing about that!"

He gave me a long look.

"I wanted to give you a happy surprise," says I.

"Yeah, it's a happy surprise, all right," replied Milton. "You mean that you're gonna turn over half of the mine to me, Mr. Dugan?"

"That's what I mean to do," says Slope. "I've had the conveyance drawn up. When I say 'I,' I mean to include all three of us. We agree on the matter."

"Sure we do," said Blondy, choking as he leans over to fix his boot.

Slope takes the big envelope out of his side pocket.

He's smiling like a charm, the dummy! "I have it here for you, Mr. Milton!" he says.

Milton, he shook his head a little.

Then he said: "Well, Dugan, the other day you looked white to me, and you sounded white to me, but honest, I never thought that I'd ever be able to get what was coming to me without a gun fight!"

Now, it just so happened that he kinder touched Slope on the wrong spot with that wrong remark. Maybe you ain't noticed, so far, that Slope was the kind of a gent that could be led with a thread, persuaded or wrangled, joked or fooled, into anything that you had in your mind. But if you tried to make him do anything, that was a lot different. Yes, sir, even if you strung a steel cable around his neck and hitched a team of twelve mules to it, he would just plant his heels and either break his neck or the cable. He was that kind of a gent! Simple as a fool, and smooth as silk, if he was handled right; but he had a streak of bulldog in him about a mile wide.

Now he heaved up his head and said: "Mr. Milton, perhaps you imagine that you are frightening or forcing us into this act?"

Milton, he sort of swallowed and said:

"Frighten? Force? One man can't frighten three!"

He laughed a little. "I include Red as a man," said he, "because I understand that he's a good deal more dangerous than most men."

It was pretty good to hear a growed-up man, that had done his share of greaser hunting, talk like that. It puffed me up a mite, I guess. But the sharp look of Blondy, it kinder punctured me the next minute, and let all of the hot air out. He didn't seem to be near so happy.

"I'm glad that that's your attitude, Mr. Milton," says Slope. "I dare say that legally we could fight your claim. In fact, you would have a very small claim indeed, even according to Mr. Christian. But we want to do what is right. There is such a thing as a moral obligation. Therefore I'm handing this paper to you, which makes you at once a half owner of the Christabel. As for the money we already have received, we'll pay you your share.

Perhaps, however, you may care to question your half of some of the expenditures which we have made in behalf of the mine?"

"Me?" says Milton. "Why, Mr. Dugan, I told you the other day, and now I tell you again, once I'm a partner in a business I'm a real partner, and the easiest man to please in the world. It ain't smart cracks or sharp practice that I'm up on, but it's fighting for what is mine that I'm mostly experienced in. Now, I gotta say that for the first time in the world I'm getting a square deal without a fight. It's a big deal, too. The biggest that I ever was hitched up to. And I'm gonna show you that your confidence in me, it ain't throwed away, Mr. Dugan, and that goes for the rest of you, too. A pinch might come, and I reckon to be worth my salt in a pinch!"

It was a good speech, it was a quiet-spoken speech, and there was a meaning to it that got down inside of your blood and curdled it a little and started the goose flesh to creeping all over you. It made you think of a man dying for the sake of his friends and all that sort of thing.

It got the tears into my eyes, and stinging tears they were. I told myself that there was no other place in the world where the men come of the same big caliber that they done in the West. I was glad that it was my country, I can just tell you that!

Then, with a shock, I seen that Blondy was kinder keeping his head down, but from any angle I could see that he was sneering!

Yes, it was a shock. I was surprised and ashamed of Blondy for not being able to see when a man was a man and talked real man talk!

Now, Slope, he fished out papers from the envelope, saying: "Here you are, Mr. Milton, and I hope that the greatest happiness comes to you from—"

There he stuck. He looked at the papers with his eyes popping.

"Why, Blondy! Why, Red!" says he. "It isn't here!"

"Hello!" says Blondy.

Things wavered and shook before me. I did some of the fastest guessing in the world.

"Not there?" says Blondy, rising up, stern and frowning. "But it has to be there! It was put there."

Then Milton says, under his eyebrows, so to speak: "Is this a sell, gents?"

Slope breaks into a shining perspiration. "Mr. Milton," says he, "I don't know what to say. I'm humiliated. We had three conveyances drawn up. I conveyed half the mine to you. It was simpler that way. And my friends then kindly conveyed half of each of their shares to me. It made each of them a one-twelfth owner. It made me something more. You can see their conveyances! But the other paper seems to have disappeared. I'm terribly afraid that you may think that I've brought you here under false pretenses!"

Milton, he hesitated for a minute, his head down and a real mean look on his face.

Finally his head went up, little by little, and he says: "Dugan, if you're not an honest man, there ain't any honesty in the world. I know that! What probably happened is that the paper was never put in that envelope at all. It must have been left behind!"

"At the lawyer's!" said Slope with a gasp.

He mopped his forehead.

"Of course, that's what happened," he went on. "Or else could it have been jogged out of the envelope on the way down?"

"That ain't likely," said Blondy. "Because the other two are still there!"

"Yes, they are," said Slope. "Mr. Milton, I'm terribly sorry. I'll send straight back for the paper. Red, you won't mind taking Kate and riding to Pottsville to the lawyer's?"

I said that I wouldn't mind. Blondy, he said he was terrible upset, and he went outside with me, leaving Milton behind with old Slope.

"Ride hard, kid," says Blondy to me when I get into the saddle.

I looked down at him. I kinder loved him.

I said: "I never seen a fox with such long legs, Blondy!"

"Whatcha mean by that?" says he.

"Nothing," says I.

"I didn't think you did," says he. And he gives me a great big wink.

Honesty is all right, but it's gotta be kept in its right place. And I tell you what, having a man like Blondy around, it keeps honesty where it oughta be!

CHAPTER 39

I went on into Pottsville, all right, and called on the lawyer, but I wasn't surprised none when he told me that conveyance was not there.

He was a funny, bald-headed man, and the forehead wrinkles went on up all the way to the top of his head. When he asked a question, the question mark run clean to the back of his neck.

He said: "Those conveyances caused you a good deal of pain, I take it, Red?"

"Yeah," I answered. "I'm one of these here funny guys. It makes a difference to me whether I got a coupla hundred thousand dollars inside of my pocket or outside of it!"

He gave me a big grin, and the wrinkles, they played over the red top of his head like lights on water at night.

He took out a pen, like some of these indoors people do that can't think without pretending that they're writing what they say, and he says: "A very good way of keeping money in the pocket is to keep one ear close to the ground."

I looked hard at him, but he turned away, which was a sure sign that he had said all that he had on his mind just then. So I didn't ask any more questions, and went out in the street. I sauntered along until something stopped me. It was the look of that alley where I'd been trapped that other day.

I walked over, and I stepped down to the first turn, feeling like I had gone down a shark's mouth. When I made the first turn, I stopped hard and short, for there I seen, whacha think? Mr. Bonanza Chris and Mr. Joe Milton, talking hard and fast! And Bonanza, he was cussing, and Milton, he was shrugging his shoulders.

I was about to fade to the side and get under cover, so's I could see more, but just then Bonanza seen me over Milton's shoulder. And I didn't think he looked pleased. He looked like he wanted to swallow me, as a matter of fact.

A second later he made a pass at Milton's head with the flat of his hand, and Milton knocked that hand aside out of the air, and Bonanza, he stepped back through a doorway and slammed a door. Milton, he knocked at the door and shouted a few things.

I could hear him when he shouted, and what he said was good. It was just about what I thought of Bonanza, in fact.

Then he turned around and came down the alley, his face still hot and working, and he sorter stumbled into me and says: "Hello, Red! This you?"

"Nobody else," says I. "Have a nice little party with Bonanza?"

"A nice party!" says he. "I get a mysterious call to come to town, and it's this fat crook that wants to talk to me, and what he wants is to hold me up for my share of the mine. He wants a cut. He says that I'd never've got it if it hadn't been that he winked when Dugan asked him if he really had bought the whole mine! So he wants a cut."

I said: "Well, that's straight. It was his saying that that made Dugan believe everything you said!"

He looked at me aside. It wasn't much of a look. It was no more than a black-snake cut that takes the hide off of a mule, say!

"Are you riding back down the valley?" says I.

"Not for a spell," says he.

"It's a funny thing about that conveyance," I told him. "It wasn't at the lawyer's. It must of jogged out of Slope's pocket. Maybe it wasn't in the envelope at all. Maybe it was just put in his pocket loose!"

"Oh, that's all right," says he. "Dugan will make it right. I'd trust that man around the world."

I left him and went back on the mare, but even the wonderful way that Catherine the Great had with her on the road wasn't enough to keep me from thinking.

I was putting a lot of little details together and shaking my head over them. When I got back, I says to Blondy, when I got him alone, after telling Slope the bad news and after Slope had decided to go down and make a new conveyance in the morning: "Listen, Blondy," says I, "how d'you make out Joe Milton?"

"He's a hard-boiled sourdough," says he. "But he's all right. If he wasn't all right, he never would've got such a fool idea that he could still collect a share in that Christabel. He'd see that he was already ruled out and had lost out."

I said: "You think he's honest? Well, I just seen him talking with Chris in an alley in town, and he says that Bonanza was trying to hold him up for a share in his split of the mine. He talked pretty mad. But I dunno. I've seen him dealing himself five sets of poker hands, as they looked to me, and nothing but the tree squirrels to look over his shoulder and see what he was getting. And I've heard him talking a lot about south of the Rio Grande. The good little prospectors that I've heard about, they don't play in Mexico's back yard so much of the time, it seems like to me."

Blondy got hold of his long nose and wabbled it slow from side to side, which was a way that he had when he was thinking hard. And then he says: "I dunno. I call him square, but I dunno. I may be wrong. He comes from Buffalo Creek. Where's Buffalo Creek?"

"That's what I'm gonna find out," said I.

"Where?"

"I'll find out," I answered.

I went over to the Ledbetter mines, where there was about five hundred bohunks working. Every time anybody got busted in Pottsville and he didn't have no handy bank to rob, he'd go down and get work at the Ledbetter, because the place was so big that they was always taking on new hands that way.

It was a mean-looking layout, with dumps everywhere, and hand-truck lines. The air was filled with the high, whining drone of labor and cursing. Your nerves all pulled up tight when you got near the Ledbetter mines and heard the muffled clanging of the drills deep down in the shafts. Whole tons of gold were coming out of those holes in the ground. I reckoned that somebody from every section of the world was there; if only I could find the right one.

I tried five groups of bohunks, one after another, and none of them had ever heard of a place called Buffalo Creek. Then I sat down, tired of asking questions, and glad to watch a donkey engine working at the mouth of a shaft. It snorted and shuffled, and groaned, too, but it lifted a lot of weight along the way.

It was amazing to see the way that the piston jumped back and forth, then slowed up when the load seemed to get heavier and struggled, like a human arm putting out more power to make a lift. I said so to the old fellow that was in charge of it.

He had a big smear of axle grease over one eye and running down into the bristles of his eyebrows. His face was hot from the heat of the fire, and every now and then he gives his forehead a swipe, and with every swipe his face gets blacker.

"You're right, kid," says he. "A donkey engine is about the most complicated thing that there is, next to a woman! But you ain't old enough to know about females."

I said: "I got a worse job than running a donkey engine."

"Maybe I'll believe that when I hear about it," says he.

"I'm trying to find out about a place called Buffalo Creek," says I. "And I can't do it!"

"Because you ain't asked in the right place. That's all,"

says he. "But when a donkey engine or a woman bust down, there ain't any right place to go and ask about 'em!"

He grinned and seemed happy about his joke.

I simply said: "Well, where should I go to ask about Buffalo Creek?"

"Ask at a post office," says he.

I give my left shin a good hard kick with my right heel because I hadn't thought of that sooner.

"You're right," says I. "I should've gone to the post office in town."

"But you won't get much information in the post office, even," says he.

"Won't I?" says I.

"No," says he.

"Why not?"

"Because there ain't much information to be had."

"Look here," said I. "Maybe you've heard about Buffalo Creek your own self?"

"Yes, I have," says he.

"Why didn't you say so?" I asked him.

"Because you didn't ask me if I knew anything about it."

I laughed, and he laughed, too.

And he says: "I lived about three years close to Buffalo Creek. I know everybody in it except the half-breed across the water."

There I had my information on tap, just about when I was gonna give up asking in the Ledbetter mines. It often happens that way. Luck turns when you don't expect anything but another kick in the face.

I said: "What about a man named Joe Milton?"

"I know Joe," said he.

"Do you?"

"Yeah. Pretty well."

"Prospector, ain't he?"

"Yeah," says he, "a prospector, and a sheep-herder, and a puncher, and a lot of other things. Why?"

"Been down to Mexico a lot?"

"He tells a lot of Mexican yarns," says the old gent.

This all stacked up pretty accurate with what I knew for my own self about Milton.

201

At last I said: "What sort of a looking man is he?"

"Whacha wanta know all this about?" says the old fellow. "Think that Joe Milton stole a pair of your shoes? Why, Joe is middle-aged. Forty something or other. Kind of gray."

It tallied perfect.

"Nothing funny about him," says I hopelessly.

"Not a dog-gone thing," says he, "excepting the scar over his left eye."

I looked hard at him.

"Big scar?" said I.

"The kind that a horseshoe makes," says he, "when you been kicked by it and the horse has gone and forgot to take his foot out of the shoe!"

He laughed good and hard at that stale joke, which I got up and didn't even thank him for his information. I was just in a dizzy trance, because I knew every inch of my Joe Milton's face; and there was no sign of a scar anywhere about it!

CHAPTER 40

Kate, she was off to a considerable distance, because I hadn't wanted to bring her too close to the donkey engine. When I climbed into the saddle again, I looked back, grateful, toward the donkey-engine driver, and there I seen, standing and talking to him, my Joe Milton!

It give me the coldest chill that I ever had in my life.

It made everything perfect. It finished out the picture.

This fellow in Potts Valley, he was just a plain crook that was wearing the name of the prospector that had really found the Christabel.

And I could understand why he had been talking with Bonanza Chris up that alley that day.

It was because Bonanza was in on the deal. Yes, that was why Bonanza had been willing to admit that he had crooked Joe Milton.

It got clearer and clearer. The light, it fair rushed into my brain, on the way back toward the shack. I seen everything. Bonanza's plan had been beautiful, so perfect and so simple. It was all built up on the dumb-fool honesty of Slope. You couldn't force money out of Slope's hand with a gun. But you could win it out of his heart easy.

So Bonanza, he finds him a crook that looks something like the real prospector, whose name would be known. And he makes the play, and everything goes perfect; and by thunder, a half of the Christabel would've been on the loose right that moment for Bonanza and the fake Joe Milton to split up between them, except that Blondy had used his fine long fingers to steal the conveyance out of the envelope!

Think what a slick scheme it was, and what a simple one! It looked too easy, too foolish. But it was planned and made for a mighty foolish man!

Well, I rode along home slow, with my head hanging so far to one side that I got a crook in my neck; and I kinder woke up mighty late and found that I'd let Kate get off the track, because I was thinking how easy it was for a crook to make money if he had any brains. Yes, and he let other folks take all the chances and the risks, while he sat pretty and collected big profits. Only a fool would pitch in and work with his hands, it seemed like.

So finally I got that mare across the woods and into the right trail. My head was still full of crooks and their ways, and I was mighty thankful that I had unraveled this one, when I come in sight of the house.

That wasn't all that I came in sight of, because just then up comes the fake Joe Milton and a girl alongside of him. He hadn't wasted any time. When he found out, as he must've done, what I had been talking about to the donkey-engine man, he went right quick to make his last play. There he was ahead of me at the house. I

203

gritted my teeth together and damned myself for dreaming away the time on the way home.

Then I galloped up, and I come on this kind of a picture. It's Blondy and Slope standing in front of the house, and Joe Milton standing there with the girl in his arms, saying, grand and deep in his throat: "Gentlemen, I'm called away by a great duty, and I'm leaving behind me my little girl. She'll be waiting in the shack over there, my friend. And if there's anything coming to me from the mine, which I leave entirely in your hands, Mr. Dugan—"

"You can leave it in mine, too," I hear Blondy say through his teeth. "I'll see that you get your share, Milton!"

It nearly bumped me out of the saddle to hear old Blondy talk up like that—Blondy, that had a brain in him like a knife edge when it come to seeing through things!

"Thank you," said Milton. "That means a lot to me to hear you say that. A mighty lot. Goodby, Mary! Goodby, my child! I won't be gone long!"

He kisses her and pushed himself away from her, and she holds out her hands after him.

By Jiminy, I seen her fair and square for the first time, then, and it was a wonder to me that any man could let her hold out her hands after him that way. Take her by and large, she had every other girl in the world stopped. I mean, there was more eyes to her, and more sweet smiling, more gentleness, and more rose and gold. I didn't need more'n half of a look at her to pick her for mine, I tell you! I mean, the kind that I would like to grow up and get. I knew that there'd never be another like her. There couldn't be! She was the one and only, that Mary Milton!

And I heard her cry out "Daddy!" in a tone that just jerked the tears right out of my heart and stung my eyes with them.

And him? Why, he swung around in the saddle and he held out one arm toward her, and he sings out: "God bless you, Mary, darlin'. Don't worry. Everything's gonna be all right!"

Then he turns and gallops fearless, with raised head, into the blazing glory of the West, if you know what I mean. I mean to say, it was just like the wind-up of one of them books that has a sad ending, sad and noble, and the devil take the hero.

Well, off goes Milton, and it was into the sunset that he rode, all right, and into the dark of the trees. And the girl, she gives a little, wild, sad, terrible cry, and she runs to her horse and grabs the reins and starts to mount it.

It was a funny thing how both Slope and Blondy got there in front of her, and at the same time I heard them telling her that she'd been left in their care, and she would be all right. And what was the trouble that took her old man away?

In the middle of these questions, when she tried to answer, the words just wouldn't come, but a terrible burst of sobbing comes over her, and she shook and wabbled.

They had to assist her into the house, and right smart they done that assisting—Blondy on the one side, and Slope on the other. They was plumb tender with her. And she went on crying, right into the house.

It was a mite sad, and still it was a mighty musical thing to listen to her crying like that, and I stopped in the doorway and dried my eyes up before I went inside.

But I didn't need to be so mighty particular about my eyes, because Slope was already seeing kinder dim.

But what about Blondy? What about that hard-boiled egg?

Well, I'll tell you! Blondy had a cold in the nose; at least, he was sniffing enough!

They had got her fixed up in the best chair, they had put a blanket behind her head, and they had poured out a cup of coffee, which Slope was holding the coffee and telling her to have a drink, and Blondy was holding her hand and telling her not to worry.

Yes, they were terrible cut up about her, I tell you! I was cut up, too. It didn't seem right or nacheral that anything so beautiful and good as her should suffer like this.

Says Blondy: "What's happened? What's called him away?"

"Oh, my poor brother Dan!" says she. "Oh, Danny, Danny, how could you!"

She gets into an ecstasy of grief over this, looks at the ceiling, wrings her hands, and the tears, they turn right on down her face. It was a terrible, and still a beautiful, thing to see. It made my heart ache and my lips tremble.

"What's he done?" says Slope.

"Oh, Danny, Danny!" says she. "He's broken into the jail at Buffalo Creek, and he's set a friend of his free. Oh, Danny, how could you do it! And now daddy will certainly be caught trying to set him free, and they'll both be killed—and then—"

Tears stopped her again. By thunder, I thought that Slope would begin to cry, too. And the coffee cup shattered on the saucer that he was holding.

But my own tears had dried up all at once.

And why? Because with the name of that town, all at once I remembered and realized that her "daddy" was no more Joe Milton than anything; that she must've knowed it, and, therefore, that she was just a plain crook, no matter how pretty her face was!

It was a hard sock for me to take. It started the room spinning all around me. But I knew that it was the truth. She was simply another one of the wires that Bonanza Chris knew how to pull.

What a man he was!

CHAPTER 41

Blondy said that he would go after Joe Milton and stop him. But she got almost screaming excited about that, and she said: "No, no! For Heaven's sake, don't try to do that. He'd kill anyone who tried to keep him away from his boy! He lives for Danny!"

"Then," says Blondy, "I'll go and help him get Dan out!"

"No, no!" cried "Mary Milton," busting into her weeping again, rocking back and forth. 'Oh, don't you see? Don't you see?"

"See what?" says Slope.

"There, there, there now!" says Blondy, his voice melting all over the place. "Don't you be worried. Don't you be excited. Just you sit calmly and quietly here and you tell us, and Blondy's gonna help you right out of trouble. Yeah, and your father, too, and your brother, Dan. I'll manage all things for you."

"And so will I," says Slope. "I'll do everything I can for you! Can you try to believe that? Only tell me what to do!"

She stopped crying.

And a funny thing was that all of the tears hadn't swelled up her eyes. Her face was wet, but under the wet it was as cool and sweet as you please.

When she stopped crying, she suddenly held out her hands, one to each of them; and she looked at both of them at the same time, and kept on looking in a way that made me sort of dizzy to watch; and she talked to them both at the same time, making herself special for each of them at once.

I never seen such a wonderful girl!

She was saying: "Oh, don't tell me that I've found two friends such as you seem to be. But are you what you truly seem? Can you be real?"

Her eyes went out on 'em and fondled 'em, looking at 'em like a calf at its ma. I seen them two grown-up men eat it right up and get happy, soft in the face, and foolish-looking.

I've gotta admit that there is a lot of weak cogs in the machine of a growed-up man! About a smile and a half is all that girl needs to wreck the machine.

"You can trust me," said Slope. "And I know that you can trust Blondy, too."

"You can trust me to the finish," says Blondy, with a terrible scowl for the rest of the world and a terrible smile for her.

"Oh, Mr. Dugan," says she. "Oh, Blondy!"

"Oh—" says I to myself.

I didn't finish off the rest of that sentence. I didn't dare to, partly because I couldn't write it down here and partly because I was pretty sure that if they'd heard me, either Blondy would have killed me or else Slope would've been saddened about me the rest of his life.

But I was beginning to get pretty sick of that sloppy scene.

I stood over by the stove and leaned my shoulders against the wall. I looked and looked. The more I looked, the more I couldn't believe my eyes—those two big, hard-boiled men turned into limp sweetness.

"Yes," I hear the girl saying soft and slow, "I know that you are both my friends."

"We are," says the chorus.

"And oh," says she, turning up her eyes to the ceiling, "if only you could know how rich it makes me feel, and how strong! Two friends and at such a time, and in such a terrible need."

"Oh, bunk!" says I to myself, and I turns around and makes a noise, jamming the poker into the fire box of the stove.

Blondy, he bawls out: "Red, where was you raised? Whacha mean making all of that clatter?"

And Slope he says: "Red, I think it's really a little inconsiderate of you!"

Slope, too! I expected that Blondy would sink his claws into me, but not Slope. I never expected that he'd turn.

But I tell you what; a woman would turn any man, the best man. And sour is what she'd turn him!

"That coffee is getting cold," says I. "I'll throw it out and fill up the cup."

I took the cup out of Slope's shaking hand. He didn't notice nothing. He was like a sleepwalker. I stepped on Blondy's toe. But his foot was marble, and he didn't feel nothing. I give him a hard right jab in the ribs and made him lean his ear over toward me. I poured out a fresh cup of coffee, and I says to Blondy:

"Cheese it! I've got the whole yarn. Milton's a crook. He ain't Milton at all. And the kid, here, knows it!"

And what did he do? He just leaned his head back toward her and gives her another sweet look.

He hadn't understood a word I said. He was just unconscious. My Jiminy, how I wanted to make him unconscious in earnest just then. I would've used a mallet to turn the trick!

Old Slope, he was saying: "You see, Miss Milton, if you'll tell us how we can help—"

"Oh, Mr. Dugan," says she, "I can't tell. I only know that I'm the only thing in the world that can stop my father once he has begun. No one else could turn him. Anyone else would only infuriate him. Oh, his passions are terrible once he commences! Some of his frightful temper was inherited by poor Danny. Oh, poor, dear Danny!"

She sobs a coupla times.

"Then, if that's the way of it," says Slope, "we'll take you to him! We'll start now, if you know the way!"

"Of course I know the way," says she. "But I can't go. I've given daddy my promise. I can't dare go. I have to stay here, and I'm going to go mad, I'm going to go mad. Oh, Heaven," says she, holding up her hands, "teach me what to do! Oh, teach me what to do."

"Take your hands down and rest your arms," says I.

But nobody heard me, which maybe was lucky for me! Then something reached out and found me.

It wasn't the hard hand of Blondy, which I had been half expecting, but it was the glance of the pretty girl, and it was as cold and bright as the eye of a bird. She saw me and noted at once that I was a pretty black splotch in the picture.

But there was Slope, saying: "What is it that keeps you here, Miss Milton? What prevents you from going?"

"It's that wretched mine," said the girl. "Oh, I wish that I had never heard its dreadful name! Because I told daddy that I'd stay here and receive the conveyance for his share of it. While I wait here, he's riding on and on. He's riding to his death! Oh, and Danny, too! They'll die together—while I wait here."

It was getting dark. I went over and lighted a lamp, because it seemed to me that the atmosphere might be a lot less thick if we was to have some light on the whole subject.

"It's the conveyance," Blondy says, as though he was translating the thing to Slope. "She needs the conveyance. Quick, man!"

Yes, that was Blondy speaking. And that was me over by the door, sort of hanging onto things and trying to believe my ears, that Blondy had gone so crazy!

Yes, and there was Slope, hurrying over to the table, taking up a sheet of paper, sitting down in the lamplight, with its glow over his lion's head, his honest brow puckered, his big hand working away carefully with the pen.

The first word he wrote was a big, sprawling "Whereas," that went halfway across the page. It sickened me, all right.

The girl was saying that she had to go at once, she couldn't stay, and it was only her promise to her daddy that made her pause a single instant.

I got hold of Blondy and pinched him. He turned around on me. And I said: "Blondy, will you step outside with me one minute? There's something wrong with Kate. I want you to see her. She's dead lame. I'm terrible worried!"

He shrugged his shoulders.

"Kate?" says he. "Well, a horse is only a horse."

"Ah, don't say that, Blondy," says Slope, looking up from the paper. "I'll come out and see her in just a moment, Red."

"Go on! Go on and write it out!" shouts Blondy.

And he went outside with me.

The sunset was dying fast. There was still drifts of gold dust filling up the channels among the trees, though, and the broadest yellow moon that you ever seen was lifting in the east and balancing itself on the tip end of a pine tree.

"Where's that darn mare?" says Blondy.

"She ain't a darn mare," says I, pretty hot.

"Well, well, what's the trouble with her? Where is she?" says he.

"The trouble's in your own thick head," says I.

He gives me a mean look. "Come out to the point," says he.

"The point is," said I, "that you're too thick. I've been around and made inquiries. The real Joe Milton has got a scar from a horse kick over one eye. And the fellow that's been pulling your leg is a plain crook, and he's working with Bonanza, like I guessed that he was!"

"Eh?" says Blondy, looking like a man that's feeling his way through a pretty dark spot.

I went on fast and hard: "If he ain't Joe Milton, then that girl's name ain't Mary Milton, neither, and she's as bad a crook as the rest of 'em, and just one of Bonanza's tools. She's getting the conveyance out of Slope, after all, and you, like a fool, are making everything easy for her!"

He raised up his fist. It looked as big as a whole bundle of clubs, but I was so mad that somehow I almost hoped that he'd brain me with it.

But he didn't. He lowered it slow and careful, like he had to be sure where it dropped.

Then he said: "Red, you're a bright kid. You're real smart, and you got your good points. But this thing that you've just said, it shows what you are. You're low. You ain't got the right kind of a soul in you, or you couldn't lay up language like that agin' the kind of a woman that's sitting in there, that any born creature would take its hat off to."

I had a kind of a quick flash of horses and dogs and other creatures taking off their hats and kotowing to "Mary Milton."

He went on: "I dunno that I ever wanta see you ag'in. Red, keep out of my way. I'm kind of deep down disgusted with you. It ain't easy for me to keep my hands offn you."

"You puddin' head," says I. "If I was half an inch taller and two pounds heavier, I'd lay in and knock the spots off of you. That's all that I gotta say!"

He just looked at me, and then he turned around and walked back into the house.

Yes, he was hypnotized, and the worst case that I ever seen of the thing. I've seen kids on the stage so blind hypnotized that they thought they was on the edge of a swimming pool, and was all ready to jump into the water, and started to peeling off their clothes. But old Blondy, he was worse than that!

I stood there, sick and beat. Then out they come, Blondy and Slope. Slope was waving the paper to dry the ink, saying in a fool, happy way, that now they were on the right road, and that everything would soon be all right. "Oh, Mr. Dugan," says the girl, "it's nothing to me. The wretched mine! If it wasn't for that, I'd be this moment at daddy's side, but he said that he would never rest content until there was some provision made—"

But she took the paper, all right, and give it a look, and I heard Slope saying: "I know. He's a man with a heart, and he thinks of his children, as a man should. If there were more men in the world of his sort, Miss Milton —wait one minute! I'll soon be back with the horses. Come on, Blondy. We have to ride fast, and we have to ride far!"

And off they went. The girl, when they were out of sight, looks to me, and she says: "Aren't you the little fellow my dear daddy has spoken to me about? Aren't you Red?"

"Has that alias told you about me?" says I.

"Alias?" says she real sweet.

"Yeah, alias a lot of other names," said I. "You got that pair buffaloed, but you ain't got me, beautiful. And I'm gonna spoil the deal for you and Bonanza and your fake father. Don't forget it. I ain't through. You tell 'Mr. Milton' that when he makes up for a part, he oughtn't to leave out the scars. There's ways of building mighty fine fake scars, and he oughta know how to do it before he gets onto the stage."

At that she lets out a little laugh: "Red," she says,

"you're a whip, that's what you are. If either of them had the brains of a doughnut—but neither of them has. And if you try to tell them the truth, just see how far you'll get!"

"I know," says I real mournful, "you got them dancing, all right, but the game ain't finished till the last card falls!"

"That sounds like a book," says she. "This fellow Dugan, have you known him long, the poor, simple fellow?"

"Don't pity him," says I. "Even for a thing like you to look at Slope is too good for you. He's got the biggest heart and the strongest hand that ever I seen. But he's too good to be smart. That's all. Coyotes and mean foxes like you and your tribe, they can eat the soul out of him. By Jiminy, when I think of what a thing you are!"

I held up my hosses after that.

There was no use talking, and yet it surprised me to see her looking at me and not saying a word. Then out came Blondy and Slope, and they was on their best hosses, and they had another for her, and mounted her.

"Why, Red," said Slope. "Ain't you and Kate going? Is she too lame?"

"I'm gonna meet you later," said I. "I'm going by a short cut to the same place!"

They didn't argue. They just all three rode off.

CHAPTER 42

Well, it made me feel lonely and small and weak to see the three of them go off like that. But I meant what I said, that I would find a short cut and get to the same place quick.

I didn't hurry none. I just went and leaned my head

against the mane of Kate, and she turns her head around and nibbles at my sleeve.

It ought to've made me feel a lot better, but it didn't. It only made my heart ache a lot more. There's times like that when kindness is a lot worse than meanness, when you're feeling real down.

What had hurt me the most was the way that Slope went off without arguing with me to come along, without trying to persuade me, or without asking me what I meant by a "short cut," because then I could have started talking. But no! That girl had everything her own way, and I could be as sick as I pleased, but it didn't do me no good at all.

After a while I got on Kate and I turned her straight toward the place where "Joe Milton" had been hanging out. I'd seen him ride off very grand in the opposite direction to save his "Danny," but just the same, I expected to find him there in the shack by the worked-out-mine, and I expected to find fat Bonanza Chris with him.

A little distance off I got my first gleam of hope, and it was a real gleam—the beam of a lamp or a lantern, and I come closer and cached Kate away among the trees, and went sneaking on. Pretty soon I rounded up at the edge of the window, not the door. Because somehow folks expect to be looked at through a doorway, but they don't never think that a window is anything more than a part of the wall.

Well, I got there to the window, and through that window, which didn't have no glass in it, and never had, I seen and heard everything pretty good. There was aplenty to see and hear, believe me, because in there was sitting just the pair that I expected. Bonanza Chris was smoking at a cigar, and "Joe Milton" was sitting near him.

Bonanza was saying: "Slip, I think that you've planned a good job, and that you've tried to do a good job, but I can't say that I think so much of the way that you've let a snip of a red-headed brat look in on you!"

"Joe Milton," alias "Slip," he says: "What was I to do? Wring the brat's neck, or drop him down a shaft? I'd've done either of them things, too, but he kept looking.

He's got eyes in the back of his head. When I found out that he's been talking about Buffalo Creek with a fellow that knew the place, I guessed that hell was about to pop, and I made up my mind that there would have to be a strong play and a quick play. That's why I went on the run to gather in Mary."

It kind of surprised me that her name was really Mary.

"Well, Mary is all right. If she wasn't all right, I wouldn't've let you have her for this job," says Bonanza. "What kind of a daughter did she make?"

Here Slip scowled.

"She didn't have much use for me," he said. "She's a high-toned and—"

He stopped himself.

"She talked down to you a little, did she?" says the fat man.

"Yeah, she talked down to me, all right," says Slip. "I wasn't good enough for her to wipe her shoes on."

"I told you she wasn't common stuff," said Bonanza. "She's a high-class crook, is what she is. She's a lady; if only luck had given her enough money to live on after her taste. But not getting the cash by her luck, she got it by her brains. She's turned some big deals."

"I hope she chokes on 'em," says Slip bitterly. "She's a pretty devil. I take hold of her hand the first day and tried to be friendly. 'Don't be so easily amused,' says she to me. Like that! Why, I tell you I wanted to—"

He stopped himself again.

"You need a sense of humor, Slip," said Bonanza. "Whether you like her or not, you'll realize her value before this night's over. She'll come back here, and she'll bring half of the mine with her. I wouldn't be surprised if she brought the whole thing!"

He leaned back in his chair until it creaked, and he laughed deep and soft, his two or three double chins fluffing in and out as he puffed and blew.

"Oh, she's a beauty!" said he. "She cuts the wind, all right. And she finds the money. Clean as a snake's tooth is what she is! I never knew a girl so dependable, either. You know, she does what she says she'll do."

"Will she take a percentage?" says Slip anxiously, making himself a cigarette.

"Of course, she will. Ten per cent or ten thousand is what I guaranteed her. Of course, she'll want the percentage, if she has any sense at all. That leaves for you and me, apiece, over twenty per cent each of the whole value of the mine. Call that value two and a half millions—you never had your hands on such a deal as this before in your life. But you should have done a better job."

"I had everything lined up," says Slip, alias Joe Milton. "But the brat of a kid, he stepped in and spoiled things. It's all up to the girl, now. I played the fond-father stuff, all right. You can trust me for that."

"Yes, I'd trust you for that," admitted Bonanza.

I had pulled myself up to the sill of the window, so that I could sit there comfortable and see and hear everything, and not be seen or heard, but just then I slipped.

I dunno how it happened, but I do know that I slipped, and came down onto the ground with a whang. I could have dropped three times that far without hurting myself, but this happened so quick that I wasn't prepared. I gave my knees a bad bang, and my head slammed against the side of the house.

I knew that trouble would be following me pretty fast, and I up and cut for it. At the same time, I seen a shadow dart out through the door of the shack and come around on the whirl after me. It come fast, charging, and it came low, like somebody that knows how to sprint.

I tried to make my legs work, but I had banged the knees pretty bad, and they were sorter numb.

The runner come whizzing up behind, and I knew that it was Slip, and I knew that he'd as soon kill me as not.

When I felt through the nerves in the back of my neck that he was reaching for me, I slipped flat to the ground, and then got up and tried to run back the other way.

It was a good dodge. I'd worked it before a lot of times. But this fellow, "Joe Milton," he seemed ready for it, and he rounded in behind me just as I started running again.

He picked me up in the hollow of an arm. As he did

216

that, I twisted about and seen his face as I struggled. The moon was full upon it, and he looked hard as iron twist. I never seen a worse expression on a man's face.

Then he lifted up his free hand, bunched his fist, and smashed me in the face.

I felt my skin spilt and the blood run. I looked right through the pain at him and watched the devil twist at the corners of his mouth. Then he hit me again, in the jaw, and suddenly everything went half dark.

Things cleared up again a good deal when he packed me into the shack. I mean, I could see the way you do through a rain mist, the rays from the lamp being all split up, and shining one by one.

"You've found the little treasure, have you, Slip?" says Bonanza.

"Yeah, I found him," said Slip.

"You've hurt him," said Bonanza. "Or did he hurt himself when he fell at the window?"

"I hurt him," says Slip, mean and low. "And I wish that I'd murdered him. It's what I got in mind, anyway!"

"It's rotten to think about," says Bonanza.

He crossed his legs and knocked the ash off his cigar and shook his head.

"I don't like it a bit," says he.

"What else is there to do? Let the brat blab?" says Slip.

"Kid, will you blab?" says Bonanza.

"Listen, you fat stuff," I said to him, "if I told you that I wouldn't, would you believe me?"

"How directly you come to the point, Red," says Bonanza. "You're a fellow after my own heart. In fact, I'm horribly afraid that I shall regret you when you're gone. But it seems that go you must, Red. I hate to say so, but you simply know too much. Your little brain is too active. It dodges about and gets into too many unexpected corners. You understand, I guess?"

I hated him so much that I don't think that I was much scared. I just glared back at him. I felt my lips working. I guess that I didn't look very pretty.

For suddenly Bonanza, he turned his back on me and says to Slip: "Tie the brat up, and gag him!"

"No sooner said than done," says Slip.

And he did it just about that quick, too. He had some strong twine for tying. There ain't anything so hopeless to get away from as twine. It fits right into the middle of your joints when it's pulled tight, the way that Mr. Slip knew how to pull it.

He stuffed an old bandanna into my mouth.

Bonanza had walked to the door of the shack, his hands behind his back.

"Well?" says Slip.

"Well," says Bonanza. "I'll ride on down the road a piece. I'm an older man than you are, Slip, and my nerves are not quite so strong. Let him lie where he is, or else put a bullet through his head. If you drop a match on the floor of this old tinder box, it will burn up the evidence, I dare say. Old ashes are not sifted very carefully in this part of the world!"

Slip grinned. I seen his grin. Yes, sir, he liked that dirty job.

And out went Bonanza, and I heard his horse carrying him away. Then Slip said: "After all, kid, it was a rough day for you when you went up agin' a growed-up brain. A smart brat you been, and a tough one, but you stretched yourself too far. And now there's gonna be an end to it. You hear?"

He stirred me in the ribs with the toe of his boot. He stirred me slow, grinding the toe in so that it would work the flesh against my bones.

But I kept the groan back. I was telling myself that I'd breathe in the fire deep when it come my way. That's the way to get the pain over the quickest.

Somehow I seen and thought of only one thing just then. And that was Slope! I mean, I thought of his honest, dull face, and all the kindness in it.

Then a gun come into the hand of Slip. "I dunno," says he. "But I think that I'll make you sure before I drop the match. I couldn't trust you even to fire, kid!"

As he spoke, I heard a wild, horrible, thick, great sound from the door of the shack.

It wasn't no human thing. It was the roar of a wild beast. And I looked across, and there was Slope rushing through the door toward me, with both arms flung out.

CHAPTER 43

Let me try to put it down item by item. If I hurry it, everything still gets black before my eyes, like it done then. I was half blind. All the way through what followed, I was trying to scream out, and the effort, it puffed the flesh around my eyes, and my wits were spinning.

Well, I say that Slope charged, and that Slip, he turned around and faced him with a little laugh, as cool as you please. And he pulled the revolver up and took a steady aim.

Slope was as good as dead against a marksman like that, of course. So I wriggled over and jammed my heels into Slip's nearest shin. He hopped and let out a short howl, like a scared dog, and I knew that the bullet he fired went wild.

Then Slope reached for him.

By a fraction of a second he missed, and Slip, dodging back, shot straight into Slope's back!

And I gotta lie there and see it all!

Slope, he turned right around, and I saw the awful pain in his face, and he rushed in on that thug without a word. I wouldn't say that he was looking fierce or savage—only terrible and kinder grand. I never seen anything like it.

As he run in, slow, deliberate, and calm, Slip drives a bullet through his body again, and I see the impact twist Slope half around—but he lunges on in.

He picked the gun out of the hand of Slip as though

219

he was taking it out of the fingers of a baby a week old.

And he picks up Slip, sorter folds him up. I seen the blood gushing and bursting out of the body of Slope, but I couldn't help and I couldn't speak.

I could only lie there and watch him dying for me.

Then I seen a mighty awful thing. As I say, he was folding up Slip, and a frightful scream burst out of Slip's mouth as the giant that was in the body of Slope suddenly begun to break him.

At the sound, I heard Slope say: "I don't seem able to do it, but I know that you need to die, Mr. Milton."

Like that he said it, slow and careful.

Then, as he held his hand, he staggered. For the loss of blood was draining right out of his heart, and he was dizzy with it, I guess.

And that hound, that "Joe Milton," suddenly was able to kick his way loose, run across the room, and gather up his gun. Then he turned, his face like a maniac.

He was in pain, all right. I mean, something must've really been broken in his body by Slope. Slip was moaning and drawing in his breath with a slavering sound that you wouldn't hear even in a zoo.

So he turned on Slope and pulled the gun down on him again. Slope, resting a hand on the edge of the table, had his head bent. He seemed to be thinking, and his eyes, they dropped toward me with a far-away smile, very sweet and gently. It was heart-breaking. Right then I heard the sharp, high sound of the girl's voice, calling: "This way, Mr. Murderer Slip! This way, if you please!"

When I turned my head, I seen her there in the doorway, slim and whitish, the little revolver bright as a diamond in her hand. To my eyes it was like a sort of searchlight turned on everything and changing everything.

"You damn sneak!" shrieked Slip at her. "I'll teach you, then—"

Yes, sir, he turned, and would have shot her down, but her bullet landed through the legs. His own hummed past her head, and I still carry it over my heart—the little lock of hair that the slug cut neatly away.

Well, as he twisted, he fell, and his spinning arms,

they hit the table and knocked it over. Down goes the table, crash, and the lantern with it, shattering and throwing oil and flames clean across the floor.

I nearly went mad, but I know what happened.

Slope got to me and picked me up and carried me out. And he started back for Slip, and fainted on the way. There was no good going for Slip, anyway, for that house was what Bonanza had called it, just a crazy tinder box. It went up with a whoop.

The most good it did was to give a light while me and Mary tied up the two great wounds that were killing Slope. We were still at work when Blondy came in and stood silent by us. He fetched some water. That was about all that he could do to help now, and giving Slope a shot of whisky, which was poured down his throat. Then he sat and looked at the crumbling red of the fire, away from us.

"I missed you, Mary," he said. "It was only the light of the fire that brung me back here."

"You missed me from the first," said Mary. "I'm a crook, as Red knew. I came back here to give the conveyance to Bonanza and Slip—whom you called Joe Milton."

Blondy said no more; there wasn't anything to be said. He just sat and watched the dying fire. And it stained everything red—Blondy's face, Mary, the trees that were about us, and even a cloud that hung down low.

Once I thought Slope was dead. It was way past midnight then, and with my ear agin' his breast, I didn't feel nothing.

I reckon I kinder busted down. And I felt the arms of the girl come around me.

"You leave me be—you!" said I.

And she let me be.

Along toward the morning I heard Slope say, "Mary!" And she was already there, on her knees.

"Poor little Red," says Slope.

"Red is all right. He's here. Don't you see him, Slope?" asked Mary. He said that he couldn't but he held out a hand, which I took.

"That's better," said he.

And he went back to sleep. Blondy, he never budged. He just watched the ashes of the fire under the soft moonlight.

Well, the moon died, and the morning came, and Slope began to breathe without no moan in his sleep. I went over to Mary, and I took her face in my hands and I looked down at her and I said: "I reckon you saved him."

"It was you, Red," said she, "if he is saved."

"Are you a real bad one, Mary?" said I. "No, you ain't. But would you stick it out? His dumbness, I mean. Because he ain't noways smart."

"I'll supply the smartness," says she.

She smiled, but it wasn't much of a success, that smile. Then Blondy got up for the first time.

"I reckon I'd better get some coffee over here and some bedding," says he. "Goodby, Mary."

I wonder what he meant, saying goodby like that, when he came back so soon. But, from that day, he was a quieter kind of a man, like he is today.

Well, that's about all there is to say. Of course, Slope got well, slowly pulling uphill. As Blondy said: "He couldn't die. Things had to be kinder fixed up aloft, burnished up and got ready for him. So they left him down below for a little while."

Mary, she agreed. She still agrees, I reckon, though she loses patience with Slope just a mite now and then. But, then, he'd wear out the patience of anybody in the world except one. I mean me, that seen him living and dying on his feet for me.

I should say something about Bonanza, but there ain't anything to say. He faded out, and he never was seen no more, that I know of. It must 'a' got too hot for him. Somewhere, with a new name, I reckon, he's still inviting people to get rich quick.

Well, the three of us don't live together no more. But we meet up now and then. Whether we're together or apart, it ain't much difference, because we're still tied pretty close, more or less.